# A Narrow Exit

# A Narrow Exit

*Faith Martin*

ROBERT HALE · LONDON

© Faith Martin 2011
First published in Great Britain 2011

ISBN 978-0-7090-9204-9

Robert Hale Limited
Clerkenwell House
Clerkenwell Green
London EC1R 0HT

www.halebooks.com

2 4 6 8 10 9 7 5 3 1

Typeset in 11/14½pt Palatino
Printed in Great Britain by the MPG Books Group,
Bodmin and King's Lynn

# CHAPTER ONE

It was nearly six o'clock, and the evening in early May was trying to be mellow but not quite succeeding. Detective Inspector Hillary Greene glanced out of her office window at the view across the village of Kidlington, looking towards the city of Oxford, but it was too far for her to pick out many of the fabled dreaming spires.

Either that, or she needed glasses. And with the big five-O looming on the horizon, she supposed gloomily that the latter was a distinct possibility. With a sigh she made a mental note to visit the opticians once she was retired.

She shifted uneasily on her chair, and forced herself to repeat the phrase in her mind, yet again. *Once she was retired.* It was funny, but no matter how many times she forced herself to use the phrase, she still couldn't make it stick.

But leaving she was, and soon her last day at work would arrive, with the usual little celebratory drink with her colleagues, followed by a few uncomfortable speeches, and a gold watch. Or whatever the modern equivalent was these days. Maybe then it would finally get through her thick skull that her working career as a cop was over.

There were many things that Hillary was determinedly scheduling for when she retired; they ranged from the sublime to the ridiculous. From a long list of boring chores, such as the latest addendum, the eye test, to setting off on her narrowboat, *The Mollern*, for a long leisurely tour of Britain's waterways.

Well, those that were still navigable anyway. Thing was, she wasn't sure which way to go – west, and into Gloucestershire, maybe up through Wales? Or south – maybe get on to the Thames. Not that she really fancied ending up in London – cities were not her favourite thing. Maybe she should just head north – follow the canals till they ran out, then turn round and come back again.

For some reason, the aimlessness of this agenda, instead of imbuing her with a sense of freedom and spontaneity, left her feeling just a little flat.

Sometimes she indulged herself with the fantasy of maybe writing a book, probably fiction, possibly crime. After all, a lot of other cops had done the same, and been successful. True, that happened more often across the Atlantic than at home, but so what?

At other times an extended holiday in a more exotic clime clamoured for consideration. A world cruise? A safari? A tour across Asia, being careful to avoid backpackers and students in their gap year?

But more often that not, the chief thing she felt whenever she contemplated her early retirement from the Thames Valley Police Force was a vague and cool uneasiness that could border on dread.

With a mental sigh, she snapped shut the folder she'd been reading, which was DC Mark Chang's report on the hijacking of a lorry near the Pear Tree roundabout, in which a batch of hi-tech computers had gone walkabout. The constable clearly suspected an insider in the computer firm, and Hillary agreed with him. Someone in the firm must have tipped off the hijackers – especially since the routes were always varied, and even the drivers got shuffled around at the last minute without warning. She couldn't fault the firm's managing director in his attempts to keep the business's insurance bills down, and he must be spitting nails at this latest setback.

She wondered, idly, how much the shipment had been

insured for, contemplated an inside job combined with insurance fraud, then felt her interest wane. It was really Gemma's case anyway; she was merely keeping a watching brief. Since she'd handed in her notice two months ago, she'd gradually been dwindling down her workload in preparation for leaving. The last thing she wanted to do was leave with too many cases outstanding. She had too much professional pride for that.

She got up and reached for her jacket – a rich dark green, it matched her slender skirt and complemented the cream blouse she was wearing. The whole ensemble suited her longish bell-shaped cut of dark-chestnut hair. And since she'd lost nearly a stone in weight during the last couple of months she attracted more than her usual share of male glances as she made her way out of the large open-plan office and down the stairs into the foyer.

She made her way across to the reception desk, where a hefty desk sergeant, counting down the minutes until he was relieved, saw her approach and grinned a welcome.

'Can't say as I miss that old DC of yours,' he said affably, by way of greeting. 'You know, that long streak of wind with the ginger mop? He was all right usually, but the last few weeks he was going about with a face like a long wet weekend.'

Hillary smiled wryly. There was no point in explaining that Keith Barrington, who'd left the force a few weeks ago to join his lover on the pro-tennis circuit, had certainly had more than enough on his plate to warrant the long face.

Keith was gay and had been in the closet; having a wealthy boyfriend had not exactly been an asset to a young DC with ambition. The son of a titled man and recently convicted felon, the boyfriend had ambitions to be the next Andy Murray, and the suicide of his father whilst being held at Her Majesty's pleasure had given him the opportunity to go chasing his dreams. He'd been determined to take Keith with him.

Not surprisingly, Gavin Moreland had no love for the police, and had probably been determined for some time to winkle the love of his life out of the arms of the men in blue, and into the more rarefied atmosphere of the well-to-do, footloose and fancy-free brigade.

Hillary still secretly believed her young constable had made the wrong choice in leaving the force to become a sports agent, but she was hardly in the position to advise anyone on anything. Either on matters of the heart, or career options. Hadn't her own choices landed her in the position in which she now languished? With no other option but to resign, and with the prospect of a boyfriend about as remote as her becoming the next lottery winner.

'I had a postcard from him earlier this week,' Hillary responded to the desk sergeant's jibes. 'From Monte Carlo, I think it was, where it's ten degrees hotter. He was sipping pina coladas around the pool and pocketing a nice little cheque after bagging his second signing – some minor-league-football hopeful who's just been bought up by Swansea.'

The desk sergeant blew a raspberry. 'Swansea! Who the hell cares?' But he had a faraway look in his eyes that looked a lot like envy to Hillary, and she was careful to hide her smile.

'See you tomorrow, Bill,' she said drily and turned towards the large, modern set of swing doors that led out to a featureless car park.

The desk sergeant watched her go and sighed. No two ways about it, it would be the end of an era when Hillary Greene left. He still couldn't believe that she was actually going. Nobody could. Everyone kept on thinking that something was going to happen to change her mind. But so far she was staying grim-faced and stoical, and her leaving date grew slowly but inexorably nearer.

Outside, Hillary made her way to Puff the Tragic Wagon, her ancient Volkswagen Golf, and wondered what she'd do with the car if she did take to the canal system for any length of time. It hardly seemed worth garaging it somewhere, but on the other hand she was loath to sell it. Over the years she'd grown used to it, and it seemed like one wrench too many to say goodbye to the contrary old rust-bucket.

She shivered in the cool evening air as she fiddled with the door lock.

Once inside, she switched on the ignition and turned the heater up to full. Not that it would do much good, she realized philosophically. She only had a five-minute drive at the most ahead of her. By the time she reached the small hamlet of Thrupp, just on the outskirts of Kidlington, the heater might just have started to blow lukewarm air on to her toes. If she was lucky.

She didn't know it, but from his window on the top floor of the building, the newly promoted Commander Marcus Donleavy was watching her leave, his grey eyes darkening as they followed the progress of her car until it was out of sight.

Then he went back to his desk, and pressed the intercom switch. He knew that his secretary, who could have left at five, would still be at her desk. She always waited for him to leave first – unless there was some sort of crisis on, and he was pulling an all-nighter.

'Can you ask DCI Danvers to come in, please?'

There was a murmur of consent, and then static. Marcus sat back in his chair, steepling his fingers together in an unconscious habit that told anyone who knew him well that he was thinking hard.

And planning something.

A few minutes later there came a knock at the door, and a handsome, fair-haired man walked in. He was in his late thirties, and when he greeted his chief, he spoke with a soft northern Yorkshire burr.

DCI Paul Danvers had fancied Hillary Greene ever since he and another detective had been assigned to investigate Ronnie Greene, Hillary's late and unlamented husband, for corruption. Everyone knew that Danvers' partner had had his suspicions that Hillary must have known about Ronnie's illegal animal-parts smuggling ring, but she had, of course, been cleared of all suspicion.

But it had hardly been the best of introductions for Danvers. Hillary was hardly likely to look kindly on a fellow detective assigned to investigate her own private and financial dealings. It hadn't helped that Danvers was several years younger than she either. Or prettier, as she'd once been overheard to say to someone at the office Christmas party.

Marcus Donleavy waved the man into a chair and smiled across at him. He was wearing his trademark silvery-grey suit and an electric-blue tie. With grey eyes and silver hair he looked as though he'd just stepped out of an advert for a Saville Row tailor.

'Paul, all set for the move?' he asked amiably.

Paul Danvers nodded warily. 'I've been packed up and living out of boxes for the last few weeks, sir,' he said flatly.

'Yes. Sorry your transfer was delayed. You know how it is.'

Danvers smiled wryly. He knew.

'But I've just got the final piece of paperwork confirmed,' Donleavy continued smoothly. 'You go at the end of the month.'

'Good. The lease on my flat runs out on the first of June – and I didn't fancy trying to rent a bedsit in Oxford to see me through.'

Marcus shuddered. 'Perish the thought.' He smiled. 'No, don't look so worried, it's not your transfer that I wanted to talk about.'

Danvers relaxed marginally, and began to look less wary and more curious.

'It's Hillary,' Marcus said. 'She's still determined to go?'

'Seems so,' Paul said, with real regret. He might have accepted that he and Hillary, as an item, was never going to happen, but he still cared, very much, about what was happening to her.

When he'd left Yorkshire for Thames Valley, he'd been determined to press for the job as Hillary's immediate boss. And since then he'd pursued her carefully but determinedly, without success. Eventually, when he realized that his obsession with her was interfering with his work, he'd taken the decision that it had to stop and, biting the bullet, he'd applied for transfer back to York.

He'd been as shocked as anyone the day she'd walked into his office and handed in her resignation. He still didn't understand it. Hillary was a workhorse, and a woman so suited to her job that they seemed joined at the hip. He'd racked his brains to think of any reason for her decision, but had come up empty. It was deeply frustrating. Nor was he alone – all of her friends and colleagues had tried to talk her out of it.

Her only response was tight-lipped silence and a refusal to budge.

'And she still hasn't given you any real explanation?' Donleavy demanded.

'No. She's sticking with her story. She says that with her team disintegrating, and after Mel's death, she just feels it's time to go,' Danvers said quietly.

And there was probably *some* truth in what she said, Paul mused. Her team had sort of crumbled around her recently. First Keith had left to chase the good life, then her sergeant, the super-efficient, kick-ass Gemma Fordham, had announced her marriage – to a lord, no less. It was hardly surprising that she'd consequently been promoted after passing her Boards, and was off for pastures new, chairing the latest brainchild of the chief constable. He rather doubted that Gemma, a martial arts expert, would be doing much hands-on work from now on. Riding a desk and learning all about paperwork, budgets, and conferences was probably going to be her lot from now on. He'd discussed this with Hillary, who was sure that Gemma still hadn't cottoned on to what her latest promotion truly meant. And once she did, Hillary was sure there'd be fireworks.

But, as she'd pointed out to Paul with a dreary sigh, that wouldn't be her problem any more.

'I know she thinks the new boy, Chang, is shaping up nicely, but he's still wet behind the ears. And he's hardly going to make up for Barrington and Gemma, is he?' Paul pointed out.

'That's just an excuse,' Donleavy said dismissively. 'I've got a whole line of officers lined up who'd jump at the chance to work with Hillary. Sam Waterstone for a start, and he and she have always got on.'

Paul nodded. 'Mel's death did hit her hard,' he pointed out.

Marcus sighed. DCI Phillip 'Mellow' Mallow had been Hillary's best friend, and immediate superior officer for nearly fifteen years, before he'd been killed in front of Hillary's eyes less than a year ago.

'She's solved two murders since then,' Marcus pointed out. 'She's took leave, and got herself sorted out. She's too much of a fighter to let the bastards wear her down. No, it's nothing to do with Mel. That much at least I'm sure of.'

Paul Danvers shifted uneasily on his seat. He had a nasty idea he knew where the commander was headed with all this, and he didn't want anything to do with it. He was heading back home, a little heart-sore, and maybe with a hint of his tail between his legs, but for all that, he didn't want complications now.

But under Marcus Donleavy's grey, heavy-lidded gaze he felt compelled to speak.

'You still think it's Vane's fault?' he asked reluctantly.

Detective Superintendent Brian Vane had replaced Mel as Hillary Greene's superior, and it had proved to be a disaster within a very short time. Marcus, who'd learned too late of some of the reasons behind Hillary and Vane's mutual antipathy, shrugged.

'I can't see what else it can be. The inquiry into Janine Mallow's shooting of Myers cleared both her and Hillary of any culpability. And the publicity was never centred on Hillary anyway.'

Paul nodded. Janine Tyler had been Hillary's sergeant in the old days, before she'd married Phillip Mallow and had his daughter. When she'd shot dead the man who'd killed her husband in somewhat uncertain circumstances, Vane had accused Hillary of somehow covering up for her. It had been the first public sign of the depth of Vane's antipathy towards Hillary, and it hadn't gone unnoticed.

'But Vane's off to Hull this month, isn't he?' Paul said. 'So Hillary knows that he's out of her hair. All she had to do was wait.'

The powers that be didn't take kindly to superintendents who rocked the boat when there was a delicate and very public inquiry going on. An officer of Hillary's experience would know that.

Marcus sighed heavily. 'You and I both know Hillary Greene's one of the best investigative officers we have around here. She's even turned down promotion so that she can continue to be SIO on the big cases. It's in her blood.'

Paul promptly agreed. So far, Hillary Greene's success rate on homicide cases was second to none.

'That's why I've called you up here. It's come to my notice that Hillary's winding down her case load – passing it on to Gemma or Sam Waterstone, or anyone else who's willing.'

Paul frowned. 'Well, that makes sense. She's leaving in three weeks, so she wouldn't want to be in the middle of anything big. You know the kind of headache that's involved in handing over a complicated case.'

Marcus Donleavy smiled grimly. 'Indeed I do. That's why I want you to assign her to the next big case that comes up.'

Paul Danvers opened his mouth to protest, then caught the steely glint in the commander's eye and snapped his jaw shut. 'Yes sir,' he said, after a moment's silence. He knew as well as Donleavy that Hillary would hate to leave in the middle of an unsolved murder case. But would it be enough to make her postpone her leaving? For some reason Paul Danvers doubted it.

Donleavy nodded with a brief smile of satisfaction. He was known at the nick for getting his own way, and now Danvers understood why.

With a sigh, and a premonition of trouble ahead, the Yorkshireman left his boss's office.

It was pitch-black at midnight. The moon, which had previously been full and beaming a cold, frost-laden gleam across the ground, had suddenly been swallowed up by cloud, and the temperature was beginning to rise just a little.

This was a fact which Frank Ross, night watchman at the Aynho Islip Business Park, was only too happen to acknowledge. Not just because it made his nightly rounds that much more comfortable, without the cold biting at his hands and face. But because of the loss of the light, which would make his main task of the night that much easier.

He shone his torch on to his watch face and stood in the centre of the large, messy, modern yard, glancing around.

The business park, newly and purpose-built on the outskirts of the village of Adderbury, which was itself a near-suburb of the large market town of Banbury, was silent and dark. The nearest houses, an estate of modern little boxes on the north border, were also reassuringly dark. No little squares of light suggested that someone was abroad for a midnight pee, or that a mother was up with a teething toddler.

Although it was unlikely that they'd bother to look out of their windows in the small hours, Ross still felt better on seeing that the darkness was almost complete. There was no street-lighting here, of course. The six unit-holders had voted not to have the added expense, although their insurers had insisted on some security – hence Frank's meagre pittance of a wage.

Still, for once, Frank had reason to be glad of the stinginess of the business park's owners.

Not only had it provided him with a job – if it could be called that, he snorted to himself – but it had given him the opportunity to indulge in a nice little earner on the side.

Any time now, he thought, glancing again at his watch. The lorry was due in at 1 a.m.

He could do his rounds before then, he supposed, and make sure that everything was shipshape and all locked up nice and tight. The thought made him laugh. But on the other hand, why bother? Nobody but himself ever got up to anything in this dead-end hole.

But there, as it so happened, Frank Ross was wrong. Dead wrong.

It was not, it has to be said, an altogether unusual occurrence.

Hillary Greene had no idea what woke her. Everything was dark, and the boat was still. Occasionally, some mad boater would cruise the canals in the dark and cause *The Mollern* to rock gently but with some protest at her mooring.

Usually boaters who had a pressing need to be somewhere had miscalculated the time needed to arrive at their destination. There was a four mph limit on the canals, and newcomers to the narrowboat fraternity could be caught out. Mostly the offenders were holidaymakers, who needed to get their hired boat back to the boatyard before their fourteen days were up. Hillary shuddered at the thought of how expensive boats were to hire, and she usually felt a sneaking sympathy for those who needed to travel in the dark to avoid swingeing late-penalty fees.

But the night was quiet, and the boat was still. She supposed it could have been the call of an owl that had woken her – she knew there was a nesting pair of tawnies in the small wood beside the canal.

She sighed and rolled on to her side, the familiar and comforting scent of the canal drifting in through the small round porthole above her bed. She faced facts.

It wasn't the owls that had awoken her, just the usual malady.

For the past few weeks she'd been finding it hard to get a full night's sleep. A psychiatrist would hardly need to break sweat to point out the reason why.

She sighed, rose, and made herself a cup of hot chocolate. She glanced at her wristwatch as she sat back on the edge of the bed drinking it.

It was two minutes past one.

She sighed.

In Adderbury Frank Ross heard the first faint rumble of the lorry engine. He walked quickly to the large, double-width gate that covered the entrance to the park.

The whole park was surrounded by chain-link fencing, nearly fifteen feet high, and topped with razor wire. The gate was also alarmed, the control panel being placed in Frank's warm control booth, which was set a few yards back from the main entrance.

He'd turned off the systems from there barely five minutes ago.

Now he waited until he could see the small lorry's indicator flashing orange in the night, then he opened up the padlock and pulled the gates across. It made a lot of noise, and he glanced around instinctively, but the distant houses remained dark and incurious. Even if some insomniac was aware of the activity in the park, he doubted it would arouse suspicion. It was a business park after all, where business and industry was conducted. And with the recession still biting people worked where and when they could – sometimes even in the middle of the night. So there was nothing unduly suspicious in that.

Frank nodded to the driver as the lorry pulled up in front of Unit 4. A metal inscription over the entrance to it bore the legend HODGSON & SONS, and showed up clearly in the headlights.

Frank locked and closed the gate, careful to refit the padlock. He grinned as he did so. After all, he didn't want any of the local thieves butting in on his action and bringing unwanted attention down on them.

He watched as two men jumped from the back of the lorry, one of them with the keys to the builder's yard's private entrance. Frank had no such keys to any of the businesses –

which was just how he liked it. It meant that no one could say he had access to the premises themselves. Just in case things turned nasty, it was nice to have full deniability.

It was his job to patrol the public areas of the park, and report anything suspicious to the police. Nothing more.

Frank went back to his comfortable booth. It wasn't his job to do manual labour either, he thought with a cocky grin, as one of the men shot him a dirty look.

Hillary turned off the light and closed her eyes. It was nearly 2 a.m., and she doubted she would sleep now.

Instead she began to plan the exotic holiday. The Seychelles, maybe? Or one of those islands that was going to be swamped when global warming finally caught up with humanity. Better see it now, while it still existed.

The fact was, she'd sold her house years ago, when property was booming, and the money had been sitting in the bank ever since, earning interest – when interest rates had been high.

Furthermore, she'd worked out a mutually agreeable middle path with the pensions office, which would see her drawing enough money each month to tide her over without too much scrimping – providing she didn't go buying any diamond tiaras.

So she was, according to most people's estimation, relatively well-to-do. She also now owned *The Mollern* outright, since buying it from her uncle, so her overheads were low.

She could do anything that she wanted, within reason.

So why the hell couldn't she sleep?

Frank Ross waved the lorry goodbye, metaphorically rubbing his hands with glee over the thought of his cut. It would enable him to back a few winners at the racecourse, pay for a few prossies, and see him drinking Stella Artois at his local for a couple of weeks, easy.

He repadlocked the gates and headed back to his booth. There he turned the security systems on again, and settled down in his chair. The dim internal lighting glowed a pale green, giving his face the look of a drowned man. He poured himself a cup of coffee from his thermos, settled himself down on his chair, and closed his eyes with a small smile of well-being.

Hillary Greene was up at five. Dawn was gleaming through the willow trees and the clouds of the night were reluctantly giving way to a pale rose-pink.

In Adderbury Frank Ross too began to stir. He poured the last of the coffee from his thermos, grimacing at the tepid, stewed tasting liquid, and took the plastic cup outside where he stretched, scratched his groin and looked around.

It wasn't fully light yet, but he couldn't be bothered with the torch. More to stretch his legs than anything else, he began to do his rounds.

Because of the layout, he started at Unit 6, a large auto-repair shop, and went in a semicircle back towards the entrance.

He passed various businesses as he strolled casually in the sharp dawn air. Doyles, a scrap-metal yard, earned his careful attention. There was a lot of money in scrap metal nowadays. If they could find someone inside who wanted to earn a bit of extra cash perhaps he and the boys could do some business of their own. After all, a lorry could leave carrying metal as well as building supplies.

He whistled thoughtfully, barely glancing at the shoe depot that provided trainers and high heels to half the shoe shops in the home counties, then made his way back to the beginning and his booth again.

The last of the premises, in Unit 1, belonged to a newspaper-delivery depot, which specialized in local papers. They were due to receive a big delivery of *Banbury Cakes* (the newspaper, not the famous comestible) within the hour. Luckily he went off at six, and it would be Billy's job to let them in. He peered over the top of the high wooden gate that was the entrance to the lot, and frowned as he noticed the light spilling out of the ground-floor window.

Shit! Surely nobody had been working late in the office?

Frank felt a cold sweat break out at the mere thought of it. Because of the angle of the building and the height of the gate, the light hadn't been visible from the booth.

He cursed as he realized that he should have done his rounds just before midnight after all. Then he'd have spotted this potential problem.

The depot was surrounded by rough wooden fencing about six feet high, and as he leaned on the gate he felt it move easily with his weight. He realized it was slightly ajar.

Damn and double damn! It was the sort of thing he was supposed to notice and report. He had a list of telephone numbers for all the unit-holders, and he was supposed to report possible problems to them, in case of emergency. He pushed the gate open slowly.

'Hello there – it's just me, Frank Ross. Night security.'

His voice sounded a shade thick and uncomfortable, but nobody answered, and after a while he let his breath out in a shaky sigh of relief.

Some careless twit had simply forgotten to switch off the lights and shut and lock the gate behind him, that was all. And why not? It wasn't as if anyone was going to nick a hundred tons of tabloids, was it?

Besides, didn't the park have good old Frank Ross to make sure that no ne'er-do-wells pilfered any goodies from the park?

Frank glanced around the faceless block of the unit. Unattractive orange-yellow bricks stared back at him. There were very few windows in the building, and those that had been installed were mostly on the ground floor near the front. Almost certainly they indicated where the offices were.

Vaguely curious, Frank walked up the path, and veered across a scrubby lawn towards the lit room. There he cupped his hands to the window and looked inside. An empty, normal-appearing office looked back at him.

Frank shrugged. He'd make a note of it in his log – back-dated of course. He'd say he noticed all this on his 'first' round, just to cover his arse.

He turned, and stopped dead.

In a patch of shadow provided by a bank of shrubs that had been planted to relieve the unrelenting brickwork and tarmac, he could see a definite shape on the ground.

Slowly, Frank, an ex-copper, walked towards it, already half-knowing what it was.

He began to swear softly and comprehensively all the way across the patchy piece of grass until he was standing just a few feet away.

On the ground in front of him lay the body of a man. It had a red mess where one side of his head should be. And lying beside him on the ground was a short plank of wood, with nails sticking out of it.

The wood had probably come from the builder's yard. No matter how old man Hodgson tried to keep his area of the park tidy, there were always stray bits of wood, sawdust, nails and what-have-you littering the ground area around Unit 4. Anybody could just pick them up.

The nails on this particular piece of two-by-four were sticky and red.

In the growing dawn light, Frank recognized the corpse at once.

He carried right on swearing.

And sweating.

# CHAPTER TWO

Hillary Greene pulled out of Thrupp on to the main Oxford to Banbury road, and hit the worst of the rush hour traffic just after crossing the railway bridge a scant minute later. At this time in the morning the traffic going into Oxford made even her tiny commute a matter of patience versus stress. Behind her, a man in a Mercedes talked illegally on his mobile phone, and Hillary sighed heavily, trying to catch his eye so that she could glare at him in the rear-view mirror.

Would the idiots never learn? If they'd had to attend as many RTAs as she had when she was still in uniform, they'd think twice. Hillary had only had to see one mangled body being dragged from a crushed car to promise herself never to drink and drive – a promise she'd never yet broken. And she never used mobiles whilst driving either, always pulling over whenever she felt the need or, more often than not, when its annoying trill summoned her.

She wound down the side window and breathed in the cool May air. Then she coughed on exhaust fumes from the laden Volvo in front of her as it revved on the accelerator. She quickly wound up the glass again, swearing wearily. Grimly, she told herself that when she retired she wouldn't have to suffer even this inconvenience. From now on, she'd start listing all the good points about leaving the Force, whenever they occurred to her. Somehow, it didn't fill her with optimism.

The traffic moved another couple of feet, then stalled, and she patiently eased Puff the Tragic Wagon onwards.

Ten minutes later, she was passing by the Kidlington library, the sight of which reminded her to make sure that all her books were taken back before she left. Then she winced as a young boy on a bicycle cut in front of her, narrowly missing going under the wheels of a taxi idling at the traffic lights. He was in school uniform and probably late for class. She wondered, idly, if she'd ever get out of the habit of noticing petty wrongdoers. She somehow doubted it.

She eventually made it to the large car park outside Thames Valley Police HQ, and made her way across the cracking asphalt to the main doors. Once inside, she held up a hand to acknowledge the desk sergeant's greeting, and headed up the stairs. She never took the lift, and thanks to her recent loss of weight, arrived on the second floor without too much unsightly puffing.

She'd barely pushed through into the large, open-plan area where she and team worked, however, before she noticed the door to Paul Danvers' cubicle shoot open. He stepped halfway outside and beckoned her in. Instantly, she diverted from her progress towards her desk and once outside his door, poked her head round it.

'Paul?'

Danvers reached across his desk and picked up a piece of paper. 'This is just in. A suspicious death at a business park in Adderbury.'

Hillary stayed firmly by the door, making no move to go further inside, let alone reach for the slip of paper. 'And you're waving it around at me – why, exactly?' she asked. 'You know I go in three weeks' time. Even if it's just an industrial accident, the case could drag on longer than that.'

Nearly all unexpected deaths reported to the police were designated as 'suspicious' until checked out. Most turned out to be the result of accident or suicide rather than murder, of course.

But this time her 'spider' sense was tingling and she eyed the piece of paper in her superior officer's hand with a mixture of loathing and longing.

'You're up,' Paul insisted.

Hillary blinked. 'You've got to be kidding!' She heard the hint of a whine in her voice, and inwardly cringed. Hastily, she modified her voice to a reasonable grumble. 'I'm winding my cases down, not looking for a major new one. Can't Sam take it? Or DCI Rollinson?'

'They're busy,' Danvers lied, and rattled the piece of paper impatiently. 'Come on, don't take all day about it. The sooner you're started, the sooner you'll be finished.'

Hillary snorted at that piece of useless logic. She reluctantly took the details and headed back to her desk. As she walked, she thought it over, and it didn't take her long to figure out what was behind it all.

Paul, who was due to go back north himself any time now, wouldn't have assigned her the case off his own bat. And Superintendent Brian Vane would rather slit his own throat than hand a potential murder case over to Hillary. Which meant it had to go even higher than him, which could only mean Donleavy. And that made sense.

Hillary gave a mental smile and shook her head. She had to admire the man's tenacity. At first, he'd refused to accept her resignation, then he'd had her in his office almost every day for a week trying to talk her out of it, and get to the bottom of her decision and reasons to leave.

She had, of course, kept her mouth firmly shut about those. The less Donleavy knew, the less he'd have to worry about. As it was, she was not sure that the sky wouldn't come tumbling down around her before she had the chance to go. A lot of it rested on the shoulders of that incongruous pair, Detective Superintendent Brian Vane, and DI Janine Mallow. And the last thing Hillary wanted to do was to bring down trouble on her colleagues and the job she loved.

23

She'd quite like to leave with some dignity intact, if it could be managed.

Since Donleavy had been rather quiet lately, she'd hoped that he'd finally accepted the inevitable, and was resigned to the loss of what he considered to be one of his more able detectives. She should have known better.

As she approached her desk two heads turned to swivel her way; they couldn't have been more different. One was female, topped with spiky blonde hair so pale it was almost white. Gemma Fordham, still languishing in the rank of sergeant until she started her new job as DI out near Aylesbury, watched Hillary approach with a question in her eye. She'd obviously scented the hint of excitement that was even now making Hillary walk with a lighter step.

She was wearing her usual trademark trouser suit, this day in dark chocolate brown, and her voice, left husky after a child-hood accident, came clearly across the space as Hillary approached the desk. 'Guv, what did Danvers want?'

The other head watching her was male, dark, and belonged to a young oriental of rather startling male beauty. DC Mark Chang's black eyes sharpened at the look of grim amusement on his boss's face.

'We have a suspicious death out near Banbury way,' she said, her gaze encompassing them both. 'Get your stuff. Gemma, take Chang's car. No need to add to our carbon foot-print by turning up in three vehicles. And no doubt we'll be out there all day.'

Gemma grunted, but glanced at the clearly excited young Chang with a more or less affectionate eye. It was his second big case, and she could just about remember what that felt like.

Hillary waited at the exit to the car park until she saw Chang's respectable and reliable little hatchback pull up behind her, with Gemma, not surprisingly, at the wheel. Gemma Fordham, a martial arts expert, was definitely the sort who liked to be in control, and although protocol had it that the junior officer always drove, she couldn't see Gemma relinquishing her place behind the wheel, no matter whose car they used.

As she drove north towards the large market town of Banbury she wondered, with just a hint of despair, and not for the first time, just what she could get Gemma for a wedding present.

Her wedding was due at the end of May and was to be held at a large and prestigious church in north Oxford. Her groom was a blind and well-heeled music don, who had lately come into a title, and therein lay the problem. She could hardly turn up with a set of bog-standard crystal glasses or set of superstore-bought tableware.

Something antique perhaps? But she wasn't sure that her sergeant was into that kind of thing. Maybe something off-the-wall; police-related memorabilia perhaps. That way the cost of it would be immaterial. Mind you, that was hardly a good choice for nuptials.

She sighed in defeat and pushed the problem to one side. She was consulting the piece of paper that Danvers had given her, which was now lying on the passenger seat beside her, when she was stopped by a red light at Hopcrofts Halt.

The Aynho Islip Business Park. It was a somewhat confusing name, she thought with a frown. She knew the village of Aynho could be reached by turning right at the village of Adderbury, but Islip, another anciently named village, lay many miles away, and in the opposite direction, not far from Oxford itself.

She gave a mental shrug. Oh well, it shouldn't be that hard to find. And in that, she was quite right.

Adderbury was one of those odd places in which only a small part lay on a major road, in this case, one that linked Banbury to Oxford. Consequently, the majority of people passing through it only saw a fraction of the village – the pub on the main road, and the newly built houses near the set of traffic lights. The rest of the settlement lay out of sight down a dip in the road, but it was one of the prettiest of Oxfordshire's villages that Hillary knew of. Perhaps, if she had a moment's peace during the day, she'd drive through it and reacquaint herself with it.

She turned right at the traffic lights, figuring that the Aynho Islip Business Park would actually be on the road leading to one of the named villages, and found the entrance to it about a quarter of a mile from Adderbury itself. It was marked by two police patrol cars parked either side of it; she pulled up in front of the further one, and climbed out.

She was wearing a dark-blue skirt and matching jacket, and a pair of flat sensible shoes. Another thing to look forward to in retirement – she could wear pretty shoes.

She smiled wryly at the thought, and glanced across at the uniformed constable who was standing stiffly beside his patrol car as she approached. He looked young and self-important, and obviously didn't know her. Before he got the chance to ask her to move along she spared his blushes by reaching for her card and displaying it.

'DI Greene – I'm SIO.'

'Yes ma'am.' The youngster seemed to resist the urge to salute, then gulped audibly like a cartoon mouse when he spotted Gemma emerging from the other car. The tall, striking-looking woman didn't seem to notice this homage, however, as she briefly flashed her own card at him. Hillary looked on, amused, as the constable hastily noted their names and time of arrival down in his logbook.

'Straight in, ma'am. You'll see the activity down at the bottom end – Unit 1, ma'am; it's a newspaper-delivery depot.'

Hillary nodded a wordless thank you, and set off slowly through the high gate, now standing open, which was set in an equally high chain-link fence. She glanced instinctively at the padlock hanging from one hasp, and saw that it hadn't been forced.

It was barely 8.30 in the morning, and although there were some signs of human activity in a few of the units, the place had a quiet, waiting air, and seemed curiously deserted.

Nevertheless, it was a typical business park – smaller than average, but with the usual mishmash of unattractive buildings. A scrap-metal dealership was chock-a-block with piled up scrap and wrecked cars, which looked, to her untutored eye, about to fall over with a noisy crash at any moment. Planks of discarded wood littered the area around a builder's yard, whilst in contrast another unit looked impeccably spick and span.

She had no trouble finding the little knot of activity in the unit concerned, and stepping through a wooden gate, found herself in a small, unimpressive space that she supposed was meant to pass for a garden or recreational area. Newly greening shrubs looked apologetic against the backdrop of an ugly brick building, and scrubby grass was rapidly being turned into mud by the number of feet trampling over it.

Beside her, she could feel Gemma and Mark crowding in for their first look.

A photographer was busy snapping pictures of something lying on the ground not far from one of the few windows in the otherwise featureless building, whilst several SOCO personnel, dressed in their distinctive white overalls and with white hoods raised, bent down over the grass, collecting evidence.

Hillary, still standing at the entrance to the unit, made no move to join them. No duck-boards had as yet been laid, and she knew better than to interrupt the forensic staff at their work.

She turned as she heard the familiar throaty purr of a MG pulling up behind her, and smiled as she ducked back outside to watch as Doctor Steven Partridge parked his nifty little sports car just outside the impeccable unit. Trust the dapper little medico to find the neatest and cleanest space, she thought with a grin.

Steven Partridge was probably nearing sixty by now, but you'd never guess it from his expensive suit or near-black hair. Hillary wondered what brand of hair dye he used, but would never ask him. She wouldn't be so cruel, and besides he had the kind of sharp wit that would almost certainly cut her down to size if she tried it!

'Hillary! I'm surprised to see *you* here. The brief I got was homicide victim.' He greeted her with his usual cheerful smile and genuine pleasure. Over the years, they'd worked successfully on many murder cases, and had a deep and mutual respect for each other's professionalism. They also quite liked each other, which was nice.

'Not as surprised as I am to actually *be* here,' Hillary said darkly.

The doctor, drawing level with her, shot her a quick, surprised look, thought about it for a moment, then grinned. 'Donleavy up to his usual tricks?' he asked quietly, so that the rest of her team, who were still inside Unit 1, couldn't hear.

'I wouldn't be surprised,' Hillary agreed calmly.

Steven nodded. It was well known that the newly promoted commander had always rated Hillary Greene highly, and didn't intend to let her go without a fight.

Like everyone else, Steven Partridge had been shocked to the core when he'd heard that Hillary Greene was taking early retirement. And he'd been convinced, until hearing it from the horse's mouth so to speak, that the rumour was unfounded.

Unlike most, however, he didn't waste time speculating about the reason for it. He knew Hillary to be the kind of woman who knew her own mind and had a damned good reason for everything she did.

'So. Decided what you're going to do with all your free time yet?' he asked instead, pausing outside the entrance to the unit to take a white overall from his case, and don it. This he did with neat, economical movements, and without the hint of a waver. He did, however, have to lean against the wooden fencing to slip little plastic bags over his shoes, and Hillary glanced away, in order not to answer the question.

'I haven't seen the scene close to myself yet, and it looks as if SOCO will be here for some time, so if you could keep your eyes peeled for me and give me an oral report it would be a great

help, yeah?' she cajoled instead. 'I know you like to make yourself useful.'

Steven Partridge grinned. 'Don't I always?'

In his little security cubicle Frank Ross slowly got up from the
floor and peered over the top of his chair. He'd been trying to be
invisible since the first uniforms had arrived, and was mainly
succeeding.

The first thing he saw was the chestnut-haired woman
standing and chatting with the slice-and-dice man. He felt as if
someone had just thumped him in the guts.

'Oh shit,' Frank Ross said, as he stared balefully at Hillary
Greene, unable to believe that Fate was playing him this particular card. 'You have got to be bloody kidding me,' he growled,
banging his fist down hard on the control panel, and making the
cheap plastic casing groan in protest.

He reached into his holdall underneath the knee-well, and
drew out the bag. From the bottom of it, he extracted a bottle of
cheap whisky and took a long swallow. At that point, he didn't
give a rat's arse who smelt alcohol on his breath.

Harry Welles felt his foot reaching automatically for the brake as
he spotted the police cars up ahead. Like most drivers, it was an
instinctive reaction when out on the road. Then he realized that
they were actually parked up right at the entrance to the park,
and felt a cold sweat break out as he pulled up opposite them,
indicating to turn left into the park itself.

The constable on the gate crossed to the driver's window of
the car as Harry pressed the button that had the glass automatically rolling down.

'Is there a problem, officer?' He heard himself speak the cliché
and tried not to wince. He was a good-looking man in his early
fifties, with classic salt-and-pepper hair and a rather daringly
full moustache, which he'd worn despite his wife's nagging for
the past twenty years or so.

'You have business here, sir?'

'Yes. I'm Harry Welles – I own the shoe warehouse Hermes' Wings in Unit 2. Has there been a break in? Or a fire?' he glanced around, as if looking for smoke, and told himself not to be such a twit. There was obviously no fire, so why mention it? His hands felt slick on the wheel.

'No sir, but there has been an incident. I have to ask you to park just inside the gate and wait in your car until someone can speak to you.'

'But I have to get to the office. My morning staff will be arriving soon – we've got a big shipment of last year's remainders from Bicester Village to sort out.'

'I'm sorry sir, we'll try not to keep you,' the PC said blandly. Walking away, he tucked the radio on his collar more firmly against his mouth and said something Harry couldn't quite catch.

A moment later he waved Harry through, and indicated a parking space next to his own shoe warehouse, where a smart-looking classic MG was already parked and taking up much of the room, looking superior and smug.

Harry parked his own more modest BMW a shade awkwardly next to it, and turned off the engine. His hands, he noticed absently, were shaking.

Not for the first time, Harry Welles told himself not to be such a wimp.


From her vantage point still at the entrance to the unit, Hillary watched Steven Partridge kneel carefully beside the body on the ground. With the parting of the SOCOs to allow him room she caught her first good look at what appeared to be a white male, probably of middle age, lying on his side in a crumpled position.

She turned as an older uniformed officer approached her.

'Excuse me, ma'am. The owner of Unit 2, the shoe place, a Mr Harold Welles has just arrived. We've parked him by Doctor Partridge's car. He's the first of the managers or owners to appear.'

Hillary nodded. She glanced across and gave a brief toss of her head to Gemma, who nodded an acknowledgement, then trotted off to interview him. Chang watched her go, wondering when he'd be given his first assignment – and what it would be.

He had been bitterly disappointed when Hillary Greene had dropped the bombshell of her early retirement, since he'd only been assigned to her for a short while. He knew she had a lot more to teach him.

So, being assigned to what looked like another murder case was an opportunity to be savoured. For as long as it lasted.

Hillary waited patiently as Steven did a brief examination of the body. When he'd finished he rose lithely to his feet, nodded to the chief SOCO, then turned and walked her way. At this stage in the proceedings he was only obliged to confirm death, but very often she could rely on him to give her at least a hint of which way things were shaping up.

She'd heard on the grapevine that Steven liked to swim every day; he was also one of those small-built men who liked to run a half-marathon every now and then. Since he was devoted to a beautiful wife many years his junior, gossip had it that he had to keep young and fit, or lose her to some Lothario half his age.

Hillary, who liked his manners, wit, and intelligence, doubted that his wife would be so stupid.

'Well, it's a murder case all right.' His first words put paid to any hopes Hillary had that some poor soul had just dropped dead of a heart attack outside his office.

'Death due to blunt force trauma with, I would guess, the plank of wood lying beside the body. It was covered with blood and hairs, and had nails coming out of it that match several puncture wounds on his skull. Mind you, I might get him on my table and find he'd died of arsenic first, you never know,' he warned cheerfully.

'Oh don't.' Hillary shuddered. 'Bashed over the head will do to be getting on with, thank you very much. White male?'

'Yep, about his mid-forties, I'd say. Wearing a suit, which was damp, by the way, so I'd say he'd been lying out all night, and the dew got to him. It didn't rain last night, did it? From rigor and body temp, I'd put his death at sometime between eight and midnight last night – give or take. But don't quote me on that either just yet.'

'As if I would,' Hillary drawled.

Steven looked at her closely. 'You look tired,' he said, almost accusingly, and Hillary started guiltily.

'Not been sleeping very well,' she heard herself admit before she could stop herself, then scowled at him, as if daring him to comment.

Steven merely nodded, then began to peel off his protective clothing again.

'Well, must get back. I've got a death-by-drowning to autopsy, and then I've got to do a second PM on a disputed old woman who was found dead in a nursing home. The relatives suspect foul play.'

Hillary grimaced. 'Rather you than me, Doc,' she said, as the medical man gave her a cheerful wave and went on his way.

Harry Welles sat up straighter behind the wheel as he saw the stunning blonde woman approach. Surely she wasn't coming to his car, was she? But yes she was, he realized a moment later, as she knocked on the window beside his head.

He pushed open the door and she obligingly stood aside, watching him climb from the car with curious eyes.

'Mr Harold Welles? You're the owner of the shoe warehouse – Unit 2, I believe?' She glanced down at a small black-leather notebook that she held in her hand.

Harry's eyes widened at the sound of her voice. She sounded a bit like the singer Bonnie Tyler, but with even more of a rasp. She sounded throaty and sexy as hell, but he wouldn't have taken her for a smoker. She looked as fit as a butcher's dog. But how else did she get that amazing voice?

He was aware that she was looking at him patiently, a

vaguely amused look on her bony, striking features, and felt himself blush. He'd always been awkward and shy as a boy, and some of that had, much to his annoyance, rolled over into his adulthood. Nowadays it was apt to raise its ugly head when he found himself in the presence of attractive women.

'Er, yes. Look, what's going on? Why can't I get into my office?' He tried to sound in-charge and was aware that he merely sounded belligerent. And foolish.

'I'm afraid that at the moment most of the business park is being regard as a crime scene, sir,' she said mildly. 'Can you tell me what time you left yesterday afternoon? I take it you were at work?'

'What? Yes, I was. What do you mean a crime scene. What sort of crime?' He heard his voice rise almost hysterically, and forced himself to calm down. He peered ahead and saw that most of the activity was surrounding Wallace Deliveries.

'Is Jack all right?'

'Jack who?' Gemma asked sharply.

'Jack Wallace, the man who owns the unit.'

Gemma turned to a new page of her notebook and lifted a sharpened pencil. 'What can you tell me about Mr Wallace, sir?'

'Jack? Well, I don't know really. What do you want to know?' Harry asked helplessly.

'Let's start with a physical description, shall we, and go on from there?' Gemma suggested with a patience born of much practice.

'Well, he's an old man – the oldest one of us here, actually. I expect he's about sixty-five or so. Thinish with grey hair.'

Gemma nodded. Not their vic then, she thought to herself. Probably one of the employees.

'You say you were at work here yesterday, sir. What time did you leave?' She asked the question again.

'Must have been about six, I suppose,' Harry said cautiously.

'Did you see anything suspicious at the time? Anyone hanging around you didn't know – cars or other vehicles that you'd never seen before?' she prompted.

'No, no I don't think so. I called goodnight to Hodgson's boy.' He nodded across to the messy timber yard and builder's merchants. 'He drove out just ahead of me.'

'So he'll be able to vouch for the time you left?' Gemma said routinely. She didn't, at this point, have any reason to suspect Welles, but the way he gulped and paled instantly drew her attention.

'Yes, of course. And so will the security guard – he makes a note of that sort of thing. The times we check out and come back, and deliveries, that sort of thing. He'll be able to confirm it too.'

Gemma didn't miss the way Harry Welles rubbed his damp palms on the sides of his trousers. Here was a man not happy about something, clearly. He was nervous and obviously sweating.

Still, that in itself meant nothing, as Hillary had already taught her. Lots of people looked and felt guilty when talking to the police.

'Do you know many people by sight, sir? I mean people who work in the park?' she asked pleasantly.

'Yeah, I suppose so,' Harry Welles said, clearly taken by surprise by the change of direction. 'We've been up and running nearly a year now.'

Gemma nodded. So he might be able to identify the vic, if need be. She didn't know, yet, whether any ID had been found on him. She'd better report back to Hillary, she supposed. 'Please wait in your car a moment sir,' she said.

Harry glanced across longingly at the entrance to his unit. He had a bottle of fine gin in his desk, and he could almost taste in on the back of his throat now.

He watched the blonde woman walk away, then slumped back down behind the wheel of his car.

'Gemma, just in time,' Hillary said, as the chief SOCO beckoned her over.

She, Gemma and Mark Chang walked single file over the newly laid boards to where their victim lay on the ground.

Hillary studied him closely. He was lying at an awkward angle, half on his side and very nearly face down. His head was battered and bloody, but she could still see that, in life, he'd probably been a handsome man. His hair, though matted and dark with blood, had once been thick and blond, and she suspected he'd have the blue eyes that usually went with it. He was wearing a decent suit, and was maybe just running a little on to the heavy side – but at nearly six feet, she gauged, he probably carried it well. He was somewhere in his mid-forties, she guessed, and she noticed that his hands were clean and well manicured.

'Any ID?' she asked the SOCO, who nodded and held out a plastic bag filled with personal items, including a wallet. There was also an expensive real gold watch, and a gold-and-onyx signet ring. No wedding ring, she noted.

'Harry Welles might be able to ID him too, guv,' Gemma said, and gave Hillary a brief run-down on her interview with him.

'He seems antsy,' she concluded briefly.

Hillary nodded. 'All right. We'll hold off bringing him in on the ID though till we establish next of kin. Got a name?' she asked the SOCO man, who glanced briefly at his own notes.

'Michael Ivers, according to his credit cards.'

'OK.' She turned and walked back to the asphalt and stood staring at the unattractive building. What a soulless sort of place to work. It made her shudder.

'OK, Gemma; according to the uniforms, some staff arrived early this morning to deal with a delivery of papers. Naturally they turned the lorry away, but some bright spark took the liberty of letting the office workers into the little café area at the back. Start taking names and see if this Michael Ivers belongs here or not. You know the drill. I'll go and have a word with the nervous Mr Welles. Mark, go and talk to the security guard – get his log-book photocopied. I expect Mr

Welles will let you use his office after I've charmed him. I want to know everyone's movements from, say, yesterday noon till now.'

'Right guv,' Mark said, and trotted off.

Gemma turned back to the depot and stared at it grimly. 'Hell, what a hole. I'm glad I don't work here,' she said, uncannily repeating Hillary's own private thoughts of just a few moments ago.

Hillary said nothing.

Mark Chang looked puzzled as he approached the empty booth that was situated to one side of the main entrance. He was sure he'd seen a man inside it not so long ago.

Then he nearly jumped as the outline of a man suddenly appeared inside, like someone popping up from a jack-in-the-box. He knocked on the door, opened it, and instantly smelled cheap liquor.

So the poor old duffer had been having a quick nip. Mark couldn't say that he blamed him. It couldn't be much fun for the old man – discovering that someone had been murdered on his watch, so to speak. No doubt he'd taken this job on after retirement from some other career as a way to pad out his pension. He'd probably thought it would be a doddle and couldn't have counted on anything like this. Just a few patrols at night to show willing, then tucked up nice and warm with his thermos in the booth. Instead, he'd found a murder victim.

'Good morning, sir,' Mark Chang said politely, as Frank Ross turned and scowled at him. 'I'd just like to ask a few questions.'

'Don't try and teach your grandma to suck eggs, nipper,' Frank said unamiably. 'I used to be on the job – nearly thirty years. So I know the routine better than you do. You wanna copy my logbook, right?' He shoved the book, which he'd very carefully fiddled, into the startled DC's hands, and grinned darkly. 'Meanwhile, you'd better go and tell the queen bitch that Frank Ross sends his regards.'

Mark Chang blinked. Frank Ross. Why was that name so familiar?

Then he remembered where he'd heard it before. He opened his mouth to say something, then quickly closed it again.

Frank Ross watched the young constable walk quickly away and laughed mirthlessly. So that was Hillary's latest little recruit, was it? He looked like he should be on the telly – or posing nude in one of those magazines women liked to salivate over.

He spat on the tarmac and told himself that he felt better.

'Er, ma'am.'

Hillary Greene, standing beside Harry Welles's car, turned and saw Chang. 'Oh, Constable. Mr Welles has agreed to get his secretary to photocopy the logbook for you when she arrives. Perhaps you can take his formal statement whilst she does so?'

'Er, yes ma'am. Er, ma'am, can I have quick word?'

Hillary nodded. She'd noticed that Chang always used the more formal style of address for her when she was with a member of the public. She found it oddly touching. Once they'd stepped out of earshot of Welles's car, however, he quickly reverted.

'Thing is, guv, it's the, er, security guard.'

'Problem?' Hillary asked crisply, wondering why Chang was hopping about from foot to foot like an agitated horse.

'Yes guv. Er no. I'm not sure. He said his name was Frank Ross,' Chang got out in a rush.

Hillary stared at him, then went a little pale before throwing Chang completely by letting out a harsh bark of laughter.

She then swore, softly but with feeling.

It was the first time he'd ever heard her use such language, and he felt just a little shocked. He gaped, then quickly looked away, as Hillary strode past him, heading for the booth.

He smiled tentatively at a curious-looking Harry Welles, and only then realized that he was hugging the logbook to his chest as if it was the crown jewels.

'Perhaps we could go to your office now sir?' he said politely.

*

Hillary Greene fixed her eyes on the man in the booth as she approached, noting the grey uniform spotted with coffee stains on the lapel.

Oh yeah, it was Frank Ross all right. She smelt the cheap booze the moment he opened the door to the booth and acknowledged her with a repellent smile.

'Hey, Hill, long time no see,' he said with a sneer.

And wondered which lie to tell her first.

# CHAPTER THREE

'Hello Frank,' Hillary Greene said wearily, hearing herself say the actual words, but hardly able to believe that she was doing so. She'd thought she'd said the last words she'd ever speak to this man some time ago.

Frank Ross had been a crony of her husband, and she'd been stuck with him on her team for many years, before she'd eventually managed to force his retirement last year. Since it was widely acknowledged that he was a nasty piece of work, and was without doubt a lazy slacker even when he bothered to show up for work, nobody had mourned his loss. From the top brass on down to the most lowly constable, Ross had been universally loathed. Looking back on it, Hillary found it hard to believe she'd tolerated him for so long.

So when he'd walked out of Kidlington nick for the last time, spitting fire, whisky fumes and obscenities – in a fairly equal mix – she'd thought she'd seen the last of him. But she really should have known that she wouldn't be able to leave the job without something nasty raising its ugly head to bite her in the bum. She just hadn't expected it to be this particular snake in the grass.

'Queen bitch,' Frank greeted her, almost pleasantly.

Frank Ross was a round sort of man, with a benign, Winnie-the-Pooh kind of face that made most people who didn't know him automatically assume he was a nice man.

They didn't think that for long.

Frank, like her late unlamented and nearly ex-husband, had been as bent as a corkscrew, had filthy personal hygiene, and a toxic personality to match. She'd always suspected that he'd longed to greet her with just those words when he'd been working under her, but had just never had the guts.

Now she smiled at him sweetly. 'I see the charm school I recommended to you has worked wonders.'

Frank sighed heavily. 'Let's just get on with it, yeah? I showed your little pet Charlie Chan my logbook and he took it away to be photocopied. What else d'yah want?' he asked belligerently. He always had believed offence was the best form of defence, and she was somewhat reassured to see that he hadn't changed much. At least she knew what to expect from *this* particular witness.

Hillary settled herself against the booth, making herself comfortable. She had a feeling this was going to take some time. Frank, always supposing he wasn't involved in any way with the dead man, would delight in blocking her progress by whatever means he could, just to indulge in sheer bloody-mindedness. And if he were involved with the crime, he'd be gearing up into super-cunning mode – which was always an unpleasant sight.

Either way, it would take time to pick her way through his testimony.

'And this logbook of yours,' she said calmly, 'no doubt it'll be a picture of rectitude, neatly and accurately noted information and will give me a comprehensive overall view of the comings and goings at the park during the last twenty-four hours,' she observed sardonically.

Frank snorted. ''Course it will.'

'Right.'

She glanced up and saw Gemma coming towards her, her eyes fixed on Frank like a seagull's on spotting a bag of chips. 'Chang buzzed me to say that Ross was here. I just had to see it with my own eyes,' Gemma said as she approached.

'Well, well, the gang's all here now we've got the kick-ass

blonde bombshell.' Frank greeted her with a lascivious leer. 'Where's the ginger-nut then?'

'Keith's living it high on the French Riviera at the moment,' Gemma said, rubbing it in with pleasure. 'He left to be a sports agent. Earning mega-bucks, the way I hear it. And I've been promoted to DI,' she added, giving him a wolfish grin. Then she glanced ostentatiously around. 'And you're night watchman here,' she finished sweetly.

Frank shot her a feral grin. 'Why don't you run along, blondie? I don't have to be polite to you no more, so piss off.'

Hillary sighed, caught Gemma's eye and jerked her head slightly to one side. The last thing she wanted now was a dogfight. Gemma shot Frank the finger and walked away.

'Let's cut back on all this pleasant nostalgia, shall we?' she suggested sweetly. 'So, what happened last night. Let's hear it. Or at least, whatever version you want me to hear,' she added with a wry twist of her lips.

Frank sat down on the ergonomically designed chair in his booth and sighed. 'I got on at eight. I did the usual rounds – everything was quiet, everyone had gone home. Most of the regular grunts leave any time between half-four and half-six.'

'Flexi-hours,' Hillary said automatically. 'Nice for some.'

Frank grunted. 'The bosses can leave any time – three o'clock some afternoons, if they've got a game of golf on. Some diehards stay till seven. But usually by nine the place is deserted. It was last night.'

'And your rounds consist of?' she prompted.

'What it sounds like. I walk the perimeters,' Frank lied glibly, 'then check that each individual unit's gated entrance is closed and locked. Check the security systems are active and go back to my booth.'

Hillary looked at him with interest. 'That's a nice fairy tale. Want to continue?'

Frank reached for his nearly empty thermos and shook it. 'Look, I was supposed to go off at six. Your flatfoots have got

Billy hanging around doing nothing. I want to get off home and have some kip,' he whined.

'Then the faster you talk the sooner you can get off,' Hillary pointed out reasonably.

Frank heaved a sigh. 'My next round was at midnight. Same thing. Same result. All quiet, nothing unusual, no worries. Next round at three, then just before I clock off. It was on my last round that I noticed the gate to Unit 1 wasn't locked. It's last on my round, see.' He nodded at the business park. 'I start at six, and work anticlockwise.'

Hillary nodded. She was interested to observe that every now and then Frank kept flicking a glance over her shoulder. She turned casually to work out what it was that was in his sight line that he found so interesting, whilst pretending to check out the crime scene. He was either worried about the builder's yard or the garden-supplies depot next to it, she guessed.

She wondered why. Thought about it for some moments, then stopped wondering.

'So why didn't you notice that the gate was unlocked during the first round? Or was it locked then?' she asked sharply, turning back and watching him squirm. If someone came into the yard between his rounds, then … She stopped herself right there, remembering whom she was dealing with. Of course, Frank Ross had not done *any* rounds. He'd probably spent the night sleeping on his comfy chair in the warm and dry.

She saw his eyes dart to the left, then the right, and watched him grimace as he drank his nearly cold coffee. Whilst it was fun to watch him wriggling around like a worm on a hook as he tried to figure out the least damaging lie to tell, it was important that she got the information as accurately and as quickly as possible.

'Come on, Frank; remember who you're talking to, will you?' she snapped at last. 'If you ever left your warm and comfy little booth to do your rounds even once a night then I resemble a Dutchman's uncle.'

Frank grunted. 'OK. But don't tell the boss, all right?'

Hillary raised an eyebrow. 'And I care about helping you keeping your job ... because?'

Frank swore. 'Come on, do you want it straight, or not?'

'Straight. And here's the deal - I won't go out of my way to tell your boss what a sterling job you do, but if he asks, I'm not lying to save your unsavoury backside either.'

'Fine, what the hell ever.' Frank waved his empty plastic cup disdainfully in the air. 'Like I care if I keep this job or not,' he sneered, his eyes flickering briefly to the timber yard and then away again. 'I do a little walk around every now and then. I only noticed the gate to Unit 1 was open at just before six this morning. I wanted to make sure everything looked shipshape before handing over to Billy.'

What he meant was, he wanted to make sure that no signs of the midnight raid were visible. Billy Bainbridge was as straight as a die, and would report anything suspicious in a heartbeat.

'Right,' Hillary said drily. 'Was the gate standing open?'

Frank blinked. He felt an embarrassed wave of heat rise up in his neck as all the times he'd interviewed witnesses when on the job suddenly rose up to haunt him. He couldn't count the number of times he'd mentally cursed and jeered at them for not being able to remember accurately any damned thing of use. Now, with one simple question, Hillary Greene had made him feel about two inches tall by making him one of their number.

'Shit, I can't remember,' he heard himself admit miserably. 'It may have been a little ajar. Maybe I saw some light in the crack. I dunno, but something made me try it anyway.'

Hillary sighed heavily but nodded. 'Go on. So you pushed the gate open and went inside.'

'Yeah. I saw a light on in the office window and thought someone must be pulling an all-nighter. I went to look, then saw the body on the ground, and came back to the cubicle to report it.'

''Course you did,' Hillary said agreeably. 'Did you touch the body?'

'Now who should remember who they're talking to?' Frank hissed, suddenly venomous. ''Course I didn't touch it. I didn't go anywhere near it.'

'Now that I believe,' Hillary said. 'You recognize him?'

Frank hesitated, thinking it through. His first instinct was to deny it, but then he realized how daft that would sound. He'd worked here for six months – of course he'd know the main office workers by sight.

'Come on, Frank, just answer the damn question and stop trying to figure out an angle,' Hillary snapped impatiently.

'Yeah, I thought so. I couldn't see the face all that clearly like, but he looked to me like Mike Ivers.'

Hillary nodded. 'He work at the newspaper-delivery place?'

'Yeah. Second-in-command. Well, really, he runs the whole show, but an older geezer actually owns it and he likes to show up unannounced every now and then to make sure that none of them are slacking off. You know the type.'

Hillary did. 'So, Frank, you're a trained observer. You haven't been a cop for twenty years without noticing things. What did you notice about Ivers – when he was alive and kicking, that is?'

For the first time Hillary felt genuinely curious. Provided Ross had nothing to hide or gain by Ivers's death, she could probably rely on him for a relatively accurate portrait of their vic.

Ross snorted. 'Thought of himself as a right Lothario. Liked to dress smart, and play the big man, know the sort? The kind who could brag about getting you in at a ritzy casino in London. Knew someone who owned a yacht in Cannes. But for all that, he was a petty-minded bastard. Nobody liked him, I can tell you that much.'

Hillary nodded. 'His job pay well?'

'Yeah, but not *that* well. He had a rep as a successful gambler. I'm not sure I entirely believed it.' Frank grunted. Other people's good fortune always made him feel sour. 'Mind, he seemed to live above and beyond, know what I mean? 'Course,

44

he could have had something going on the side, but nothing that he was running out of here. I'd have noticed.'

Now *that* Hillary had no trouble in believing. Frank Ross had a nose for criminal profit. He'd helped her bent husband amass a fortune from an illegal animal-parts smuggling operation, after all.

'Drugs?' she asked. It was the most obvious route to explain somebody who had more money than they earned.

'Maybe. But on the other hand, the gambling thing might just be true. He was a jammy bastard, I'll give him that. You know, he always seemed to get all the luck.'

Hillary laughed drily. 'He didn't look all that lucky the last time I saw him,' she pointed out.

Frank smiled and shrugged. 'You gotta know when to fold 'em …'

'If you start singing Kenny Rogers songs,' Hillary warned darkly. 'I'll get the armed response unit out here to shoot you. So, what else about Ivers?'

Frank's eyes gleamed briefly, and Hillary forced herself not to react. There was something juicy to be had here, she could just feel it.

Frank shrugged again. 'How should I know? I'm just the night watchman here. I only got to say hello and goodbye to the bloke a few times.'

'Come on, Frank,' she encouraged. 'A small place like this has got to be a hotbed of gossip. Spill it.'

Frank thought about it, then realized that the more meaty a bone he could throw her, the less likely she was to concern herself with his doings. 'Well, like I said, he fancied himself as a James Bond character, right? The flash suits, sports car, a woman on each arm and a spare in the cupboard?'

'He married?'

'Was. Getting divorced, or is divorced, or separated or what have you.'

'And this is relevant … how?'

Frank snorted. 'This is getting to be just like the old days. You always did expect me to do your job for you. And did I ever get the credit for it?'

Hillary, who knew for a fact that Ross had spent over fifty per cent of his working days at Thames Valley in the local pub, blinked and bit her tongue.

'Frank.'

'All right, all right. Apparently, he and Twinkletoes's wife had a bit of a ding-dong not long ago. Right hot and steamy it was.'

'Twinkletoes?' Hillary said, then glanced at Hermes' Wings. 'Oh right. The shoe-shop man. Welles, Harry Welles?'

'That's right. If you want to speak to someone who had reason to want Ivers dead, you need look no further. And now, I'm off to get some kip. You don't like it, arrest me.'

'Don't tempt me, Frank,' Hillary said softly, a hint of real yearning in her voice. 'Don't tempt me.'

Ross hastily slammed his cubicle door shut and mouthed something anatomically impossible at her.

Back at HQ Superintendent Brian Vane sat in his office, a pile of paperwork in front of him. He was due to go to Hull next week and looked to be the picture of a busy upper-level management police officer painstakingly clearing his desk.

He was, in fact, diligently searching through Janine Mallow's files. More specifically, her list of paid informants.

Before marrying the late Superintendent Phillip 'Mellow' Mallow and leaving Kidlington HQ for Witney, Janine Tyler had been Hillary Greene's sergeant. Like all sergeants, she'd assiduously built up an impressive list of stool pigeons, which ranged from respectable people working in banks and the IT industry, to skells who'd sell out their grandmother for a snort of anything white in powder form.

He'd managed to get hold of Janine Tyler's old listings without anyone knowing about it, but it was hard going. Not surprisingly, she'd been very protective of her informants – all cops were – and none of them was listed by his or her proper name. Most were referred to by codewords only.

Some he'd managed to track down and decipher – Ma Belle, for instance, was a woman who worked at BT, and could be relied upon to pass on any criminal-sounding things she overheard to her old school-friend Janine. For a fee, of course.

Others were professional criminals who had nick-names that were easy to guess from their *modus operandi*. One skell Janine had listed as Burke, and a trawl of her past collars had unearthed one she'd lifted for grave-robbing, back when she'd been in uniform. This charming individual liked to dig up bodies after a recent funeral and relieve them of wedding rings, jewellery, even their suit, if it was a good quality and would fit him. No doubt, if he'd had a partner, Janine would have named him Hare.

But some of the codewords frustrated him.

However, he'd been working on this for some weeks now, and he was narrowing it down. What he really needed was someone who had access to street shooters; someone who'd been out of prison during the right time-frame – around the time of the Clive Myers shooting – and someone over whom Janine Mallow had a strong enough hold to be sure that he would keep his mouth shut.

With criteria like that, it would be only a matter of time before Vane tracked him down. And when he did, Hillary could kiss her nice, cosy, honourable withdrawal from the police force a sad goodbye.

When Janine Mallow had shot and killed the man who had murdered her husband there had been found along with Clive Myers' rifle and knives, a handgun. Myers, who was ex-army, had not surprisingly opted for army equipment when he went on his revenge killing spree, but the handgun was a piece of East European crap, a weapon that a man like Myers wouldn't have been caught dead using.

In a manner of speaking.

Which lead Vane to be almost positive that the gun had been brought to the scene by Janine Mallow herself, who'd then used it to kill Myers and pull her phoney 'self-defence' plea.

All he had to do was link the gun to Mallow and he'd have her. And if he had her, he had Hillary Greene too. There was no doubt in his mind that Hillary had covered up for her one-time sergeant out of friendship for the dead Phillip Mallow. He could bring both of them down – Janine for murder one, and Greene for aiding and abetting after the fact, thus heaping embarrassment on the heads of those who were exiling him to Hull and flushing his once-promising career down the toilet.

With a sigh, he pulled the next file to him and opened it up. It was code named 'Winklepicker.'

Vane groaned, and started to trawl the files for anyone Mallow could have arrested or known who might have earned such a name.

Gemma looked up from her notebook as Hillary walked into the tiny canteen. It was nearly eleven o'clock now, and the room would soon be filling up with hungry employees. At the moment it contained only her sergeant, and someone who was shovelling oven chips into a large industrial cooker behind the self-service counter. She was a large, middle-aged woman, who kept looking at them keenly.

By now all the workers at the business park must be holed up in their respective offices, eagerly discussing the latest sensation. They probably all knew the murdered man, at least superficially, and would all have their own theories as to whodunnit and why. There was a whole team of uniformed constables doing the rounds and questioning them, and she could only hope that one or two might come up with a snippet of information that would prove positively useful.

Gemma, by now, would have talked to all the employees at the depot. Hillary wanted her preliminary report first.

She joined Gemma at a small, square table topped with yellow formica. It had been wiped clean, Hillary was glad to note, as she sat down on a folding wooden chair.

'So what did Ross have to say?' Gemma asked, agog with curiosity. Like everyone else at HQ, she'd been glad to see the last of the layabout Ross. 'Think he's involved?'

Now there was a thought, Hillary mused with a knowing grin. Although she didn't think that Ross was the killer, or necessarily had even had anything at all to do with Ivers's murder, there was no way she could be sure. Which meant that she could use it as a conflict of interest argument. All she had to do was go back to Danvers, tell him that her ex-sergeant was on the suspect list, and use it as an excuse to get pulled off the case. Under the circumstances, Danvers could hardly refuse.

The trouble was – damn him and Donleavy both – she was now reluctant to give up the chase. She was already hooked.

'I doubt it,' she said at last, realizing that Gemma was still patiently waiting for an answer. 'No doubt he's been up to something, though,' she added darkly. 'He wouldn't be Frank and not have some scheme on the go.'

'What – bit of petty larceny? Goods going missing and getting sold off the back of a lorry in Liverpool?' Gemma suggested with a wry twist of her lips.

'Something along those lines,' Hillary agreed. 'He told me Ivers was something of a Jack the lad. Liked to live it high – wine, women and song, with gambling thrown in.'

Gemma was already nodding. 'Yeah, that fits in with what I'm getting around here,' Gemma waved a hand around to encompass the building. 'The men didn't like him much – envy, I reckon. Some of the women liked him only too well, although some were sour. Probably the ones he didn't fancy and didn't flirt with. Though he seemed to chase anything in a skirt, more or less as a reflex action, so far as I can tell.' Gemma snorted.

'What's your take on him? Was he actively disliked, or was he a charmer with it?' Hillary asked curiously.

Gemma sighed. 'Hard to tell, guv. I've been running up against the whole "don't-like-to-talk-ill-of-the-dead" kind of thing. But there's a nasty undercurrent running around somewhere here. I can't quite pin it down yet. But I will. I get the feeling the vic was pretty much loathed, though.'

Hillary nodded. 'OK. Keep on it. According to Frank, Ivers had a hot and heavy affair with the wife of our Mr Harry Welles.'

Gemma whistled between her teeth. 'He wasn't scared to foul his own nest then, was he?' she observed. 'No wonder he got himself topped.'

Hillary shot her a sharp glance, and Gemma held out her hands in appeasement. 'Sorry, sorry,' she muttered.

'Do I really need to remind you we're here to represent the victim, DS Fordham? I don't care if Michael Ivers was the most despicable human being on the planet. Someone murdered him, and I want that someone caught.'

She heard herself sounding like a trailer for some bad American cop thriller and grimaced. 'Oh hell. You know what I mean,' she finished, a shade shamefaced.

Gemma did. 'You're already feeling the pressure to get the case solved before you go,' Gemma said softly. 'I know how you feel. I want it solved before the wedding too. Otherwise I'll be going over and over it while I'm on my damned honeymoon,' she concluded glumly.

Hillary couldn't help but laugh.

Ten minutes later and back outside, she noticed with some relief that a new man was in the booth as she passed. He nodded to her politely as she walked past him on the way to Hermes' Wings.

She stood at the entrance to the large shoe warehouse and contemplated the name. Hermes was the winged messenger of the ancient Greek gods, and was usually depicted in classical art with a pair of nifty little wings on his sandals. Mercury, his Roman counterpart, was depicted in the same way. Also, Hermes had a ready-made image in most people's minds, because they always thought of high fashion and the expensive scarves.

So at least Harry Welles had shown some imagination in naming his business. Unless, of course, he'd had some PR company do it for him. But she doubted he'd have gone to that expense. Or maybe his wife had chosen the name? If so, did that mean that they had been close, once? Had she been an active member of the business, for instance?

'Enough speculating,' she muttered to herself, and went inside. She immediately became the centre of attention to the two women seated in a small office space. Something in their sudden and profound silence told her that she'd just interrupted them in the middle of an animated discussion.

She reached for her ID and introduced herself. 'Detective Inspector Hillary Greene. I'm the senior investigating officer for the incident over at the newspaper depot.'

The two women shot each other a knowing look, and instantly Hillary realized that the affair between the murder victim and the boss's wife was hardly a secret.

'Oh yes.' The one on the left, a tall brunette with unfortunate buck teeth, smiled briefly. 'I've just finished photocopying a logbook for that handsome young constable. But he's just left.'

'Not a problem. I'd like to speak to Mr Welles, please.'

The other woman, a bottle-blonde, made a little squeaking noise and looked terrified. She looked as if she was expecting Hillary to take her boss away in cuffs at any moment, leaving her jobless and destitute.

'Er, I'll just make sure he's in,' the brunette said, in a valiant effort at secretarial efficiency. Hillary decided to let her get away with it, and waited patiently whilst she disappeared behind a door.

The whole office had a plywood look about it, and a curiously echoing acoustic. It took her a moment to realize that the whole building was probably just one massive space for the storage of shoe-boxes, and that the office was constructed as a mere box within a box, to house the limited admin needs. This guess was vindicated when she was shown into Harry Welles's office, and she saw through an open door in the rear wall a vast cavernous space, where fork-lift trucks were busily at work stacking vast columns of boxes.

Imelda Marcos would have thought she was in heaven inside there, Hillary mused wryly.

Harry Welles shut the door, and turned to her with a brief smile. For just one moment she had the strange feeling that Welles had been tempted to run out to the back and hide amongst his thousands of shoes. If so, he'd obviously changed his mind, for he was now smiling at her amiably, if a little nervously.

'Mr Welles. Thank you for the use of your secretary and the photocopier. I'm afraid I need to ask you a few more questions however. We've now identified the victim as a Mr Michael Ivers. He worked as the manager at the newspaper depot.'

'Under-manager,' Harry Welles heard himself correct pedantically, then he flushed.

So, Hillary thought, interested. The antagonism he felt towards his wife's lover was so deep-seated that he couldn't let even the littlest of things pass.

'Ah yes. Under-manager,' Hillary agreed, pulling out a chair in front of his office desk and sitting down, without being asked. She didn't think Welles's neglect in not offering her a seat had been designed as a power play. He simply had other things on his mind.

With a start, he took his own seat behind the desk and began to fiddle with the laptop on it.

No wonder Gemma had picked up on his nervous vibes. Had he already known that Mike Ivers was lying dead outside his office?

'We're treating this as a murder case, Mr Welles,' Hillary said calmly, and saw Welles swallow hard.

'Oh.'

Hillary crossed her legs and fished out her notebook from her briefcase. She pretended to consult her notes. 'From our preliminary interviews, it seems that Mr Ivers was something of a character.'

Harry Welles gulped again. 'Er, yes,' he concurred unhappily.

'A bit of a gambler, it seems. Liked to dress well, take high-class holidays, drive a flashy car. A bit of a ladies' man, too,' Hillary added, letting the concluding words drop into the silence like pebbles into a pond.

Harry Welles nodded, his eyes fixed to hers like those of a rabbit hypnotized by car headlights.

'It's been suggested that your wife was one of his conquests, Mr Welles,' she said quietly. She had no desire to be cruel, but right now this man had to be a prime suspect and she couldn't muck about.

'Er, yes,' Harry Welles mumbled. 'My wife, Honor, and I … well, all's not been as it should be in our marriage for quite some time now. We've been married a long time, you see, and … well, I suppose boredom sets in.'

'On your part as well sir?' she asked curiously, and he blinked at her blankly.

'What?'

'Do you indulge in the occasional affair as well?'

He gulped again. 'Er … well, I'm not …' He trailed off and shrugged.

'So you knew about the affair with Mr Ivers?' Hillary asked, letting it pass for the moment. In her notebook, however, she made a memo to get Chang to find out whether Welles also played away from home.

'Yes. Well, I sort of guessed, and she didn't deny it. They met at the Christmas party. Good grief, isn't that a cliché? I feel quite embarrassed to say it.'

Hillary nodded gently. 'Was it still going on?'

'Oh no. I think it fizzled out after a few months. Well, Michael isn't the kind to … you know, he likes variety. He has a younger woman now, I think,' he added, with satisfaction.

And I bet you enjoyed rubbing Honor's nose in that, Hillary thought, but didn't say. It was interesting too, that he used the present tense, Hillary thought. Had he really not fully realized that Ivers was gone?

'I imagine you didn't like Mr Ivers, sir,' Hillary said mildly.

Harry Welles blinked and gulped. 'Er, well, no. Not really.'

'Did you kill him?'

'Ay? No! No, of course I didn't kill him. What sort of man do you think I am?' Harry Welles squeaked.

Hillary smiled patiently. 'I don't know what sort of man you are, sir,' she pointed out reasonably. 'We've only just met.'

Harry gaped at her, then gulped again, then nodded. He was sweating visibly. 'Well, I'm a civilized man, Detective Inspector Greene,' he managed at last. 'Ask anybody who knows me.'

*Oh, we will,* Hillary thought, vaguely amused.

'Can you tell me what you were doing last night, sir? Begin with when you left your office here. What time would that be? And did you see Mr Ivers to speak to?'

'I'm sure it must on the log the man in the booth keeps,' Harry Welles said. 'I think it was some time around 5.30. And no – I hadn't seen Ivers for some time. I went out of my way to avoid him, truth be told.'

Hillary nodded. Frank Ross had come on at eight, or so he said. So the chances were it had been Billy, the day man, who logged Welles in *and* out. Which was a bonus. Unless, of course, he was as unreliable as Frank Ross.

Which was hard to believe.

'We'll check it, sir. Did you drive straight home?'

'Er, no. I called in at the Duck and Anchor for a drink. Near the Banbury marina.'

Hillary nodded. The Oxford Canal ran through Banbury, and

the area around it had recently been given a massive and expensive face lift. It was now all trendy bars, a museum and a new shopping mall. She'd send Chang around to check and see if anybody remembered Welles being in there.

'And how long were you in the pub, sir?' she asked, then noted down the times in her book. 'So you got home about eight?' she clarified.

'Yes. Somewhere around there.'

'And your wife was in?'

'Yes. I ordered Chinese from a little place I like. We watched some television and then went to bed around eleven or so.'

Hillary nodded. As an alibi it was hardly watertight. Even if he was remembered at the pub, nobody would have been watching him constantly. He could have slipped out, bumped off Ivers and returned to the pub. He could have waited until Billy, the man who'd have been in the booth at the time, was doing his rounds and then slipped in. According to Gemma, all the unit-holders had access keys to the main gate.

Alternatively, he could have slipped out once he'd got home. He might have reason to believe his wife would lie for him and say he was at home with her all night. Until she'd had a chance to judge for herself how things were between the Welleses anything was possible.

Then again, people with watertight alibis always aroused her suspicions anyway. 'All right sir. That's all for now. No doubt we'll be speaking to you again. You have no plans to go on holiday anytime soon, I take it?' she asked, and although she smiled pleasantly as she said it, she heard Harry Welles gulp again.

'Oh no. Not until June. We're going to the Scilly Isles,' Harry heard himself say. Then he flushed. As if she'd be interested in that.

Hillary nodded, aware of his colour change, smiled pleasantly again, and left him to his little plywood office.

A socially awkward man, without doubt. Nervous by nature,

almost certainly. But even the most timid and inept of people could kill.

She would be very interested to see what the unfaithful Honor Welles had to say about it all.

CHAPTER FOUR

Hillary dialled the Welleses' home phone number after asking one of the agog secretarys for it, but there was no answer. Hillary sighed and hung up. There was no good reason, of course, for the unfaithful Honor Welles to be waiting at home just for her phone call, but it irritated her nonetheless, and she walked back to her car, holding her mobile phone thoughtfully.

Mark Chang found her outside the entrance to Unit 1, and handed her his photocopy of the security logbook.

She thanked him and told him to start work setting up the murder book; she could only hope that he was ready for the responsibility. 'And from now on, it's going to be up to you to keep it updated,' she warned him firmly.

Whenever she ran an inquiry she insisted that everybody logged everything they'd done and discovered into one folder, in order that any one of them could consult it and get the latest news, and an overall view of how the case was going. It was a vitally important task, and she saw Chang hastily hide a happy smile as he walked away, lightness in his step, pleased to have earned her trust at last.

Hillary watched him go with a small sigh. Soon he would be transferred to someone else's team, and she wanted him to have at least a good founding in the basics. But she'd have Gemma keep an eye on the book too – just in case.

Hillary flipped through the logbook slowly, getting a feel for the business park's coming and goings. Most of it was totally irrelevant, of course, but it helped her build up a mental image of the place, and start to get a feel for the workforce. Margery Dawson, for instance, the owner of the garden-supplies company Greensleeves regularly checked out at fortnightly intervals at two o'clock on a Tuesday afternoon. Probably a standing hairdresser's appointment, Hillary mused.

As Frank had said, several of the more senior men left at one o'clock and were gone for the entire afternoon – probably off to the golf club.

One or two, mostly middle-management types, were extremely diligent, always or nearly always clocking in before nine, and leaving after six. Chasing promotion, no doubt. But the victim, she noticed, wasn't one of them. He seemed to arrive more or less at or around nine, and leave at or around five.

Except for last night.

Yesterday evening Michael Ivers hadn't checked out at all. Well, not out of the Aynho Islip Business Park at any rate. He'd certainly well and truly checked out in other ways.

For a moment she was surprised that the incoming night watchman hadn't noticed and checked on this circumstance when it got so late. Then she remembered, with a mental head-slap, that the night watchman in question had been Frank Ross. And he almost certainly wouldn't have even checked over the day man's reports. Or cared a toss about what Ivers had been up to if he had.

OK. She ran through the list of unit-owners, and all their members of staff, trying to keep track of them, but soon got cross-eyed. Once she could have done this sort of exercise in her head. But she was getting old. Time she was put out to pasture.

She reached for her mobile and rang Gemma's number.

'Where are you?' she asked crisply.

'Unit six, guv. Talking to some of the mechanics. Apparently, the vic gets his car serviced here – a nice little Aston Martin, no less. One of the grease monkeys does him a real good deal on the costs. My guess is, he just wants to get his hands on a classic car to have the kudos of saying it was the kind of thing he works on to his girlfriend.'

Hillary smiled. 'You're probably right. Look, I've got the security logbook here. Grab a bright-looking uniform and get him to come and pick it up for me will you? I'm at the car. I want you to check off the leaving times for every member of the park.'

Gemma groaned.

'I know, but it has to be done. And do me a time-line, would you, starting with the first one to leave, and ending with the last. Our vic was never signed out at all. Then get the uniforms to give you their interview notes – see if any of them remember seeing Ivers, and at what time. Oh, and while you're at it, ask the uniform to bring me your prelim report.'

She relied on Gemma to gather all the immediate and relevant facts as quickly as possible, and set them out in some sort of order. It was something she was very good at.

'Right guv. And where will you be if I need you?'

'Informing the next of kin,' Hillary said flatly. 'Wanna come?'

'Hell no,' Gemma snorted, and rung off.

Hillary smiled grimly. She didn't blame her sergeant for giving it a miss. Breaking bad news to grieving families was a duty that everyone hated. Which was why she mostly reserved it for herself.

In this case, the next of kin seemed to be the ex-wife. Ivers, according to what she'd be able to glean so far, had no living parents or siblings. She looked back through her notebook, and tapped the relevant page, just to remind herself of the details.

Madeleine Ivers, divorced for two years, with just the one child – a son. She had an address in Bodicote – which was barely a stone's throw away. The proximity of it made Hillary wonder.

Just then, a uniform trotted up and gave her Gemma's summary. Hillary handed over the logbook, repeating exactly what she wanted done with it.

Bodicote had probably at one time been a pretty little village, miles away from the centre of the sprawling medieval market town of Banbury. But now the town's suburbs had spread, incorporating the village like a greedy sponge soaking up the gravy.

She found the house right on the outskirts, overlooking a field where some sheep grazed on a sloping hillside. As she climbed out of her car Hillary noticed a gleam of water somewhere below, and wondered what the name of the river was. Could it be the Cherwell, this far north?

She shrugged and walked along the pavement, checking out the neat, small houses. Several were bungalows that had had their lofts converted and now sprouted windows like eyebrows, reminding her of surprised old maids caught showing their ankles. Some were old stone cottages. Most were late 1940s houses, built in the housing boom just after the war. There were many weeping flowering-cherry trees and neat gardens, playing host to the last of the dying daffodils and bright tulips.

A just barely affluent area, she'd have said. Whatever Ivers had spent his money on, it hadn't been on a posh residence. Unless of course, he'd kept a more substantial house in the divorce, forcing Madeleine out into the more mediocre suburbia. But somehow she doubted it. She was beginning to get a feel for their vic, and she was sure he'd have had 'better' things to spend his money on than providing a big home for his wife and kid.

She hadn't been to Ivers's own place yet, and had in fact assigned Gemma to go over it once she was finished back at the office, but she'd have bet anything that the dead man had moved into some swanky bachelor pad, maybe one of those overlooking Banbury marina. It was the sort of thing he'd have told himself he deserved.

Meanwhile the ex and son lived on here.

Number 22 was another converted bungalow with a neatly mown tiny lawn and uninspired but carefully planted shrubs in big tubs. What estate agents liked to call a low-maintenance garden.

She rang the bell and waited, fully prepared for it to remain unanswered. After all, she had not rung ahead and, like Honor Welles, there was no reason for Mrs Ivers to be at home.

Then the door was suddenly thrown open, to reveal a belligerent teenager. He looked to be about sixteen or seventeen, Hillary guessed, and had the usual problem of blackheads that clashed with his nose ring. His pale blond hair was so spiked up with gel it was made to look almost nondescript brown. He was wearing jeans so loose they were almost falling off his hips, a T-shirt that had been washed so many times that the legend written across it was illegible, and he had bare feet. His toenails were disgusting. He was chewing a piece of toast and marmalade with enough vigour to make Hillary's jaw ache in sympathy. Since it was nearer to noon than breakfast, Hillary assumed the kid, for some reason, was not at school and had only just got up.

'Yeah?'

He had small brown eyes that looked at her with growing interest, and his eyes lingered on her breasts beneath her jacket.

Hillary sighed. 'Mr Ivers?' She searched her memory for his name, and snagged it. 'Benjamin Ivers?'

'Ben,' he corrected instantly.

'Is your mother home?'

'Yeah.'

He made no move to step away from the door, and continued munching on his toast.

'I need to speak to her. And to you also. May I come in?' She held out her police ID, and he stopped chewing long enough to read it. It was as if he couldn't chew and read at the same time, and he put her in mind of a dim-witted billy-goat chewing the cud. Then she reminded herself that she was here to tell this lad that he'd lost his father, and gave herself a mental kick up the backside for being so damned insouciant.

'Cops? What for? We ain't done nothing.'

Hillary, an English Literature graduate, fought the instinct to tell him that he'd just spoken a double negative, which meant that he had indeed done *something*, and gave herself another mental ticking-off.

'If I might just come in?' she asked, with forced patience. 'I'm sure your mother wouldn't want to discuss private business out here on the doorstep.'

He shrugged and stood aside, and Hillary moved past him into a narrow hallway. Hearing sounds from the left, she pushed through and found herself in a kitchen. A radio was playing Radio Two, and by the sink a woman was washing up what looked like breakfast dishes.

Even from behind and stooped over the sink she looked tall and painfully thin, and when Hillary cleared her throat she looked over her shoulder, revealing brown eyes to go with her brown hair.

'I'm Detective Inspector Greene, Mrs Ivers. I just need a quiet word.'

'Oh, hello,' said Mrs Ives, somewhat blankly, her eyes going over her shoulder to where her son stood behind Hillary, her eyes asking the obvious question.

'Nothing to do with me,' Hillary heard him say defensively. Too defensively. It set her radar twanging. Unless she missed her guess, this wasn't the first time this woman had had the police come calling on her doorstep. And it didn't take Hillary long to guess the reason. As soon as she got out of here, she'd have Chang run both mother and son through the police database. She was sure that Benjamin Ivers, for one, would have some kind of form. Almost certainly petty, juvenile form. But you never knew.

'I'm afraid I have bad news, Mrs Ivers,' Hillary began cautiously. 'Perhaps you'd like to come and sit down?'

The kitchen was small, but it had room for a tiny table and two chairs, pushed up against the far wall. The lanky teenager leaned against the doorjamb and finished off his toast. His mother rinsed off her soapy hands and wiped them nervously on a towel.

She was dressed in a turquoise jogging suit, but for some reason Hillary felt that the woman had never jogged in her life. The suit was probably just cheap and comfortable.

As if in confirmation, Madeleine Ivers reached into the pocket of the jacket as she approached and brought out a packet of fags and a cheap lighter. As she sat down she reached behind her and brought a large ashtray, full of fag ends, and placed it on the table between them.

Hillary's nose twitched, but she said nothing. This wasn't her house, and it wasn't her lungs.

She waited until the other woman had her cigarette alight, and had taken a hefty drag. She was probably around forty or so, but she had the lined, tired face of a woman much older. Hillary would have bet almost any amount that their vic had traded her in for a younger model at the sight of the first wrinkle around her eyes.

'It's about your ex-husband, Michael,' she said, watching the woman closely. 'I'm afraid he was found dead at the business park where he worked, early this morning.'

'Good.' The word came from just to her right, and Hillary flicked her eyes at the teenager.

'Benji,' Madeleine said, but without much heat.

'Well, it *is* good, isn't it?' he asked sulkily.

Madeleine flushed as she caught Hillary's eye, as if the policewoman had spoken some criticism out loud.

'Sorry. But it's not as if Mike was his father or anything,' she said, by way of apology, making Hillary sit up and really take notice.

'Not his father?' she asked, checking her notes. She wished now that she'd taken the time to read Gemma's notes as well before coming here. She'd bet her extremely competent sergeant had more detailed knowledge on the vic's home life.

But how could she have got it wrong? Or was Madeleine Ivers confessing to having an affair. And if so, had the victim known he wasn't the boy's natural parent?

'I was married before, see,' Madeleine Ivers said, dragging on the cigarette and quickly bringing Hillary's surmises to a quick halt. 'But Bernie died when I was just twenty-three. Benji was barely out of nappies. Bernie had his own business repairing tellies and radios, washing machines and whatnot. Had his own van and everything, and we'd just taken out a mortgage on this nice little place in Cropredy. You know, where they have the music festival? That's where Bernie was brought up. But when he died, well, things got bad. I couldn't afford the payments on the house, and I lost it, and had to get a job, waitressing like. It crippled me, it did, having to pay Benji's nursery fees and whatnot. Then I met Mike. He was like a breath of fresh air. Like someone out of the films, he was. So good-looking and clever and everything.'

Her voice became wistful.

Hillary nodded. 'I see,' she said. And did. Madeleine had obviously been brought up in a working-class environment, and if she'd thought Bernie, with his own van, had been something of a catch, no wonder a seasoned Casanova like Ivers had found her such easy pickings.

'Tosser,' Benjamin snorted.

Hillary glanced at him, then said softly, 'So you're name isn't Ivers?'

He mimed gagging. 'No way! I'm Ben Hardwicke.'

'He and Mikey never seemed to get on,' Madeleine Ivers explained helplessly, and rather unnecessarily. 'At first, Mikey tried to be a good father to him, but it never really gelled.'

'Tosser!' growled the boy from his doorjamb. It seemed to Hillary that either it was the only word in his vocabulary, or he deliberately used it in front of his mum instead of using something even worse. 'Tried to teach me tennis when I was six, so he could impress his friends at the bloody country club.' Ben snorted. 'But I wanted to play footie with my mates down at the sports centre, didn't I? Then he promised me he'd give me driving lessons when I was sixteen, but the sod had gone off by then with a chick my age.'

'Benji, he didn't. She was in her twenties.'

'Tosser. He left us high and dry, didn't he?'

'We got the house. And the car.'

'A crappy Mini. Right. I saw him down town the other day, driving this swanky … Well, anyway he was a tosser.'

Hillary, by now, had the idea. Michael Ivers was a tosser.

'You've been divorced for two years now?' Hillary got the interview back on to a more formal footing.

'Must be that, yeah,' Madeleine agreed, stubbing out her cigarette and immediately lighting another one. 'We were separated for some time before then, though. He helped me get a job at Nash's. You know, the bakery shop, serving in the café there. He knew the manageress and put a good word in for me.'

'Shagging her more like,' Ben put in. And added the inevitable 'Tosser.'

'Ben! It was nice of him to care. Most men, they get divorced, and pretend you don't exist. It was good of him to help me get a job.'

Ben snorted, then turned to Hillary. 'So, why are you here then,' he surprised her by asking suddenly. 'You're a full DI, right? Was it an industrial accident?' he suddenly asked brightly. 'Is Mum gonna get some compensation. Insurance, like?'

'No,' Hillary said flatly. 'We're treating your stepfather's death as a murder case.'

Madeleine choked on her cigarette. The boy blinked, looked surprised, then confused for a moment, then gave a long, slow grin. 'Really? Cool. Wait'll I tell Barry! Shit, I gotta log on to Face book.'

Before Hillary could stop him, he spun round and disappeared. A few seconds later they heard him galumphing noisily up the stairs.

Madeleine blinked a few times, her eyes brightening with unshed tears, and shakily continued smoking her cigarette.

'When was the last time your saw your ex, Mrs Ivers?'

'Oh, ages ago. Probably around Christmas time. He dropped in for a drink. Gave me a bottle of perfume. Nice stuff – Yardley.'

Hillary nodded. 'So your divorce was amicable?'

'What?' Madeline asked, puzzled.

'You parted as friends?'

'Well. Yeah. I suppose,' she said doubtfully, her voice hardening. She stubbed out her cigarette with sudden anger, and sighed. 'Well, I wasn't best pleased, obviously,' she added. 'And I'm not really all that sorry he's dead, truth to tell. It's just … a bit of a shock, innit? You don't think someone you know is going to get murdered, do you? But he wasn't never what you could call a good husband.'

'Your son's right then,' Hillary said softly. 'He *was* a bit of a tosser?'

Madeleine smiled tremulously. 'Yeah, I suppose he was.'

'Have you ever been to Adderbury, to the business park where he worked, Mrs Ivers?' Hillary asked quietly. She hadn't seen her name listed in the logbook, and she'd flipped through it all the way to the end of last month. But it didn't hurt to check. 'It's not that far away,' she pointed out.

'Oh no,' Madeleine denied it at once. 'No reason to, had I?'

'And can you tell me where you were last night? From, say, five o'clock onwards?'

'Well, I left work at six – we stay open till then, 'cause lots of people pop in for some bread or sausage rolls or whatever on the way home from work. I got here about quarter past – I take the bus, it's easier and cheaper than parking the car somewhere. Ben was in,' she said, with careful emphasis, which Hillary didn't miss, 'and I made us some dinner. Ham and eggs and chips – Ben's favourite. Then we watched telly – *Eastenders*, and Ben watched the football match. I mostly dozed, really. I'm not into sport. Then we went to bed when it was over – about half-ten I suppose it must have been.'

Madeleine Ivers's chin came up just a little as she ended this recital. She met Hillary's gaze with unblinking eyes of her own.

She's lying, Hillary thought at once. Whilst she was prepared to believe that most of it was true - the part about coming home from work, putting together a makeshift dinner and watching the soap, she doubted that her teenage tearaway son had been anywhere in residence.

Of course, that could just mean that he was getting up to his usual brand of mischief elsewhere. But who could say?

Ben Hardwicke had certainly hated his stepfather. Maybe he blamed him for his mother's crappy life, and resented living in the respectable little bungalow while his stepfather drove an Aston Martin and boasted about his gambling and his women. It was, after all, exactly the sort of lifestyle that a teenage boy dreamt about. Had he resented Michael Ivers so much he'd taken a two-by-four to his head?

'Well, that's all for now, Mrs Ivers,' Hillary said quietly. 'Do you know who Michael's closest blood relative is? We need to arrange a formal ID, and there will be funeral arrangements and such. Unless you…?'

'Oh no. He's got an uncle, lives in Cassington. I still send them a Christmas card. Just a sec, I'll get you the address.' She went to the drawer furthest from the sink, rummaged around, and then came back with a tiny blue address book. Hillary made a note of the name, address and phone number, thanked her and left.

Outside, she sat in the car, supplementing her notes, and making memos to herself. Then she read Gemma's notes. As ever, it was an impressive précis, giving her a much more complete biog of the vic, and a more detailed overview of how the business park was run.

What she needed to do was to get back to the office and start making up a list of all the things she wanted done.

Priority one was to confirm her hunch that young Ben Hardwicke had form – and exactly what kind of form. If he was known to be light-fingered, for instance, perhaps he and what-ever gang of misfits he ran with had decided to do a bit of thieving from his stepfather's workplace. It was probably the kind of thing that would appeal to him. Nick the computers from the office, trash the place, make the old man furious. And perhaps Ivers had caught him at it. A desperate, angry young teenager might have taken a swing at him, not meaning to kill, but not knowing his own strength.

If their victim had been felled by only one blow, that was. For all she knew at this point, Michael Ivers could have been hit over the head several times. It was a sobering thought, and she warned herself not to get too far ahead of herself.

She leaned back in the seat, trying to stretch. Her stomach rumbled, and she decided to go and have some lunch.

And she knew just where to find it.

The Nash's bakery shop where Madeleine Ivers worked did indeed sell some delicious sausage rolls, and Hillary brought one as she chatted to the senior serving woman behind the counter.

It was too early for the shop to be very busy, and the woman was more than happy to confirm that Madeleine had worked up until six last evening. She'd even seen her heading towards the bus stop as she locked up behind her.

Hillary took her lunch back to Adderbury and sat in her car eating, watching the activity all around her. Of course, today the police were out in force, but even without their presence she could tell it was a fairly busy place.

And yet somebody had killed Michael Ivers here without being spotted. So did that mean that he or she must have waited until it was dark? Or at least dusk? That made good psychological sense, she knew, but she'd have to be careful not to get dogmatic about it. Killers might prefer the cover of darkness, but if Ivers's killing had been a spur of the moment thing, and done in a blind rage to boot, then whoever hit him over the head could have done so in full daylight and not cared one whit about being seen.

Once she knew whether all the people who worked at the park had been checked out last night, she'd have a better idea of whether it was an inside job, or if someone had come to the park from outside. But surely, if it had been someone from the business park, they'd make sure they checked out with the man in the booth. Otherwise they might just as well tattoo a big 'X' on their forehead to make them stand out even more.

Of course, there was nothing to stop someone from checking out, then sneaking back in later. Hillary sighed heavily.

A lot of it would depend on time of death, too. If Steven Partridge could confidently put it at around 2 a.m. for instance, where would that leave them?

With Frank Ross well and truly in the middle of the picture, that's where. Hillary sighed even more heavily and forced her thought-processes onwards.

The plank of wood. That surely put paid to any thought that the killing had been anything other than premeditated. I mean, you just didn't carry a plank of wood around with you, did you? On the other hand, she chewed her sausage roll thoughtfully, if you came to kill someone, wouldn't you provide yourself with a weapon? A knife or a gun if you could get one? No, the piece of wood suggested a course of action halfway between cold-blooded, premeditated murder, and a spur-of-the-moment killing. Someone came here, saw the wood and picked it up, meaning to do some damage with it.

Unless the killer had taken it for self-defence. Now there was a thought. Suppose the killer had had reason to suspect that Ivers himself might be a threat?

Of course, it hadn't even yet been established that the piece of wood used to kill Ivers had been picked up by the killer from amongst the jumble of debris that hung around the builder's yard. But Hillary didn't think it likely that the killer had brought it with him either. With luck, forensics would be able to match the type of wood with a batch in the yard. And at least one of her questions would be answered.

OK. She wound down the window of her car and leaned back in her seat to digest her lunch and think some more.

The killer arrives at the yard. He or she has some kind of bone to pick with Ivers. The first obstacle the killer has to negotiate is the security – in this case, the man in the booth. According to Gemma's notes, the park isn't locked up until eight, when the night watchman comes in – this Gemma had already established from Billy, the daytime security guard.

So had the killer done some reconnaissance? Did he/she know this? She made a mental note to ask Billy and – so help her – Frank, whether they'd noticed anyone who might have been taking note of the park's routines.

OK. So for the sake of argument, the killer knows when the main gate will be locked, and somehow dodges whoever is on duty in the booth. No signing in or out. Under the radar. What's the next move? Go to Unit 1, obviously. On foot, surely? Nobody was going to have the brass neck to try and drive in and park unobserved, surely?

Hillary thought about it for a moment, felt that it was sound, and moved on. OK, then what?

Ivers's body had been found outside the office. But had the killer gone into the office first, and then, for some reason, had they both walked outside again? If so, it must have been done when nobody else was in the office, obviously. Ivers, a man who usually left at five, was the last one out last night – Gemma had established that fact almost as a first priority. And several of his fellow workers had expressed surprise at the boss's sudden work ethic.

So, for some reason, Ivers had stayed late last night. Why? Had he arranged to meet his killer? It seemed unlikely. Why not meet at his flat in town? Or at a pub? And did that indicate that his death was work-related? But that didn't sound right. Who'd want to kill a newspaper depot manager? The idea of a turf war with rival gangs murderously angry at not selling enough copies of the *Oxford Times* didn't somehow ring true. Besides, this smacked of something personal. And from what they knew of the vic, she was inclined at this stage to think that it was his lifestyle which had got him killed.

But the killer could definitely have rung him at work at some point. She made yet another mental note to have the uniform boys check the telephone records, but that could take ages. She shuddered to think how many calls the depot got in a day. She could only hope, if the meeting *had* been prearranged, that it was done on the vic's mobile. That was much more manageable. She'd get Chang on to that first thing.

OK. Back to the scenario. Ivers was killed outside the office. Had the killer literally called him out? Tap on the window and beckon? Ivers, maybe surprised, comes out – and bam!

Yes. Perhaps. Hillary found it all very unsatisfactory. She didn't have anything like enough information yet. But that was always the way at the start of a murder case. She wanted to know so many things, and know them right away.

But she'd have to wait. Amass the information in dribs and drabs as it came in. Read through the initial interview reports. Wait on forensics. Wait on Steven Partridge's autopsy reports.

With a sigh, she got out of the car and headed into the business park. It was probably going to be a long and frustrating day.

Hillary got back to HQ at nearly five o'clock, going in just as most of her colleagues were coming out. She met a few of the night-shift workers on the way in, and gave the desk sergeant a salute in passing. Once at her desk, she noted that Danvers had gone, and sighed in relief. She knew she'd have to tell him about Ross sooner or later, but she'd rather do it later.

She hauled out the pile of paperwork she'd taken with her from the park and began to get it into some sort of order.

She started with the witness statements from everyone who worked at the park. They'd provide the best chance for a few meaty tit-bits.

But it was soon clear that she was out of luck. Nobody, it

seemed, had seen anything suspicious. Several of the men, Hillary gauged, would have noticed a different car had there been one hanging around. They seemed to be the sort who equated makes of cars with their own masculine appendages. There was also the fact that parking spaces were in short supply, and thus were at a premium; everyone guarded their own spot zealously. Anyone parking an unknown car where it shouldn't be was bound to earn someone's wrathful attention. It tended to reinforce her feeling that the killer had either already been inside the park, and had gone unnoticed because he or she worked there (and their car was a known entity) or the killer had walked in from the outside.

Nobody from any of the other units had admitted to seeing Michael Ivers after around three o'clock yesterday afternoon, with the exception of the people who actually worked in the depot with him, of course.

Hillary made a tick against each of them. She'd have to get Chang and Gemma to do deeper background checks on all of them. It would be a painstaking, boring, and time-consuming task, and would probably lead nowhere, but it had to be done.

She phoned Steven, who promised her he'd get around to her cadaver just as soon as he could. No promises.

It was getting dark by now, and she still had the dry-as-dust preliminary forensics to go through. Chang and Gemma came back, and she told them to get off and get some sleep.

After a moment's thought, and casting a bleary eye over the scientific prose of the fingerprint expert, she decided that that was excellent advice, and locked the reports away in her desk drawer. They could wait until tomorrow.

When she got back to Thrupp the lights were coming on in the hamlet's cottages, and a single moorhen swam around her boat, looking for a handout. Once inside, she tossed it some stale cornflakes, and warmed up a tin of chunky soup. She'd bought a farmhouse loaf from Nash's with her sausage roll that lunch time; now she cut off the crust and added some butter.

She put on lights to dispel the gloom and ate her solitary supper in silence. And told herself she was not panicking.

In little more than two weeks' time she'd leave the HQ building for the last time, and then this narrowboat would be the centre of her world.

She had to chew and swallow hard to get a lump of bread down her suddenly tight and constricted throat.

# CHAPTER FIVE

It was barely four o'clock in the morning, and Jason Vaughan was having trouble keeping his eyes open. Since he was driving his delivery van to work, keeping his eyes open seemed to him like a good idea. It would be just the way his luck was running recently for him to wrap his van around a tree, and end up dead. Or even worse - paralysed from the neck down, if his recent show with the dice was anything to go by. He'd never known such atrocious luck.

He'd had a late night last night – not due, alas, to revelry – but as a result of insomnia brought on by worry. His rent for the cupboard his landlord called a maisonette was due, and he didn't have it. Yet again.

He indicated to turn into the business park, and had to wait for the lazy git who was supposed to guard the place at night to come and let him in. Jason had never yet come into work to find the night watchman ready and waiting for him, even though he started work at exactly the same time every day. He was due to pick up a load of the weekly rag that his boss sold to half the newsagents in the county and they had to be in place before the shops opened, some as early as 6.30 a.m.

He cursed as he leaned on the van's horn and waited for the gates to open. Why couldn't he have a job that worked normal hours? Other people managed it. But then, other people seemed to manage their lives so much better than he himself seemed able to do. It was something Linda had always been griping on to him about. How he could never be normal, like everyone else.

Well, at least he didn't have to listen to the constant nagging, he mused now, finger tapping impatiently on the steering wheel as he yawned enormously and hunched himself over the steering wheel. He tried to tell himself that he was glad the missus had left, taking the kids with her. He had peace and quiet now.

Of course, the house had been repossessed, leaving her with no other option but to move back in with her mother. It had come as a considerable shock to him when his mother-in-law had flat-out refused to take him in as well.

For months he'd cadged the use of sofas and living room floors from an assortment of friends, until he'd eventually managed to find the tiny hovel he now called home. Even that was situated in a bad area of town, and once or twice he'd been mugged.

It was almost funny when he thought of it. Each time the snotty-nosed little hoodie who'd done it had got away with precisely nothing. Any money Jason managed to accumulate went like a puff of smoke. And he'd long since sold his watch and gold signet ring. And it was all that bastard's fault.

He sat back up as the gates opened at last, and he gave the night watchman the usual finger. He heard the man – Ross, was it? – let rip with some foul language, and driving the short distance to Unit 1, Jason gave him another finger in his driver's mirror. Wasted effort, he supposed, since the git probably wasn't able to see it.

He parked the small van in his usual spot, and was just about to turn off the headlights when something pale and fluttering caught his eye. It took a moment for him to realize what he was seeing, then he blinked. Tape was looped around the lawn and shrub area in front of the depot.

What the hell?

He shut off the ignition and slowly climbed out. The security light outside the building came on at his approach, and he was able to read the writing on the tape. He'd only ever seen it on the telly before, on all those crime shows they put on. Cops put it up to keep people from trampling all over a crime scene.

Slowly, Jason looked around and saw that, as usual, he was the first to arrive. Naturally, that made sense. Old man Wallace had put him on the earliest shift when he'd begged him for the overtime it brought with it. That had been back when he still had a marriage and kids to support and a mortgage to – supposedly – pay off.

Now he walked to the little inset door, carved into the big metal doors that could open up wide enough to allow a lorry to pass through them, his eyes glued to the dark patch of scrubby grass as he did so.

Yesterday had been his day off. He'd spent it at the track, trying to recoup his losses. The turf didn't have the same atmosphere or kudos as the casino, of course, but it was better than nothing. He should have known better than to hope he could win, with the way Dame Fortune was giving him the cold shoulder lately.

He walked into the office, looking around for any instructions. Usually Dave or Kevin would leave a note relaying the bastard's instructions. Ivers himself never came in until nine, of course, by which time Jason was halfway round the county delivering the newspapers. Which was how he liked it. So when the old man himself walked in from the office area, Jason felt his stomach lurch. Jack Wallace was all but retired, and to see him here so early rang the alarm bells loud and clear.

'Ah, Vaughan, good. You're on time.'

Jack Wallace was in his sixties, and was one of those men who had a fine head of thick silvery-white hair. He eyed Vaughan sharply, as if trying to read his face. It came as a bit of a shock to the young lad, who, though he was used to poker players and croupiers doing the same, felt wrong-footed to have it done to him in this environment. In the workplace, and with an old stickler like Wallace, it felt all wrong, somehow.

He shifted nervously from foot to foot. 'Something wrong, Mr Wallace?' Jason asked, his voice sounding a little tight and high with nerves. 'I saw that funny tape outside. Was there a burglary or something?'

'You didn't read last night's papers?' The local rags had run a short piece on the incident, but thankfully, details were still scarce. Wallace knew that wouldn't last long. And the irony wasn't lost on him. He'd made his money in newspapers, in playing his part in delivering them to the doorsteps of Joe Public. And now it was going to be his name, and the name of his company splashed across them. Already he could feel the acid building in his stomach. Any moment now, his ulcer would start playing up.

'No,' Jason said, and felt himself flush guiltily in the face of the old man's level, probing glance. 'I, er, don't really read 'em, sir,' he added. 'I know I should, I suppose, delivering them and all, but ...' Fact was, Jason couldn't afford to buy papers. Most days, he couldn't afford to eat properly.

'Mike Ivers was murdered here yesterday.' Jack Wallace cut across the waffle, his voice hard and precise, but something inside him seemed to unbend slightly as the young lad went deathly pale. Jason's eyes widened, and his mouth dropped open like a fish.

'D'yah what?'

Wallace let out a slow breath of relief. So it was nothing to do with the run-in between the two of them, then. Good. Of all the people who worked for him, when that striking blonde police sergeant had asked him if he knew of anyone in the company who might have had it in for the manager, only Vaughan's name had come to mind.

Of course, Mike hadn't been popular with a lot of people at the works. He tended to be a bit of a tyrant, and his tomcatting around hadn't earned him any approbation either. But only this lad might have taken a plank of wood to his head.

Now that Wallace was able to reassure himself that the kid's shock was genuine, the relief was exquisite. He'd been worried all day, and unable to get hold of Vaughan. Not surprising, of course. He had no landline in that hovel he lived in, and he'd no doubt sold or hocked his mobile long ago. Which meant he, Wallace, had had to wait around here and catch him first thing.

But it was worth the loss of a night's sleep.

'Right then. You'd best keep your mouth shut, son,' Wallace said grimly, making Vaughan pale even further. 'That's my advice.'

'Huh?'

'When the coppers question you. They'll be back today, you mark my words. You, Pete and Whacko all had yesterday off, so they're bound to want to speak to you today.'

'But I didn't do anything!' Jason heard himself whine.

'Glad to hear it, lad. But like I said, if I was you, I'd keep my mouth shut about Ivers. He was just your boss, yeah? You can say you didn't like him much, but I wouldn't volunteer any more than that.'

Even as he gave the advice, Jack Wallace realized it was probably already redundant. It was no secret how things had been between Ivers and Jason Vaughan. And although no one, as far as he knew, had told the cops anything yet, it was probably only a matter of time before they got wind of it.

Still, *keep your head down* had always been Jack's motto.

He nodded at the lad, told him to start loading up the teenage magazines waiting in bay 1, and left to go home. It had been a long time since he'd pulled an all-nighter, and he was hardly a spring chicken any more. But at least he could now be reasonably certain that whatever shit it had been that had got Ivers killed, it was nothing to do with his company.

Briefly he wondered which outraged husband, boyfriend or maybe even brother had offed his manager. If Mike had been stupid enough to mess with a Muslim girl, his death might even be the result of one of those honour or revenge killings he'd read about. Mike had considered anything in a skirt fair game, silly sod. Or maybe one of his gambling cronies had got tired of being owed dosh. Who could say?

Wallace climbed wearily into his car and beeped his horn at the gate. He'd have to advertise for a new manager, he suddenly realized, and felt a wave of weariness engulf him. Perhaps he'd just get a recruiting agency on to it. His last choice, when he'd done the interviewing himself, hadn't exactly been a raging success had it?

He scowled at the night watchman who slouched past him to open the gate. The man somehow managed to look slovenly, even in a uniform.

Wallace sighed. Perhaps he should just sell up once and for all and go live in Portugal, like his wife wanted. She'd been hinting at it for long enough.

Hillary Greene parked her slightly wheezing car beneath a large horse-chestnut tree in HQ's car park and climbed out thoughtfully. Puff the Tragic Wagon had passed his latest MOT but that had been nearly ten months ago. Who knew what ailments he'd picked up since?

She sighed, and hoped the car didn't let her down when she was out on one of the country roads. She'd let her AA membership lapse last week, deciding that she'd hardly need it if she was going to let her boat do the travelling once she retired. A bicycle would be her main mode of transport then.

She walked through the lobby, giving a vague wave to the desk sergeant who watched her progress with brooding, depressed eyes. Like most of the regular stalwarts at HQ, the desk sergeants had all agreed that seeing Hillary Greene go was like watching the end of an era. And they didn't like it.

Upstairs, there was a note on her desk to go and report in with Donleavy. Hillary read it and grimaced.

Strictly speaking, Donleavy, who was now a high-ranking commander, wouldn't normally have much to do with a mere hard-working DI on a murder case, and she wondered what he wanted. It was bound to be a pain in the arse, whatever it was. She contemplated briefly putting it off, then decided it wasn't worth the hassle.

She trudged upstairs and tapped on the door of his secretary's office. She was a woman who'd known Hillary for years, and knew how highly her boss rated her. She regarded Donleavy's promotion as her own, and gave Hillary a rather cool smile. Like her boss, she took Hillary's decision to leave as a personal slight.

'He's in,' she said, murmuring something into her intercom and nodding her head slightly towards his door.

Hillary took a deep breath and went inside.

'Hill, you're looking well,' Donleavy said in greeting, looking up from the report he was reading. He noticed she'd lost weight, in all the right places too, since her famous hourglass figure still managed to retain its curves in all the right places.

'Thank you sir,' Hillary said coolly. 'You wanted to see me?'

'Yes. The murder at the business park. How's it looking?'

Hillary let the question hang heavily for a moment. It was, of course, the sort of question Paul Danvers should be asking. Not someone who'd achieved the lofty heights of commander.

'You're asking for a briefing, sir?' she asked, letting her voice sound ever so slightly amused and surprised.

Donleavy nodded. Then he listened, his face totally expressionless, as she gave him what she had so far. Which was a lot of speculation, and as yet, very few facts.

'Sounds interesting,' Donleavy said when she'd finished.

Hillary fought the impulse to grind her teeth. Of course it was interesting. Murder cases always were – a fact he'd been relying on.

'I'll be collating the information as it comes in, and I'll start interviewing the principal witnesses today,' Hillary continued phlegmatically flatly. 'Of course, in two weeks' time I'll have to hand it over to whoever takes over the case, assuming it hasn't been resolved,' she added.

Donleavy scowled. It wasn't often that any expression marred his usually immobile face, and Hillary tensed.

'You know how I feel about that,' Donleavy said. 'Which brings me to this.' He closed the folder he'd been reading, and to Hillary's astonishment, held it out to her. She'd assumed it was some high-level management memo, something that would bore her to tears about budget levels or the latest Home Office advice on crisis management in the event of some major incident or other. Wasn't that what commanders occupied themselves with?

Hillary, caught on the hop found herself reaching out for the folder and taking it before she could think of a good excuse not to.

She glanced at the thick black writing on the front of the beige card. THAMES VALLEY CRIME REVIEW TEAM.

She knew their work, all right. 'The cold-case unit?' she asked, bewildered.

'That's right,' Donleavy said briskly. 'It contains all the details you'll need.'

'For when?' Hillary huffed.

Donleavy, who was already reaching towards his in tray for the next piece of paperwork that demanded his attention, looked up at her as if in surprise.

'For when you come to your senses of course, and find yourself adrift on that boat of yours, bored out of your skull and longing to be back on the job.'

Hillary opened her mouth, realized she was in imminent danger of blasting off at a commander, and managed to hold her tongue. Even if it was Donleavy, who always gave her a lot of leeway, and even if she was only weeks away from retirement, she could still be disciplined for insubordination.

She sighed instead, said curtly, 'Sir,' turned on her heel and marched stiffly out.

Donleavy watched her go, his lips twitching just slightly. For a moment there he'd expected fireworks. And seeing Hillary Greene let rip would have been something worth watching.

Then his amusement waned.

He was resigned to the fact that she'd made up her mind to go. Knowing Hillary the way he did, when she made up her mind to do something, she did it. So he'd abandoned his attempts to talk her around, and decided to do some lateral thinking instead.

And the Crime Review team was what he'd come up with. Once Hillary was retired, and her pension sorted, there was simply no coming back for her as a fully paid-up police officer. But she *could* still become a consultant for the cold-case team, as everyone thought of them.

These units consisted of an acting police officer – usually a DI, but sometimes a very experienced sergeant or even a DCI, if the case was high-profile enough - and ex-coppers or other useful retired people who worked on the cases on a 'consultant' basis. Forensic experts put out to pasture, medical men slowing down, computer nerds, burned-out law experts; all people who'd spent their life in the judiciary, and who found themselves with time on their hands and wanting something useful to do.

Donleavy leaned back in his chair thoughtfully. He'd give it six months. Six months for Hillary Greene to regret her decision to retire, and come back to them.

He hoped he wasn't indulging in wishful thinking.

As Hillary Greene returned to her desk, fuming, and shoved the offensive folder into her desk unread, Brian Vane was just pulling out of the HQ parking lot.

He turned right and headed towards north Oxford, where he parked in the Pear Tree Roundabout Park-and-Ride. He took the waiting bus to just opposite the iconic Randolf Hotel in Oxford itself, and walked down into Jericho. Here were mostly student bedsits and old shops run by eccentric diehards. And it was one of these, a particularly noisome pawnbroker's, that had brought him out and about – and out of uniform.

Superintendent Brian Vane pushed into the shop, wrinkling

his nose at the smell. It was a weird mixture of old musty books, metallic tang, smoke and booze fumes, and dirty carpet.

In front of him, a young woman, a student by the looks of her, was haggling out a deal with the fat, middle-aged man slouched behind the counter. Eventually they agreed the price for a little heart-shaped gold locket, and the girl left, giving Vane a hostile glance at she did so. No doubt the locket had been a gift from her dear old granny, and she was hocking it in order to get high. Or to help fund a private abortion. Or something equally degrading. Vane had a very jaundiced view of humanity, and saw no reason to start modifying it now.

'Hello Cockles,' Brian said softly, making the pawnbroker look up, surprised.

He was one of those men who, going bald, was trying to hide it with a comb-over of long hair dragged from one side to the other. He was running to fat, and his hands had a pudgy, pasty look that made Vane wrinkle his nose in distaste.

'Huh? What d'yah call me?' he demanded, trying to sound belligerent and failing.

'Cockles. I imagine it's short for "cockles and mussels", but why DS Tyler gave you that particular moniker, I wouldn't like to speculate.'

The pawnbroker relaxed slightly. 'Old Bill, are yah? You're a bit behind the times mate. I ain't narked for the luscious Janine in years.'

Brian knew this was true from checking Janine's files. He was marked inactive. But it was what he did back in the day that interested Vane.

'I heard you were the supply man to some pretty dodgy persons, Mr Quinn.'

Ian Quinn blinked. 'That was ages ago. When I was young and stupid and would do anything not to have to join Dad in the shop.'

Brian Vane wasn't interested in his personal history. Although a thought did pop immediately into his head. 'Was your dad running a fishmonger's outfit, by any chance?'

Ian Quinn began to look distinctly nervous. 'Ere, what's it to you? My old man died years ago, and the business was sold.'

Brian shrugged. 'It just occurred to me that that's why Janine Tyler labelled you Cockles, that's all.'

'Oh yeah. That. It was her bit of a joke. Gotta have a laugh, ain't yah?' Ian said nervously. He wanted to get this weird copper out of shop before some of his less-than-lily-white clientele showed up.

Vane had little difficulty interpreting his unease. 'Don't worry, Cockles, I'm not staying long. In fact, as soon as you answer a few quick questions, I'll be on my way.'

Ian Quinn wasn't sure whether to feel relieved or not. 'What sort of questions then?' he asked warily.

'As I say, you used to be a supply man. When you wanted to supply shooters, for instance—'

'Here, I never did,' Quinn lied instantly. 'Nothing like that,' he insisted.

'No, of course not,' Vane said smoothly. 'And I have no interest in who your supplier was, or even whom you gave them to, for that matter,' Brian continued with a smile. 'I only want to know the names of those who took over from you when you retired.'

'Ay?' Quinn blinked, trying to see the catch. In his experience, you had to dance very clever around coppers. They'd stitch you up quick as a wink. Bent and dishonest, the lot of them. And when they weren't it was even worse. Take Tyler, for instance. She'd caught him out with a caseload of dodgy videos once, and he'd been in her pocket ever since. He'd only been holding on to them as a favour for a mate, too. He wasn't a fence, for Pete's sake.

Or at least, he hadn't been then.

'Come on, Cockles, it's a simple question,' Vane cajoled. 'Let me make it even easier for you, then. If say, just for argument's sake, Janine Mallow had wanted to find a shooter, clean as in untraceable, and not too fussy about the quality, who would she go to?'

'Here, I ain't a nark,' Quinn said, then blinked as he realized how stupid that sounded. Of course he'd been a nark. Once. That was why this oily copper was here, contaminating his shop.

'Do you really want this place put high on my shit-list, Mr Quinn?' Vane asked softly. 'I could have the local coppers take a very keen interest in the comings and goings here. Have them park outside whenever they take their lunch break, for instance. Patrol cars have to park up somewhere, don't they?'

Quinn gulped as he contemplated the drop in his income if it got out that he'd brought down trouble on his head with the heat, and he began to whine.

Vane let him get on with it, but left a few minutes later, with a list of names. All were low-level scrotes who could get their hands on shooters.

Now all he had to do was see if he could link one of them with Janine Mallow.

In his shop, Ian Quinn sweated for a while, became slowly angry, poured himself a measure of pink gin, his favourite tipple, and thought for a good ten minutes.

Then he picked up the phone book, found the number he wanted, and reached for his mobile.

Hillary Greene attacked the forensics reports she'd put off from last night, gradually building up a picture from all the mass of scientific data so far on offer.

Preliminary reports confirmed that the blood and tissue found on the piece of wood beside their victim was indeed human, and matched the victim's blood type. But getting a DNA match would take a few days yet, or maybe even weeks. It always did. It was only on the telly, and mostly on swanky American CSI crime shows, that cops had access to instant results.

Still, it was enough to reassure her that the obvious seemed to be the way to go here. The piece of wood lying beside the victim was the murder weapon.

Moreover, the SOCO in charge of it had found that the plank of wood had enough similarities in common with several other pieces of timber found in the lumber and builder's yard to make it a reasonable match. She had no wish to read about the chemical components found in certain brands of creosote, nor did she much care about the oxidation rate found in the rust in the nails of the murder weapon.

If a man in a white coat told her it was a reasonable assumption that the piece of wood had came from Hodgson & Sons in Unit 4, then she was prepared to take their word for it.

She made a note to go through their preliminary interview reports first, but in truth she thought it meant very little. If someone from the builder's yard had killed Ivers, surely he or she wouldn't use the wood from their own site? Similarly, she'd seen for herself that the area around the unit was regularly littered with detritus from the yard – things bouncing off lorries, things only haphazardly loaded. You could probably pick up enough wood, nails, tacks, and what have you to build your own garden shed if you trawled the area regularly enough.

OK, so someone picked up a piece of wood, probably from the area around the builder's yard, then whacked Ivers over the head with it.

Unfortunately, the rest of the forensics on the murder weapon told her little. There were no fingerprints of course – rough, grainy wood was useless for holding fingerprint impressions. Morever, there were no strands or fibres on it, either from the clothes Ivers was wearing, or from any clothes the killer might have been wearing. Which made sense. If you picked up a piece of wood and hit someone over the head with it, you probably wouldn't leave any fibres behind. Unless the far end of the plank had managed to catch on your cuff or sleeves. Which, in this case, it obviously hadn't.

Apart from the DNA taken from the bloodstains, she noticed that SOCO had detected minute traces of three different sets of

DNA on the plank. She decided on reflection that that was probably nothing to get excited about. After all, the product would have had to have gone through a sawmill and then been manhandled by all sorts of people before ending up at Hodgsons.

With a sigh, she put it to one side.

It was nearly 8.30 when Chang and Gemma came in. All the planning for Gemma's wedding was now being finalized, and her sergeant was tired from working on the finer details well into the night, but she listened diligently as Hillary summarized what was in so far.

'So, what would you say was the most interesting nibble you picked up yesterday?' Hillary asked her, when she'd finished.

Chang, who was quickly updating the murder book, paused to listen.

Gemma thought for a moment, then shrugged. 'His private life has got to be what got him killed, guv. He liked women, and he liked gambling. Plenty of scope for a motive in there.'

'I agree,' Hillary said, as Chang hung on their every word. As the only male in a small team, a lot of his mates ragged him about it, but in truth, listening to the sarge and his DI talk was fascinating. They both seemed to know so much.

'I think I'll concentrate on our vic's romantic dalliances. Gemma, I want you to follow up the money trail. According to Ross, Ivers might have been that rare thing, a genuinely lucky and successful gambler.'

Gemma snorted. 'Yeah, right. And I'm the sugar-plum fairy. Ross always did talk out of his arse.'

'Exactly,' Hillary said succinctly as the phone on her desk rang. 'So follow it up. See where Ivers did his gambling, find out who runs the outfit, whom he owes, how much, and do they have a reputation for playing rough with their punters.'

She reached for the phone and picked it up. 'DI Greene,' she said, her mind on Ivers's women. She'd spoken to the ex-cum-widow. Priority one now had to be Honor Welles. Then the woman before her, and the current girlfriend of course. Wasn't their vic supposed to have a young girl in tow at the moment? She'd have to …

'Hillary? It's me. Janine.'

Abruptly, Hillary's train of thought came crashing to a halt. Automatically she tensed, her face losing all expression. Both Chang and Gemma looked at her quickly.

She listened for a moment, then said quietly. 'OK Janine. The Buttery, in ten.'

She hung up, grabbed her bag and reached for her jacket. 'Report in anything of immediate interest. I'll be on the mobile,' she said briskly.

Both Chang and Gemma knew enough not to ask her questions when she got that look on her face. Besides, it was obvious who'd been on the line – her old sergeant Janine Mallow.

And whenever she called, the shit always seemed to hit the fan.

Gemma watched her superior go, a worried frown tugging at her brows. Then she caught the same look on Chang's face, and shrugged wordlessly.

# CHAPTER SIX

The Buttery was a nondescript kind of eatery in Kidlington's small shopping precinct, a favourite of housewives out shopping, and bored teenagers who didn't want to get into trouble or have any hassles. It was the kind of place that was clean without being inspiring, and where you could buy a cup of reasonably priced tea or coffee and on the way out buy a loaf of bread or a couple of eclairs from the serving counter. It had its own bakery on the premises, and the cob rolls were often quite good.

When Hillary walked in, she saw her one-time sergeant, now DI Janine Mallow, sitting at a corner table and looking listlessly over the short menu. Toasted teacakes, scones and home-made gateaus were the main items, and just reading it made Janine feel slightly sick. She put it away immediately when she saw her old boss approaching, and smiled wanly.

Since giving birth to Phillip Mallow's daughter five months after he was shot dead, Janine had lost most of her excess weight, and had cut her normally long blond hair into a shorter, neater style. She was dressed in a black trouser suit and wore the minimum of make-up.

She looked tired.

Hillary guessed that things weren't going all that well. Although Janine had been cleared of any criminal wrongdoing in shooting dead her husband's killer before he was able to kill another serving officer, whom he'd had in his rifle-sights at the time, the press hadn't been altogether kind to her. Clive Myers's young daughter had been gang-raped, his wife had committed suicide because of the stress, and his daughter languished in a mental institution to this day. Worse, the perpetrators of the crime had walked free from court, due to a cock-up for which Myers had held Mel personally responsible. He had already killed the main rapist, a nasty teenage thug, as well as Mel and had the SIO in charge of his daughter's case in his sights when Janine shot him dead.

Myers had been ex-army, and a hitherto well-liked, respected and law-abiding man. He had many admirers in the press, and enough public sympathy on his side to give Janine a rough ride.

Hillary suspected that Janine's career was currently stalled as well, and that she herself knew it. For someone as fiercely ambitious as Janine, this must rankle. But it was inevitable. Until the fuss died down, and the brass could tell whether or not she could still be useful as a serving officer, it was hardly likely that they were going to fall over themselves to do Janine any favours. The fact that the rank-and-file members of the police force considered her to be a heroine was neither here nor there.

'Hello boss.' She greeted Hillary automatically by her old title. Janine had never called her 'guv' like everyone else had, and had never really been happy serving under another woman, mainly because she resented being seen by her jealous male colleagues as part of an all-girls-together team. Nothing, in fact, could be further from the truth. Although they worked well together, they'd never been friends. And when Janine had started a relationship with Hillary's oldest friend and boss, Mellow Mallow, it hadn't helped matters much.

But Janine had never underestimated Hillary's intelligence, or her standing at HQ. And she'd always known she could rely on her if she got into trouble. It had been one of the main reasons why she'd called Hillary after shooting Clive Myers, even though by then she was working out of the nick at Witney, and by rights, should have called her own super.

Janine didn't like to hark back to that period in her life. She'd been heavily pregnant at the time, mourning Mel and feeling distinctly emotionally unsteady. Not only had she made some bad choices, but she hadn't handled the crisis, when it came, at all well, and it was this that still gave her the most nightmares. She'd always prided herself on keeping a cool head when all around her were losing theirs. But instead of thinking things through and acting accordingly after she'd killed Myers, she'd frozen like a rabbit in the headlights, just retaining enough sense to call her old boss and let Hillary Greene do the thinking and acting for her.

And because of that she'd been saved from having to face the consequences of the worst that might have happened. Unfortunately, it also meant that the sword of Damocles that she knew hung over her own head, now hung over that of Hillary Greene as well.

When she'd heard on the grapevine that Hillary was retiring she'd been shocked to the core. She'd been convinced that Hillary would be one of those women forced into retirement at the very last possible moment, kicking and screaming.

But shock had quickly turned to guilt. Although Hillary would never say so, Janine knew the other woman's early retirement must be all down to her and the mess she'd made. Perhaps it was the strain of knowing that the full story about the Clive Myers shooting might still come out. If they were unlucky. Perhaps Hillary just felt that she had to jump before anyone could shove her. But knowing how Hillary felt about the police force, she might even have decided to go as a matter of honour. Janine wouldn't put it past her. There was a stalwart, knowing-right-from-wrong assurance about Hillary Greene that had always annoyed her, mainly because Janine knew that she herself didn't, and never would, share it. Hillary was a straight-as-a-die copper, and the sort who inspired confidence when things got hairy. There had been many a time when Janine had watched her reassure and steady a nervous uniform when things started to go pear-shaped. It was one of the many things that had made Hillary a local hero and legend at HQ.

'Janine.' Hillary greeted her with a brief smile and took a seat. Janine noticed that she'd lost weight, and her face looked paler than usual, thinner and somehow more grim. But that was hardly surprising, the younger blonde woman thought with a renewed pang of guilt. Her old boss might have decided to go, but there was no way she could be happy about it.

'I heard from an old nark of mine recently. He tells me he had a visit from Vane,' Janine said, cutting to the chase straight away. They'd never really been ones for social chitchat, and neither of them would have known how to trade pleasantries without feeling awkward about it.

Hillary nodded slowly, but didn't look as dismayed or angry as Janine had expected. 'So he's still poking around, is he? It doesn't surprise me. He's off to Hull soon, and that's a prospect that would make anyone want to spit.' And knowing Detective Superintendent Brian Vane as she did, he'd want to spread as much of the hurt around as he could.

'Serves him right,' Janine said vindictively. 'I hope he rots there.'

Hillary said nothing, but she felt worried. Janine was in real danger of becoming a seriously embittered woman.

'How's little Pip?' she asked, hoping that changing the subject to that of her infant daughter Phillippa, named after her late father, would take the sour look off her mother's face.

'Fine. I've got a nanny for her. Full time.' Janine said it abruptly and then stared hard at Hillary, as if daring her to comment. Mel had left her relatively well off, and she could afford full-time child care. But her mother had been giving her grief about it non-stop, nagging away that even in these modern times, a poor fatherless baby needed its mother twenty-four seven, and she was almost surprised when Hillary Greene didn't wade in to add her own disapproval. She could, after all, have taken extended maternity leave, and she doubted that her bosses would have kicked up any fuss.

'She crawling yet?' Hillary asked mildly, well aware of her ex-sergeant's views on the importance of her career, and not intending to wander into any minefields.

Janine slowly relaxed. 'Yes. She's into everything. Won't be long before she starts talking. Julia, that's her nanny, says that teething is the last really big hurdle, and she's over that.'

Hillary nodded.

'About Vane.' Janine brought the conversation back to the point. 'This nark, an oily little toad who runs a pawnshop down Jericho way - he tells me that Vane wanted to know about skells who could get their hands on street shooters.'

Hillary felt a cold finger of alarm touch her in the small of her back. She was about to speak, noticed the approach of a wait-ress, and held back. She ordered plain coffee, and Janine did the same. Both women resisted the waitress's bored recital of teacakes, scones, shortbread and biscuits, all baked on the prem-ises, and available at reasonable prices.

When the girl had gone Hillary sighed heavily. 'He's spotted the weak link in the evidence we gave at the inquiry.'

Janine nodded. 'The handgun,' she said.

Hillary had never asked how Janine had come to have a gun in her hand when she shot, in self-defence, the man who'd killed her husband. Nor when or how she'd acquired it. She didn't really want to know now.

'Don't worry about Vane,' she said quietly. 'I can handle him.'

A while ago she'd asked around and pulled in a few favours. This had resulted in an old colleague of hers from Vane's old stamping grounds up Birmingham way, handing her a photo-graph. In it, Vane was seen talking to a woman who was obviously a tom. Although she wasn't told the story behind it, her friend had assured her that showing Vane just a glimpse of the photograph would be enough to ensure that he'd back off.

Hillary could only hope and pray that the photograph was as all-powerful as her old pal claimed.

'You sure?' Janine asked tensely. Although, if the truth came out, Hillary might face disciplinary charges, and possibly minor criminal ones, it was she, Janine, who was in the greatest danger. She well knew that she could face murder charges. And everyone knew what happened to cops who got sent down.

'Yes,' Hillary said firmly, and with far more confidence than she actually felt. 'I haven't exactly been idle these past few months.'

Janine, seeing Hillary's usually warm, sherry-brown eyes harden, suddenly felt some of the terrible tension that had had her in its grip for the past six months begin to ebb away.

'You've got something on the bastard,' she said softly with a tremulous and joyful smile. At that moment the waitress came back with their coffees, and when she'd placed them down in front of them and retreated, Hillary reached for a packet of artificial sweetener and shook it absently.

'Like I said, you have no need to worry. Just concentrate on that little girl of yours, and the job. You had any good cases lately?'

Janine let herself be lured into shop talk. In truth, she felt a lot better knowing that Hillary Greene was still looking out for her. But still, she couldn't help but feel a nagging worry.

She'd left messages around for Matthew 'Skunk' Petersen, one of her old collars, to get in touch. It was he who'd provided her with the gun. With Vane sniffing around, it was probably only a matter of time before he hit on Skunk. And although Janine was reasonably sure that her old nark wouldn't grass her up, skells were hardly noted for their reliability. It wouldn't hurt for her to remind him of just how many years she still could put him away for, if the need arose.

She debated telling Hillary what she was doing, but then decided against it. She could look after herself, and it was high time that she started to remember that. Besides, since Hillary Greene would soon be leaving the job, she wouldn't always have her old boss to run to when the going got tough. It was time to stand on her own two feet again.

When Hillary left the café she was relieved to see that at least Janine seemed more laid-back about things, but she felt deeply uneasy. At some point there was going to be a major showdown between herself and Vane.

She could feel it.

Once again, she thought angrily, the whole Janine/Myers thing was distracting her from her proper job. She should be concentrating on who had killed Michael Ivers and why. It was precisely because things kept spiralling out of her control that she was going.

She damned well wasn't going to let her last case as SIO on a murder investigation go down the tubes. She just damned well wasn't.

She got into Puff and slammed the door shut angrily. Right then, she thought briskly. Honor Welles. It was time to see what the mistress of the victim had to say for herself.

Honor Welles, it turned out, didn't really have much to say, although she answered all of Hillary's questions fully and, as far as the policewoman could tell, honestly enough.

The Welleses lived in a mock-Tudor, detached house in a pleasant cul-de-sac, built on the outskirts of a village resigned to urban sprawl. On the north side of Banbury, the four-bedroomed house had a pleasant view over fields with grazing sheep, but how long it would be before they too were built upon was anybody's guess.

Honor Welles answered the door at Hillary's first ring. She was, Hillary knew from Gemma's impeccable notes, forty-eight years old, but she looked nearer forty. She had dark blond hair that might or might not have owed something to a bottle, and big brown eyes. Slim, wearing plain cream slacks and a white, brown and orange V-neck sweater with the sleeves pushed up carelessly to the elbows, she ushered Hillary into a tidy lounge, after a quick but careful scrutiny of her credentials.

The furnishings of the lounge, like the house, were modern

95

and looked nice enough, but Hillary couldn't have lived there if someone had paid her. For some reason the pleasant, fairly spacious room repelled her.

Maybe she was just used to living in a big pencil box, as her one-time lover, Mike Regis had once described *The Mollern*, her narrowboat.

'I suppose this is about Michael, yes?' Honor started the conversation easily, and without any apparent embarrassment. 'Please, sit down.'

Hillary took a seat in a big coffee-coloured leather armchair, whilst Honor Welles chose the matching one opposite. Between them stretched a hand-made wooden coffee table, inset with a large print of a watercolour of Highland cattle, encased in thick protective glass.

Hillary ignored it.

'Yes. I understand from people at the business park that you and Mr Ivers were close?' she began cautiously.

Honor allowed a cool, amused smile to flicker briefly over her face. It was a thin, attractive face, but something in her eyes looked dissatisfied. Hillary wondered whether she too resented this nice house, in its nice cul-de-sac on the edge of a nice village. Had she envisaged this life when she married her husband, all those years ago? According to Gemma, the Welleses were coming up to celebrating their silver wedding anniversary. No kids though. Perhaps she or her husband couldn't have children. Or maybe they'd always meant to, but now it was just too late.

Honor, according to Gemma, didn't have any specific career herself, but 'did things' in the community. Perhaps her affair with Michael Ivers was nothing more than a symptom of that classic cliché, the mid-life crisis?

Or was she a serial adulterer?

'We had a brief affair, yes,' Honor agreed simply.

'Do you have many affairs?' Hillary asked, without any inflection in her voice at all. It made the cool and collected

Honor Welles blink for a moment, then give another small, iron-ical smile.

'Actually, no. There was only one other affair, yonks ago now, with a primary school teacher from the local village school.'

'Did your husband know about the affair with Ivers?'

'I expect so. He never said, though. Harry wouldn't. He's the ostrich type. Sticks his head in the sand and hopes the world and all its troubles will go away. And do you know,' Honor said, with something approaching real surprise in her voice, 'it usually does. Take this thing with Michael, for instance. You'll find out who did it, Harry will go on pretending nothing happened, and after a while it'll seem like nothing did.'

She looked around vaguely, then gave a sharp bark of laughter. 'On the other hand, I might just up and pack my bags and leave him. But where to go, though; that's the thing. And what to do?'

Hillary, interested as she was in Honor Welle's problems, needed to get things on to a more specific level.

'Was the affair still current?' she asked curiously.

'Oh no. Three months it lasted, back over Christmas time. That was about how long all of Michael's affairs lasted, I gather. He dumped me for some young girl, oh hell what was her name? Anyway, someone told me just recently that he's now dumped her and is on to the next one. Sorry. *Was* on to the next one.'

Honor seemed to think about this for a moment, then shrugged one elegant shoulder and waited for the next ques-tion.

Hillary, beginning to get her measure, settled down to a serious question-and-answer session.

'Who instigated the affair?'

'He did. We met at a Christmas works party. All the business park lot rented a hall for a bit of a do. Michael came on to me from the moment we were introduced.'

'Were you flattered?'

'Not particularly. But I was bored. And Michael was sort of fascinating. He really did see himself as some kind of larger-than-life figure, you know. And to be fair, I suppose in a weird kind of way, he actually was. The car he drove, the fancy restaurants he knew, the names he could drop. He took me to a casino once – taught me how to play baccarat. It was fun, but it was never real. If you see what I mean?'

Hillary thought that she did. 'Who ended it?'

'He did. Well, he just stopped calling. And I never called him back. And after a while, that was that.' She gave another sophisticated little shrug.

'Did you ever see him after the split?' Hillary persisted.

'Only once or twice if we happened to run into each other in town. Banbury's hardly a teeming metropolis; it was sort of inevitable.'

Hillary nodded. 'Any animosity between you?'

'Good grief, no.'

'And what about your husband?' Hillary asked cautiously. 'Is he the jealous type?'

Honor laughed and said nothing.

'Did he resent Ivers?'

'He might have done. If so, he never said anything. Harry would never rock the boat. He'd cringe and die with embarrassment just at the thought of creating a scene.'

Hillary paused and thought back over her meeting with Harry Welles. A nervous, inept man. It all fitted in with what his wife was saying. And after nearly twenty-five years of marriage, she supposed Honor had a good take on him by now.

'Do you know whether Ivers had any enemies?' Hillary changed tack.

'Oh, loads, I should imagine. Cuckholded husbands, gullible idiots he shafted at cards, and he treated his staff at the depot like lackeys.'

'Anyone who'd want to kill him?'

Honor shrugged wordlessly.

'Where were you the night he was killed?'

'Here, at home. Where else?'

'From say, five to ten?'

'Like I said, here. All the time.'

'You never went out?'

'No.'

'Did anyone call at the house? Did you speak to a neighbour in the garden, or did anyone phone you?'

'No. I was all on my little lonesome,' Honor said, with that ironical twist of her lips that was beginning to seriously annoy Hillary. Not that she let it show, of course.

'At what time did your husband come home?'

'About a quarter to eight or so, I expect. He never comes straight home from work,' she replied. Then she glanced around the lounge again, her expression grim. *As if he'd be in a hurry to come back here,* she might as well have said out loud. 'He always stops off for a drink somewhere. A pint he makes last a couple of hours, probably, knowing Harry. He'd never drink and drive. He never breaks the rules.'

'And he stayed in after that?'

'Yes. We ate, watched some telly. Went to bed.' Her voice faltered over the boredom and helplessness of it, and for a moment her eyes were suspiciously bright.

Then she shrugged again.

She was the type of woman, Hillary realized, who could probably shrug off most of life's little lumps and bumps with those elegant shoulders of hers.

'And you never went out?' she pressed.

'No.'

'Did you kill Michael Ivers?'

'No.' Honor Welles spoke in the same level voice, but her ironical little smile came and went briefly. 'Am I really a murder suspect?'

'For now,' Hillary said, with a brief, ironical smile of her own. She left Honor Welles to her comfortable lounge and walked back outside into fitful sunshine. Lilac bushes shone like purple torches in the gardens as she drove slowly and thoughtfully back to HQ.

She wasn't quite sure what to make of Honor Welles. She wouldn't have been surprised to learn that she was a secret drinker. That lounge probably had bottles of gin and vodka scattered and hidden around it in all the strategic places. That she was bored out of her mind was a given.

Could she really have been as unconcerned about the fate of her one-time lover as she'd seemed, though? If her affair with Ivers had been meant to lead to her great escape from a stultifying marriage, she might have been really and seriously enraged when Ivers ended it. It wasn't hard to imagine that she had developed a taste for Ivers's playboy lifestyle. And if she *had* pictured herself with Ivers at some point down the line, on a yacht in Monte Carlo and living the good life, it might have unhinged her to realize that it was all so much pie in the sky.

So she might have blown her top and whacked him over the head with a length of two-by-four when it became plain that he'd tossed her back into her domestic little pool, like a fish that he'd hooked, and then decided wasn't worth keeping.

And she certainly had no alibi before 7.45 or so. Yes, on the whole, Hillary rather thought that she'd keep Honor Welles on the suspect list until or unless some new evidence came to light that took her off it.

It was lunchtime, and Gemma was starving. She glanced across the elegant table where she was sitting in the Randolph's dining room, and regarded her groom-to-be with affection.

Guy, like most blind men, chose to wear sunglasses. In his case, it was because it helped to stop his eyes drying out and becoming sore, rather than because his sightless eyes made him look disfigured in any way.

He was a tall, elegant, handsome man, not quite forty. He spoke like an Oxonian, and was everything you'd expect a

music don to be – witty, intelligent and cultured. He was everything that Gemma, the only daughter from a predominantly
firefighting family, considered herself not to be.

He was also rich, and had a title. Which was nice. Gemma had
long since been of the view that the best revenge of all was to
live well.

'So, you definitely think pinks and not carnations are the way
to go?' she asked. Along with an expensive wedding planner,
Gemma was determined that her wedding should be a significant social event. But she also wanted it to be perfect and
personal as well. And she knew that Guy, being blind, was far
more aware of his other senses than most sighted people. And
pinks, unlike their showier and more popular cousins, carnations, had a stronger, sweeter scent.

'Yes, pinks,' Guy agreed. 'I'll be able to smell them when you
walk towards me down the aisle.'

They were discussing her wedding bouquet, and Gemma, for
a moment, had to take a deep breath and let it sink in all over
again. Before this month was out, she'd be a married woman.
And a 'lady' to boot. Well, technically, and in law, if nothing else.
Mind you, there were a lot of criminals and lowlifes whom she'd
been obliged to kick in the balls from time to time, who'd laugh
themselves sick at the idea that Detective Sergeant Gemma
Fordham was in any way, shape or form, a lady.

'So, how's the boss been lately?' Guy asked, desperate for a
discussion that didn't include menus, choristers, the best type-
face for wedding invitations or the colour of tablecloth that
wouldn't look too washed-out in a marquee.

Gemma thought about it, then said tentatively, 'I'm not too
sure.'

Guy knew, better than anyone, that Gemma's relationship
with her superior was distinctly odd. Many years ago, Gemma
had had an affair with Ronnie Greene, and when she'd first been
assigned to Hillary Greene's team she'd been intent on finding
out where the now dead Ronnie had stashed his ill-gotten gains.

She'd had her self-esteem and confidence seriously dented when she realized that not only did Hillary Greene know who she was, but had also figured out what she was up to. Surprisingly, somehow, they'd gone on from that to finding a way of working quite well together, and with a kind of grudging mutual respect.

'She's still determined to leave?' Guy pressed.

'Oh yes. I think so. And Janine Mallow's still fouling up the works somehow. And now we've been given this murder case. It's crazy. With DCI Danvers due to leave for York any time now, and our honeymoon in the offing, and Hillary retiring in less than two weeks, why the hell were we given a murder case? It's mad. Not than I'm complaining, mind. But it'll leave Chang working on the case on his own if they're not careful.'

That thought made Gemma laugh out loud.

Mark Chang looked up as Jason Vaughan came into the 'interview room'. The room was, in fact, little more than a cupboard where the secretaries came to use the photocopier, drink coffee and have a crafty fag, out of the cold. Now it housed a tiny desk and two fold-away chairs, and DC Mark Chang, conducting initial interviews.

He'd already seen two of the employees at the depot, who'd been off the day following the murder, and this was the last.

In truth, the young officer was feeling a little jaded. Apart from the responsibility of keeping the murder book up to date, he felt as if he'd been doing nothing but talking to people who knew nothing, and cared less, for days now.

And he was getting writer's cramp.

'Mr Vaughan, isn't it? Please sit down, sir; this won't take long.'

Jason Vaughan sat. He put his hands on his knees, licked his dry lips and tried not to stare at the police constable. After a quick glance that told him that Chang was an Oriental, surprisingly young, and didn't seem particularly threatening, Vaughan kept his eyes fixed firmly to the wall just over Chang's left shoulder.

'You're Mr Jason Peter Vaughan?' Chang repeated his address and date of birth, and Vaughan nodded.

'And you've worked here for nearly four years now?'

'Yes.'

'And Mr Ivers was your immediate boss? That is, he was the one who ran the place on a day-to-day basis, rather than Mr Wallace?'

'That's right. But I work early shift, see, and didn't see much of Ivers. It was usually one of the other lads who relayed instructions from him, or he left notes, like.'

Vaughan suddenly clamped his lips together, mindful of old man Wallace's advice. Don't volunteer anything, he'd said. Vaughan felt himself begin to sweat, and his hands clenched on his knees.

Chang noticed it all, and felt a shiver of excitement.

'Did you like Mr Ivers?'

'No, not much,' Jason said, trying to sound nonchalant. 'None of us did, really. He was a bit of a prat.' He figured that he was safe enough in saying that. He was sure a lot of people would already have said the same.

They had. Chang nodded non-committally, trying to think what Hillary Greene would say or do next.

'Did you ever meet Mr Ivers outside of work?'

Jason swallowed hard. 'Of course not. Why would I do that?'

Chang smiled, trying to put him at ease. 'These are just standard questions, sir. We ask everyone the same.'

Jason told himself not to be such a chump. Of course they must have been asking the rest of the lads the same thing. Old man Wallace was right. He just needed to keep his head down and say nothing. He coughed awkwardly.

'Oh. Right.'

'When was the last time you saw Mr Ivers?' Chang asked carefully.

'I'm not sure. Beginning of the week maybe?'

'And he seemed the same as always? Not moody, or worried or anything like that?'

'No, he was the same as ever.' Cocky sod, Jason added silently, but didn't divert his eyes from the wall over Chang's left shoulder.

Chang went patiently through the list of standard questions, and when he'd finished and watched Jason Vaughan leave, a sense of excitement vied with a sense of frustration. He was sure that Vaughan was hiding something, but he hadn't been able to pinpoint just what it was that was setting off his alarm bells.

What was more, he was sure that either Hillary Green or the sergeant would have done better.

As soon as the door closed behind Vaughan he reached for his mobile and keyed in Hillary's office number from the memory.

'DI Greene.'

'Guv, it's Chang. I've just finished interviewing the last of the depot's staff who were off work yesterday. One of them, a Jason Vaughan was acting really jittery.'

'You think he was holding back?'

'Yes guv. I think so.'

'OK. Do a background check on him, see if anything interesting pops up.'

'Thanks guv,' Chang said, chuffed that she was willing to back his judgement.

'When you have time, Constable,' Hillary warned quickly. 'Get on with the other tasks I gave you first, and in order, mind.'

'Yes guv,' Chang promised and hung up.

Hillary, sensing his enthusiasm, sighed a little wistfully as she put down the receiver. It was hard to believe that she'd ever been that young and keen once.

But she supposed, rather sadly, that she must have been.

## CHAPTER SEVEN

Frank Ross's alarm went off at 3.30 that afternoon, its annoying electronic beep jerking him awake after what had felt like barely a few hours of sleep. He rolled over in the narrow bed and switched it off, then blinked blearily at the dial. What the hell had he set it so early for? He usually slept until six, then went down to the pub for a spag bol, or whatever was the special on offer that day, had a couple of pints, and then rolled into work, usually late, for his shift.

He lay for a moment in the off-white sheets that smelled of his stale sweat and stared at the cracks in the ceiling, frowning and swearing mildly. Since he'd retired from the force he'd also moved from Kidlington, and was now renting the top-floor flat in a converted council house. The estate was one of those where, when the wind was in the right direction, you could smell the reek from a factory producing something that sometimes smelt edible. And sometimes not. Today, he had his windows firmly shut, but he could still hear some kids shrieking in the street below, and he wondered belligerently why the noisy little sods weren't at school.

Then he remembered that he'd set the alarm because he was due to meet Ollie at the Three Ducks and he rolled out of bed, dressed in his usual Y-fronts and vest. Both garments, meant to be white, looked grey. He pulled on a pair of baggy grey slacks and a thick woollen jumper he'd got from the Heart Foundation a few weeks ago, and reached for a pair of black socks, so in need of washing that they were actually stiff. He left the flat a few minutes later, and ambled to his local pub barely two minutes' walk away. The Ducks, unlike most pubs, had largely missed the breweries attempts to 'theme' it, and it remained drab and dingy, a little rough on Saturday nights, but with a good selection of beer. It was Frank Ross's sort of pub.

When he walked in the familiar scent of stale beer, unlawful cigarette smoke and old lino hit him in the face. From the depths of one dark corner he saw Ollie look up nervously. With narrowed eyes Frank also noted the younger man sitting beside him, and sighed. No doubt about it, from the looks of him, Purple Pete was shitting a brick. Ollie was all right, but his lad simply had no guts. And no brains either.

Frank went to the bar and irritably ordered a pint of Hook Norton's finest, then ambled over to the table. Ollie nodded at him briefly, and glanced around. It was an ingrained habit more than anything else. At this time of day they had the pub practically to themselves.

'Frank, what the hell's going on at the park?' It was Pete who spoke, or rather whispered, and Frank shot him a reproachful look. There was nothing more likely to make someone actually care about what you were saying than to start whispering. Hadn't this twit learned anything?

'You know what's going on. You can read, can't you? It's in the papers,' he said dourly, his look openly scornful.

Ollie, a man a few years older than Ross, reached out and tapped his son's still nearly full glass of cider. 'Drink up, lad,' he said firmly. It was his way of telling the boy to shut up and let him do all the talking, and Pete subsided at once, like a well-trained sheepdog.

Ollie Foreman had been a dustman for most of his life, and had been 'forced' to retire with a 'bad' back when he was in his mid-fifties. A nice little disability pension helped stave off the big bad wolf, but he liked to supplement his income with a little bit of this, and a little bit of that. Helping the lads do the odd midnight run here and there, relieving places like the Aynho business park of some of their goods, were among such enterprises. He was the kind of man who didn't like trouble, and could sense that Ross was ready to pick a fight.

'So some one really offed the bloke then, yeah?' Ollie said quietly. 'The manager of the newspaper depot, wasn't it? Did you know him?'

'Only to speak to,' Ross said, taking a sip of his beer.

''Course, me and the lads are gonna lay off – you know – for a while.'

'Of course I bloody well know,' Frank said contemptuously. 'I know none of you would ever pass an IQ test, but even you wouldn't risk a run with the Old Bill hanging around. Especially with the Queen Bitch in charge.'

Ollie, who was moon-faced, with tiny button-black eyes and a five o'clock shadow, shot a quick look at Ross and nodded. 'I thought her name was familiar. Wasn't she your old boss back at the nick?'

'What?' Purple Pete squeaked, then quavered under a sharp glance from his old man.

'Oh yeah. Detective Inspector Hillary Greene,' Ross said with a snort, and took a deep swallow of his beer.

'Weren't you and her old man in on some gigs together? Before he got killed in that car crash, like?' Ollie pressed. Although he was reasonably sure that Frank Ross was not the sort to crack and drop them all in the shit, he still craved a little reassurance. 'Bent, wasn't he?'

'As a corkscrew,' Ross said fondly. 'Ronnie knew how to make a quid, I can tell you. It was a bloody sad day when he went.'

'And you were on his widow's team?' Ollie said with a grin, as if applauding the sense of humour that fate sometimes displayed. 'I hear roundabouts that she's good. Got a good track record like.'

'Oh yeah, she's good,' Frank said grudgingly. 'Which, in a way, is also good for us.'

Pete blinked and stirred, about to protest this baffling logic, then he thought better of it.

'How come?' Ollie asked, as surprised by this statement as his offspring.

'Stands to reason, don't it?' Ross said patiently. 'Somebody bashed Ivers over the head and killed him. And the sooner somebody's charged with it, the sooner the park will get back to normal.'

'Yeah, 'spose so,' Ollie said, after pondering it for a moment. Then he added cautiously, 'Young Alan's been saying that the runs will have to stop though. I mean, even if your old boss nabs her man quick, like. This thing has really shaken him up. He's terrified his dad'll find out what he's been up to and cut him out of the will, like.'

'Alan's a pissartist,' Ross said scornfully, taking another gulp of his beer, and ignoring Purple Pete's snigger. Pete, dressed in purple jeans and a maroon sweater was a waste of space, but if you wanted Ollie along, you had to have the sprig as well. And Ollie, for all his 'bad' back, could haul lumber like, well, a lumberjack.

'What's he got to be so scared of anyway?' Ross asked resentfully.

'The cops interviewed him,' Pete said. 'It put the wind up him.'

'The cops interviewed everyone who works at the park, from the secretaries down to the tea ladies,' Ross said dismissively.

'That's what I told him,' Ollie sighed. 'But he's still got the wind up. He even asked if one of us could have done it.'

Ross blinked. 'Hey, what? He'd better not going around saying that, the silly bugger. How could it have been one of us anyway? You lot were all busy loading up the gear, weren't you?'

'*We* were, yes,' Ollie said carefully, looking at his own pint of shandy, but not reaching for it.

Frank Ross thought about it for a few moments, then swore

colourfully. 'The silly sod actually thinks that *I* might have offed Ivers?' he said, his voice full of contempt. 'What the hell would I do that for?'

Ollie shrugged. 'Dunno. Because you had a run-in with him, maybe? What I think is, he's just freaked at the thought that a bloke was lying dead just a few hundred yards away whilst we were loading up the lorry. It's got him proper spooked, I'm telling you.'

Ross stared at Ollie thoughtfully. 'Then you'd better go back to Alan and remind him to keep his lip buttoned. If he starts talking about me, I can start talking about him. To his dad, for a start. Just remind him of that.'

'All right, calm down,' Ollie said soothingly. 'It'll all blow over.'

'It better,' Ross said grimly. 'And if my old boss comes to me, saying she's been hearing rumours, I'll know where to come.'

Ollie shrugged, but, in truth, he wasn't all that displeased with the way things had gone. Frank Ross wasn't going to be helping out the Old Bill any time soon, not when he himself wasn't in a position to throw any stones. And he wasn't the sort to feel any kind of loyalty to his old job either. Being in the possible frame for the murder had focused his mind nicely.

Ollie took a sip of his shandy and sighed. It was a shame about the income from the lumber yard, though.

It had been a nice little earner while it lasted.

'Gemma?'

'Guv?'

Gemma jiggled her mobile phone closer to her ear, and continued tapping on her keyboard. She was back at HQ and typing up her notes, and had the place virtually to herself. 'Where are you?'

'Still at the yard. Have you found out the name of our vic's latest squeeze yet?'

'No. Well, yeah and no,' Gemma said, somewhat confusedly.

'Apparently, he'd already dropped the Welles woman for a girl named ... hold on ...' She stopped tapping keys and reached for her notebook, shuffling back through the pages. 'Yeah, here it is. Lucy Kirke, with an "e". Want her address?'

'Yes please.'

Gemma recited it, and Hillary quickly jotted it down.

'But here's the thing,' Gemma went on. 'From the gossip doing the rounds, I reckon he'd also dumped her not so long ago, and I haven't been able to find out who his latest, right-up-to-the-minute love interest is. Either nobody at the park knows, or for some reason they're not telling. Or he might just be taking a breather,' she added sardonically. 'Even Casanovas have to come up for air sometime, right?'

Hillary smiled. 'I'll just go and have a word with Lucy Kirke, then. Everything all right your end?'

'Yes guv,' Gemma confirmed crisply. As if it would dare be anything else. Soon she'd be a fully fledged DI, once she'd take up her position on the task force liaison team that she'd been assigned to. Everything was going very satisfactorily according to plan. She was still on course to be a commander before she hit forty-five.

'OK, see you later,' Hillary said, and hung up.

The Kirke family, it turned out, lived in the village of Deddington, the next village down the road from Adderbury, heading back towards Oxford way.

As she drove through the pretty ironstone village it reminded Hillary of a murder case she'd had there not so long ago. As she parked in the shadow of the unusual church, she wondered how the parents of the murdered man were getting on. She hoped things were getting a little easier for them now. Or perhaps that was too much to ask. Maybe it never got easier for the families concerned. Perhaps they just got slowly more and more used to it until, one day, they were able to wake up and could simply ignore the pain and loss for whole hours at a time.

Number 8, Lilac Lane was a small, semi-detached house, probably built in the sixties, and was almost halfway down a little cul-de-sac of similar houses. It had a square front garden, which had been neatly tended, and a bright sky-blue door with a gleaming brass knocker in the shape of a dolphin. It looked warm and welcoming somehow, like a proper home, and was a far cry from Honor Welles's more splendid mock Tudor residence.

Hillary rang the bell, and a few moments later the door was opened by a woman in her fifties. She was reed-thin, with white-blond hair fast turning grey, and a gaunt face. Her eyes looked tired and somehow blank.

'Mrs Kirke?'

'Yes, I'm Suzanne Kirke.'

Hillary showed her the ID in her wallet. 'I was wondering if your daughter was at home?'

'Lucy? Yes, it's her day off. Luckily it's mine too, well, afternoons anyway. I work at the health centre near the canal. Lucy and me always have lunch together today. Come on in.'

She was talking too much, and explaining too much, a sure sign of nerves. No doubt she'd read about Michael Ivers's death being treated as a case of murder, and had been dreading the moment the police would come calling.

'Come on through to the lounge. Luce, it's a Detective Inspector,' she said, pushing open a door that lead into a small but pleasant lounge. It was decorated in shades of peach and mint green. A girl, sitting on the sofa and reading a magazine, looked up warily.

Like her mother, Lucy Kirke was small-boned, lean and possessed a fine head of white-blond hair. She was pretty in an unusual way, and Hillary could see why Ivers, who probably considered himself to be a connoisseur of women, had been taken with her.

On the mantelpiece were a range of family photos – one of a young Mrs Kirke and a man taken on their wedding day and a whole range of pictures of two little girls, growing up into adult-hood.

'That's my husband, Ken. He died ten years ago,' Suzanne Kirke said, seeing Hillary looking. 'And that's my other daughter, Myra.'

Something in her voice cracked a little on the girl's name, and Hillary looked at her curiously. Lucy Kirke suddenly rose to her feet from the settee and forced a smile on to her face. 'Come and sit down next to me, Mum,' she said softly. As her mother joined her on the settee Hillary saw again that there was something fragile about the older woman.

Hillary wondered whether she'd been ill recently. She took the armchair opposite them as Suzanne Kirke waved a hand vaguely in its direction.

She watched as the older woman reached out and rather touchingly held her daughter's hand. The gesture of silent support seemed to go both ways, however, for it was Lucy who squeezed her mother's hand, and took the lead.

'I take it you're here about Michael?' she said quietly. She had large, hazel eyes and a gamine face that, Hillary guessed, a camera would love.

'Yes. But let's get the boring preliminaries out the way first, shall we?' Hillary smiled briefly. She took down Lucy Kirke full name, date of birth, telephone number, and address, and learned that she was a secretary at a local firm of estate agents. With a face like hers, Hillary wondered why she hadn't tried her hand at modelling.

'That's all fine. Now, can you tell me how you and Michael met?'

'At a friend's anniversary party. Jayne, a girl at work, was celebrating her tenth anniversary, and she had me and Winnie, the other girl in the office, round to the do at her place. Michael was a friend of her husband's. We just clicked right away.'

Beside her, her mother made a little sound, and her lips

thinned. So Suzanne Kirke, for one, had not been impressed by her daughter's affair with Ivers. Hillary wasn't surprised. A man like Michael Ivers – older, divorced, and happily living the bachelor life, was probably a mother's worst nightmare.

'And you were together, how long?'

'Not long. A few months or so. It ended just last month.'

'Can I ask if it ended amicably?'

'Oh yes,' Lucy Kirke said, with perhaps more bravado than truth. Her eyes showed pain as she smiled. 'We just realized the age difference was too much and we both sort of agreed that we wanted different things. It was obviously not going anywhere.' The phrases sounded like ones she'd rehearsed many times over in an attempt to make herself believe them.

To Hillary, at least, the pain the break-up had caused was still obvious. From the way her mother's lips got even thinner, it was obvious to Lucy's mother as well.

Hillary saw Suzanne Kirke glance at the photograph of who must be the elder daughter, Myra. Like her mother and sibling, Myra was blonde with hazel eyes, but seemed taller. Perhaps she'd inherited her father's physique.

'So there was no great falling out?' Hillary pressed, sensing that things hadn't been as hassle free as this pair were making out.

Suzanne decided to speak. 'Oh no, Inspector. There was no unpleasantness. And it was all for the best.'

Hillary nodded apparent agreement with the meaningless platitudes, then turned firmly back to Lucy. 'And had you seen Mr Ivers since the break-up?'

'Oh no.'

'He didn't call you, or come round here, or maybe pop into the office where you work to see you?'

'Oh no. It was quite over,' Lucy Kirke said firmly, and once again squeezed her mother's hand.

Hillary was finding it all a little odd. It was as if Lucy was the parent, reassuring her child, instead of the other way around.

And there was definitely some sort of subtext going on between mother and daughter that she wasn't privy to.

It engaged her curiosity.

'Can you tell me where you were the night before last, Miss Kirke? I can assure you that it's a question we've asked everyone at the business park where he worked, and all of his other acquaintances as well,' she added quickly.

But, funnily enough, this leading question didn't seem to bother either of the women, and it quickly became clear why.

'Yes, I had to work late that night – we all did,' Lucy said with a wry smile. 'We had a big buyer coming in from Spain, who was looking to buy at least ten properties in the area as an investment. Me, Winnie and Jayne all stayed behind, putting together a portfolio for James – that's James Coleman, the senior partner. He was there too. We didn't finish until eleven or so. The buyer was due in on the midnight flight, and James took the portfolio to the hotel in Oxford where he was staying. Afterwards, me and Winnie went to her place for a drink and then I stayed the night, since I didn't want to drive. Next morning, we went in to work together.'

Hillary nodded, then asked for and got Winnie's full name and address. It looked, on the face of it, a pretty good alibi. She couldn't see a whole office of disparate people willing to lie for Lucy Kirke, but she'd ask Chang to interview them all, just to confirm it.

'So when did you hear about Michael's death?' Hillary asked gently, and saw the telltale brightness come once more to her eyes. But she swallowed back the tears determinedly, and managed a smile instead. Beside her, her mother shifted restlessly, and shot Hillary a very clear *I-just-wish-you'd-go* look that was perfectly understandable.

Just as understandably, Hillary ignored it.

'It was on the local radio station the next day,' Lucy answered with quiet equanimity. 'Lunchtime. Jayne heard it first, and told me, and then I listened out for it at the next bulletin. It didn't say much. Just that his b-body had been found and that the police were treating his death as suspicious.'

Apart from the catch in her voice when talking about her lover's body being found, she sounded calm and in control.

'When you were going out together, did he ever mention having any enemies?' Hilliary asked curiously.

'Oh no.'

'I mean, did he ever, perhaps jokingly, say that someone was out for his blood, or anything like that?'

'No.'

'Did he ever get any threatening letters, or strange phone calls? Did he ever hang up abruptly without speaking, or seem upset?'

'No. Michael was very gregarious. He had lots of friends, but no enemies. I mean, who'd want to kill him?' she asked, apparently in all honesty.

Hillary nodded. Perhaps Lucy Kirke was the genuine innocent she appeared to be. In which case, her mother could only have sighed in relief when Ivers had finally dumped her - even if it had been a painful lesson for her youngest daughter.

'Well, thank you, Miss Kirke. You've been very helpful. One of my colleagues might have to talk to you again at some point, however.'

'Oh, that's all right. I'll just see you out. No, you stay here, Mum, in the warm,' she said firmly, when her mother made to rise with her. 'It's a bit cold outside today.'

Hillary, who'd found the fitful sunshine outside quite warm, smiled a vague goodbye at Suzanne Kirke, and wasn't at all surprised when Lucy took her outside and firmly closed the door behind her.

'Look, Inspector Greene. If you do need to speak to me again, do you think you could come to the office? James and the girls won't mind, and Mum … well, Mum's had a really hard time of it lately, and I don't want her upset. She never did like Michael, and she's a little bit afraid of having anything to do with the police. Well, her generation, you know?'

Hillary nodded, but said nothing, and the silence, as she'd expected, forced Lucy on. It was strange how most people couldn't stand silence, and needed to fill it.

'It's Myra, you see,' Lucy said, helplessly.

'Myra?' Hillary repeated blankly. Whatever it was that she suspected that Lucy wanted to tell her, something about her sister was the last thing she'd expected.

Unless Myra had had an affair with Ivers too?

'Yes, Myra died five months ago. It was very bad. She started getting ill when she was only sixteen, and for a long time the doctors couldn't seem to find out what was wrong with her. But she kept getting weaker and weaker, and eventually they pinned it down to one of those rare disease things that hardly anybody had heard of.'

'Oh, I'm so sorry,' Hillary said, and meant it. But it explained the air of taut fragility that surrounded the woman. She was like a vase with a fatal crack in it. At any moment, you expected her to go 'ping' and shatter into a hundred pieces.

Lucy shrugged helplessly. 'Mum was brilliant. She researched it on the Internet, and got in touch with the few other families who'd been through it. They put her on to this medical facility in the States, and she was in the process of selling the house so that Myra could afford to go and get treatment. And then she died. Mum was devastated. She blamed herself for not being able to save her. Which was rubbish of course. If medical science couldn't do it, how could she? But Mum always felt she needed to look after us after Dad died. As if she could make up for him not being here, if you see what I mean?'

'I do see, yes.'

'Mum refused to let Myra go into a nursing-home, like the doctors wanted. She needed twenty-four hour nursing, you see, but Mum wouldn't have it. So I took some leave from my job as well to help out, but even so … well, as you can imagine, Mum's worn out. She was just starting to get a little colour back in her cheeks and to get some sleep at nights, and now here's this thing with Michael come along. It's something we really don't need, right now.'

Hillary nodded.

'I know it's daft, but I think she's got this fear that you're going to come and take me away in handcuffs. That she's going to lose me too. First Dad, then Myra, now me. You can see why I don't want her upset, yeah?' Lucy pressed.

Hillary did. 'Don't worry. If I need to see you again, I'll come to your office.'

'Thanks ever so,' Lucy Kirke said, then nodded and smiled, and went back inside to be with her mother, and squeeze her hand some more.

Feeling slightly depressed, Hillary Greene drove back towards HQ.


Skunk Petersen wasn't very happy. He wasn't very happy because he'd been caught shoplifting, of all things, and was due to appear in court tomorrow morning.

He wasn't happy because his girlfriend had walked out on him two weeks ago, and his room in the squat looked like shit. True, it usually did, but somehow Deirdre had made it look better.

He was not happy because someone had found his hiding-place for the bottle of vodka – he suspected it was Jim Pickett – and he was going to have to sort him out. Trouble was, Jim was big and stupid and very good with his fists. But Skunk couldn't let him get away with it. Word soon got out about stuff like that.

And now he was very, very, unhappy to have this copper in his face.

Skunk, of course, was used to having coppers in his face. From the age of eight, when he'd first been caught nicking lunch money from the other kids, to his first taste of a Secure Training Centre then the real thing, cops had always delighted in getting in his face.

But mostly the cops had been eager-beaver constables or

seen-it-all weary sergeants. This copper was a whole different breed. Wearing a decent suit and tie, the smell of high rank oozed from his very Armani-scented pores.

'Mr Petersen, you're a hard man to track down.'

Skunk, who was slumped against a wall opposite a bookies, waiting for someone he could mug to go by so that he could put some money down on the five o'clock at Doncaster, briefly considered legging it, then decided it might not be a good idea.

He'd learned fairly young that it was always best to know what the buggers wanted, that way you could avoid trouble easier.

'Oh yeah? And who's looking?' he sneered.

'Superintendent Brian Vane.'

Skunk blinked. A super? Bloody hell, what had he done? He tried, in vain, to recall any caper that might have brought this much weight down on him, but honestly couldn't think of anything.

'I understand you knew Janine Tyler? A sergeant as she was then, but now a fully fledged DI – Mrs Janine Mallow no less. She had a brief taste of fame and glory not so long ago. Ring any bells?'

Skunk felt the sweat pop out on his forehead. For now he knew exactly what had brought this smiling crocodile swimming into his pond.

And he was in deep shit.

Janine answered her phone on the first ring. She was sitting at her desk in Witney, reviewing her latest case – some kind of arson swindle at a derelict factory out Aylesbury way. She was sure the owner had paid a professional fire-raiser to torch it, but unfortunately neither she, nor the chief fire officer were having much luck proving it.

'DI Mallow.'

'It's me. Skunk. That bloke you warned me might come sniffing around. Well, he came sniffing.'

Janine felt herself go cold and she stiffened in her chair. She had to swallow hard before she could speak.

'What did you tell him?' she eventually hissed, glancing around the office, glad to see that it was almost empty. At this time of the afternoon most of the dayshift were leaving early, whilst the night shift had yet to come in.

'Nothin'!' Skunk said at once, sounding aggrieved. 'I ain't daft. I told him I never even seen you after you got me sent down that last time.'

'Did he buy it?'

'Don't think so. He kept pushing it. He threatened me with fitting me up for something. Thing is, Sarge, I've got a shoplifting case coming up tomorrow. It's nothing really – just embarrassing, penny-ante stuff. But the judge I'm going up before, he don't like me, see. And this Vane bloke, he ain't really got the clout to get me time, has he?'

Janine heard the hard-put-upon whine in Petersen's voice and felt a hard punch of fear hit her, deep in the guts. Punks like him never believed it was their own fault when it came down to doing jail time. And they were always looking for a way to weasel out of it.

'Did you do a deal with Vane Skunk?' Janine demanded, her voice sibilant with warning. 'Because if you have ...'

'Nah, nah, I swore, didn't I? Besides ...' Petersen said, then suddenly fell silent.

But Janine had no trouble interpreting it. Besides, he was thinking, he was the one who'd provided her with a gun and had then read a few days later about how she had shot down the killer of her husband. Such a thing demanded a certain amount of wary respect, even in this day and age. And especially for low-on-the-totem-pole punks like Skunk.

Petersen clearly wouldn't want to get on her bad side.

'Don't worry. Vane's just pissing in the wind,' she said, trying to reassure him. 'He's got no friends here at HQ, believe me, and he's off to Hull in a few days. Just keep shtoom, and lie low and he'll be out of your hair. And, besides, I'll deal with him if I have to.'

There was a startled silence on the other end, an audible gulp, then Skunk swore in awe and hung up. It took Janine a moment to realize why. Skunk Petersen thought that she'd meant that she'd deal with him in the same way that she'd dealt with Cliver Myers.

By killing him.

She gave a sudden bark of laughter, making her few remaining colleagues in the room look at her curiously.

Janine hung up, still shaking her head and grinning – half in genuine amusement, but with a touch of near-hysteria lurking somewhere under the surface.

She thought for a moment, and then, with a sigh, rang Hillary Greene's number.

So much for standing on her own two feet.

Gemma dressed with care that night. She was heading for London, not to have a night on the town with her intended, alas, but to pay a visit to Quixote, a discreet little casino near Chelsea.

It was, she'd eventually managed to discover, Michael Ivers's gambling place of choice.

She kissed Guy goodbye, told him not to wait up since she was bound to be hideously late, and headed for the smoke.

She had no trouble getting in, even though it was members only. Dressed in a silver-grey dress that barely covered her bum, and silver high heels, with her short blond hair at its spikiest and her eyes made up with matching blue-silver shadow, the management were more than happy to let her wander around and make the place look glamorous. And whilst she was not positively taken for a high-class call girl, nevertheless, several of the male members were happy to 'teach' her how to throw the dice at the crap tables, or let her place their bets at the roulette wheel, all the while rubbing up against her.

She didn't drink, didn't upset the serious gamblers, and was very discreet.

But she learned a lot.

Not least of all, the fact that Michael Ivers, although a mostly successful gambler, also had an arrangement with the management. It seemed that more than one member had been recruited to the Quixote by Ivers. It took a while for her to twig, but when she did, it made sense. Ivers was allowed a certain leeway with his betting whenever he brought another mug into the fold. And the richer the punter, the more leeway he got. But Ivers had recruited anyone willing regardless of their income.

At a baccarat table she flirted with an electrician who threw away every penny he earned at the tables. Another man, a down-on-his-luck chartered surveyor, had just sold his holiday home to indulge his addiction to poker; he had also been brought in as a 'guest' by Ivers. One or two high-flyers were only too happy to admit that it had been Ivers who'd intro-duced them to the Quixote; they regarded him as a real man-about-town. But it was a rather indiscreet croupier who let slip that the management rewarded Ivers for his industry with certain unrestricted gambling hours and access to the high-stakes games.

It was nearly four o'clock in the morning before Gemma left the casino, with various phone numbers in her pocket. Incidentally, she'd also won nearly £250 at pontoon.

But if the men expected a call from the stunning blonde in the days to come, they were going to be disappointed when some flat-foot copper in uniform turned up instead, and asked them all about Michael Ivers and how they'd come to be members of Quixote.

Gemma, feeling justifiably chuffed with herself, slipped into bed beside Guy just as the first robin began to sing. Her bride-groom-to-be murmured sleepily but didn't wake.

Gemma snuggled up against him, reliving her triumph, and

thought, with a rare flash of perspicacity, just how much she was going to miss this sort of thing when Hillary was gone, and she was working on a career-enhancing prestigious committee.

# CHAPTER EIGHT

Since her sergeant already knew the way, and as she had no desire whatsoever to drive in the madhouse that was the capital city these days, bright and early next morning, Hillary and her junior officer set off for London in Gemma's car. With the blonde woman happily ensconced behind the wheel, Hillary hoped they'd make good time.

Mark Chang had listened enviously to Gemma's report when they'd all trooped in to the office that morning, wishing that he had been the one who'd tracked down the lead and spent a glamorous few hours in a swanky casino. And although the blonde bombshell as she was affectionately (and sometimes not so affectionately known) must have had only a few hours' sleep at most, Gemma had, understandably, been keen to do the follow-up interview with Quixote's boss. And who could blame her?

Now Hillary leaned back in the sporty little car, which still smelt of leather and gleamed with that just-out-of-the-show-room lustre that couldn't last for much longer.

'This is new,' she said, when Gemma had eventually negotiated her way out of Oxford and could relax a little as they sped down the fast lane of the motorway towards London.

'Guy got it for me. A sort of early wedding present,' Gemma said, with satisfaction.

Hillary nodded. She'd always known that her sergeant liked the good things in life. And who was to say she didn't deserve them? She worked hard at her job, which is as much as Hillary could have asked for.

'The wedding's not far off now. Just over three weeks, isn't it? Getting cold feet?' she teased.

'Hell no,' Gemma said, a shade too aggressively, Hillary thought. She glanced at her sergeant curiously, then shrugged. Getting married was a big step, and not something that even the cool and kick-ass Gemma Fordham could take without the odd collywobble, Hillary mused, hiding a smile.

She yawned as the motorway headed into the high white-chalk cutting not far from High Wycombe and glanced at her watch. It was barely ten, and she didn't want to spend all day following up on this one lead. Tempting as it was, there was no evidence yet that Michael Ivers's murder had had anything to do with his gambling habit.

Deciding she might as well make use of her time as a passenger, she reached for her mobile and dialled Steven Partridge's direct line.

'The doctor's at the table I'm afraid, can I take a message?' A sing-song female voice answered his line, and Hillary assumed it was the latest in the pathologist's long list of attractive secretaries. Nobody quite knew why he went through so many, or why they were all so cheerful. It was one of life's little mysteries.

'This is DI Greene. I'm calling about my homicide victim.' She rattled off Michael Ivers's case number. There came the rustling sound of papers being shuffled, and then a soft sigh. 'Oh yes, I've got it. There's a note here. Doctor Partridge said to offer his apologies if you called – but your cadaver got shuffled back when a complicated case came in – something to do with a possible contagious disease. He said he'd get around to your man as soon as he could.'

Hillary sighed. In other words, don't hold your breath. For a few seconds she toyed with the idea of asking about the contagious disease case, then suddenly decided that she didn't really want to know. If there was the possibility of galloping gut-rot sweeping through north Oxfordshire in the near future, she was better off staying in ignorance.

'OK,' she said affably and hung up, then relayed the bad news to Gemma. Her sergeant, as expected, took it stoically.

'Don't suppose it matters all that much, guv,' Gemma said consolingly. 'I reckon it's a fair to even bet that cause of death was due to head injury blunt force trauma, and that the plank of wood was the weapon.'

Hillary agreed, but experience had taught her how valuable autopsies could be. They could often throw up a surprise that could change the whole course of an investigation. She imparted this bit of wisdom to Gemma, more out of habit than anything else, then reached for her briefcase and pulled out a pile of forensics reports and witness statements.

Gemma put the nippy little car through its paces once she hit town, and thoroughly enjoyed giving the finger to black-cab taxi drivers who thought they owned the road, and giving even road-savvy Londoners a run for their money.

Hillary wasn't surprised when her sergeant even managed to grab a parking space right outside Quixote's discreet front door. The fact that someone was in the process of reversing into it made little difference.

Hillary got out and left her sergeant to deal with the irate man who'd got out of the car and was prepared to argue the issue. She imagined one quick glimpse of Gemma's police badge would sort the matter out. Or then again, maybe not. It might have been years since she'd driven in the capital, but she still remembered how parking spaces were treated like gold dust and were never relinquished lightly.

Quixote, like most places that thrived at night, had a slightly sorry-for-itself appearance in the daylight. The gold lettering above the stone lintel didn't sparkle quite so much without neon, and the pale-stone building looked dirty from the city's

accumulated grime. Nevertheless, the place was open for business, and as Hillary awaited her sergeant in the discreet foyer,
she could see, through open doors, the splash of green baize and
hear the clatter of the roulette wheel. Even at 10.45 in the
morning, punters were still eager to throw away their money, it
seemed. Quixote was obviously a twenty-four-hour a day establishment.

A man, wide and tall, and looking just a little puzzled,
approached her on large silent feet. Hillary understood his
bafflement. He probably had a good feel for the suckers who
frequented this place, and his radar was telling him she wasn't
here to gamble.

As he approached her, she heard Gemma walk up behind her.
She reached for her ID.

'DI Hillary Greene, Thames Valley Police, Sergeant Fordham,
ditto. We'd like to speak to the manager please,' she said crisply.

The man didn't even so much as blink. 'Certainly, officers.
This way.'

He lead them up a wide carpeted staircase, past a landing
lined with fake antiques and copies of famous paintings to a
second staircase, this one much less well appointed, and on up
into the attics of the building. Here the noise came from the
tapping of keyboards and the ringing of telephones. He went
through to the end office, knocked, gestured to them to stay put
and briefly disappeared. He reappeared a minute later and
ushered them past a curious-looking secretary, and then into a
large, modern office.

The man who rose from behind a desk was about Hillary's
age, slim and dark, and he reminded her, for some reason, of her
old headmaster.

'Inspector Greene. Oliver Chisholme. I own Quixote. I do
hope there isn't a problem. I can assure you all our licenses are
up to date and health and safety regulations are all adhered to.
We've never had trouble with the law here ever since we
opened, ten years ago.'

Hillary smiled vaguely, glanced coolly at the large man, who still hovered beside her and met her gaze blandly. He did, however, cast a quick questioning look at his employer, who must have given him the nod to leave, since he left quietly and without another word.

'Please, won't you sit down?' The casino owner indicated two large leather button-back chairs that fronted the desk. Behind that large expanse of oak, Hillary could make out a large screen that seemed to show the share index of various countries at various times. It made her wonder whether Mr Chisholme liked to gamble as well – not downstairs in his own rooms, but on the much wider stage of the stock market.

'It's about one of your regular clients, sir. A Mr Michael Ivers.' She came straight to the point.

Oliver Chisholme nodded, sitting down in his black leather swivel-chair and making a steeple of his fingers. These he then rested slightly against his chin. The gesture seemed unnecessarily flamboyant and immediately irritated her.

'Oh yes. Mike. I heard about him on the news. Terrible. A real shock,' Chisholme gave his head a vague, sorrowful shake.

'You didn't think to come forward and volunteer information about him, sir?' Hillary asked.

'Oh no. Well, it could hardly be relevant, could it? And here at Quixote, we guarantee our clientele complete discretion.'

Hillary smiled briefly. 'Not relevant? A gambler is murdered and you don't think that we, the police, would be interested to hear from you?' She allowed her voice to sound just slightly chiding.

Oliver Chisholme spread his hands and smiled amiably. 'Come now, Inspector. We're all civilized people here.'

Hillary heard Gemma snort softly beside her. The casino owner was also meant to hear it and obviously did so, for his amiable smile cooled just a little.

'What sort of client was Mr Ivers, sir?' Hillary asked.

'A very valued one. And successful too, believe it or not. It's a widely held belief – and a totally erroneous one – that gambling is a mug's game. If you know what you're doing, and you have a gift for luck, as some people do, then believe me, you can actually make a lot of money in this game. And Mike was one of those lucky and smart ones.'

Hillary sighed softly. 'And here was I thinking the house always wins.'

Oliver Chisholme laughed softly. 'Well, we always do, in a way, Inspector Greene. Like I said, only those who know what they're doing, and are blessed with good luck, get to walk away the winners. But that is only about nought-point-nought-point one per cent of the total. The rest of our clients tend to fall into that other category.'

'Mugs you mean?' Gemma clarified sweetly.

Oliver Chisholme spread his hands again. 'People like the thrill of gambling. What can I say? Am I responsible for human nature? Here at Quixote we at least provide them with a genial and safe atmosphere in which to do so.'

Hillary lips twisted. How very gallant of him, she thought sourly. 'So how much, on average, would you say Mr Ivers won in any given month?' she asked, her voice as bland and polite as that of a politician.

She fully expected the odious man to demur and say he couldn't possibly guess, so she was somewhat taken aback when the slick operator turned to his keyboard, tapped some keys, nodded, tapped some more, did some obvious mental calculations, then turned back to her.

'Well, last month for instance, he was up nearly two thousand. The month before that a little less. Last March he had a real run, and relieved us of more than twenty-eight thousand.'

'I'll bet you just loved that,' Gemma said sardonically.

Oliver laughed. 'As a matter of fact, Sergeant, we did. You see, when a client hits a lucky streak like that, it really galvanizes the other players. You'd be amazed how much seeing someone else win big can loosen the purse strings. The house takes in more money when somebody's winning big than when it's just an average night.'

Hillary, who had a basic grasp of psychology, could well believe it. 'But that was exceptional, even for Ivers?' she pressed.

'Oh yes.'

'And he couldn't always be winning, obviously?' she added. She wondered, cynically, if sometimes the owner of Quixote gave his croupiers permission to let someone win big. After all, as he'd just admitted, it made sound business sense. If so, was it always Ivers who benefited? And if it was, what had the murdered man done to deserve such largesse?

'No. Some months he lost overall,' Chisholme admitted modestly.

'And when he did, how did he pay you? Cash, cheque, the watch off his wrist?' Hillary asked pleasantly.

'We had a gentleman's agreement, naturally,' Oliver said.

Beside her, Gemma audibly gave another soft little snort of disbelief. Oliver shot her a quick look. Good, she was getting under his skin, Hillary thought with approval.

'Did Mr Ivers ever incur any sizeable debt that he couldn't then honour?' she swept on, not giving him a chance to rally.

'Oh no. Like I said, Mike was a professional. He never bet more than he could afford to lose, and if he ever did find himself on a rare losing streak, he had enough sense to quit. You'd be amazed at how many people don't.'

'No I wouldn't,' Hillary said. 'Do you know if Mr Ivers made any enemies here?'

Oliver Chisholme shrugged helplessly. 'Not as far as the management is concerned, of that I can assure you. All the croupiers, my accountancy staff, and myself, naturally, had nothing but a professional and friendly attitude towards the man. Whether or not he might have made enemies among the other clients I'm not at liberty to say.'

Hillary nodded. She wasn't at all surprised that the oily casino owner was trying to pass the buck on to his paying customers. 'You think he may have set up private games amongst them and fleeced them for himself then? Surely you, the management, would take exception to that,' Hillary said drily. 'After all, he'd be undercutting you.'

'Oh, I'm sure Mike never did any such thing.'

'Then why would he have made enemies of some of your punters, Mr Chisholme?' Hillary asked reasonably. She knew the answer of course – Gemma had already sussed it out last night. But it would be interesting to see whether Chisholme was willing to confirm it.

And it did indeed seem to be the case that having his casino come to the attention of a murder inquiry was enough to turn him into a solid citizen - for a brief moment anyway.

'Well, Mike knew that he could always pay off his debts in a variety of ways. Some months he might not have the cash readily available.'

Hillary nodded. 'In which case?' She let her voice rise in an open-ended question.

'In which case, his debt could be deferred or reduced in return for certain services.'

'And what services did Michael Ivers perform for you, Mr Chisholme?' Hillary asked, deadpan, and saw the man give a wince of distaste. She was, like Gemma, deliberately provoking him, just because she didn't like him. And although she'd phrased her question with care, she didn't really suspect that Ivers had been gay, or that Chisholme himself was that way inclined either.

'He would sometimes bring in the punters,' Oliver Chisholme snapped. Then he realized that he was letting the mask slip slightly, and turned on the amiable smile again. 'That is,' he corrected smoothly, 'Mike liked to introduce newcomers to the casino. First-time gamblers or novices. Both men and women could be drawn to Mike, you see. They envied his lifestyle and he'd act as though he was doing them a favour, giving them an intro into the in-crowd, so to speak.'

'And you reaped the benefits,' Gemma said coldly.

'Gamblers will always find a way to get their fix, Sergeant,' he said smoothly. 'They could bet at the races, they could play the scratch cards, or on-line bingo or poker, or even go to the dogs. At least here at Quixote they get to sample the whole casino experience whilst being fleeced. Some people appreciate a touch of class.'

Hillary was beginning to feel depressed. This little chiseller and the truth of his words combined with the atmosphere of decadence and despair that seemed to stain the very air, were combining to bring her down.

She shifted restlessly on her seat. 'I need a list of all the people whom Mr Ivers introduced to this casino,' Hillary said firmly, and held up a hand as the man made to speak. 'And if you feel that you can't manage that, then I'm afraid I'm going to have to have a word with my friends in Vice. And I don't care how squeaky clean this place is, you don't want your name added to their shit-list, do you?'

Chisholme didn't.

He tapped a few more keys and a moment later they heard the discreet hum of the printer. He handed over a list of names and Gemma reached for it. Without another word, Hillary got up and left.

Once outside, she waited for her sergeant to point her car keys at her latest acquisition and when the car obediently beeped back, she opened the passenger door and slid inside.

Gemma got behind the wheel and shuddered. 'I feel like I need a shower,' she said bitterly.

'Yes, he's a real charmer isn't he?' Hillary agreed.

Back at HQ, Gemma photocopied the list, put one copy in her own files and handed the original over to Chang for the murder book.

'How many were there roughly?' Hillary asked, sitting down behind her desk and scowling vaguely at her in tray, which was so full its contents were threatening to topple over.

'Nearly thirty in all, I reckon, guv,' Gemma replied, then paused as Chang suddenly bounded up from his chair.

'Guv, this name. I recognize it.' He was tapping the list Chisholme had given them, his face alight with triumph. 'Jason Vaughan.'

'Vaughan? Isn't he one of the van drivers at the depot? The one who set your alarms off when you interviewed him?' Hillary asked sharply.

'That's right, guv,' Chang confirmed happily.

Hillary nodded. 'Well caught then,' she said. 'We'd better start with him.' She glanced at Gemma, who was obviously keen to sit in on it, and sighed. 'Gemma, you get started on the others. Once Chang and I have finished with Vaughan, he can give you a hand.'

Gemma sighed, but supposed Chang deserved the break. Although she was loath to let anybody else have a choice titbit, she could – just – remember what it was to be an eager-beaver young detective constable hungry to gain experience and learn from a master.

'Right, guv,' she grunted.

Chang, who was already on his feet and all but hopping from foot to foot with excitement, beamed at her. Gemma hid a smile and turned back to her computer.

Another day at the office – another day of eye-strain.

As Hillary drove Puff the Tragic Wagon back towards Adderbury, she asked Chang to go over his impression of Vaughan once again.

'I haven't been able to do much background work on him yet, guv, but I've learned a bit,' Chang said, when he'd finished. 'I know he's married, but separated from his wife. Another van driver told me that he thought Vaughan was living in a caravan on a mate's allotment, but later on, when I checked with the mate, he told me that there'd been complaints to the council and he'd been moved on. He gave me an address for Vaughan that matched the one Vaughan gave me himself. I haven't been there yet, or questioned the neighbours, but a mate of mine who lives in Banbury tells me the area is a real cesspit. He reckons the place Vaughan is living in is probably little better than a squat.'

'Sounds as if Quixote wiped him out,' Hillary observed. 'In which case, Ivers was responsible for the break-up of his marriage, the loss of his home, and who knows what else.'

'Sounds like a motive for murder to me, guv.'

'Try not to get ahead of yourself, Constable,' Hillary warned gently. Although she knew how much Chang must long for Vaughan to be guilty, it wasn't very often it happened this easily. And although it would be a feather in the young constable's cap if it panned out, and he *was* responsible for a break-through in the case, it didn't do to get blinkered vision.

'We'll talk to him, then you can get on to questioning his neighbours. What's his alibi again?'

Chang didn't need to consult his notes. 'He was vague, guv. Said it was his day off, so he slept in late, then went down the pub for a sandwich and spent the afternoon watching telly on a mate's set. He's got Sky, but the mate was at work – he lets him use his gaff if there's a match on he wants to see. Later he went to the chippie for some fish and chips, then back to the pub, went home about elevenish and into bed.'

Hillary nodded. 'So no alibi, in other words.'

'Right, guv,' Chang confirmed happily.

Jack Wallace looked up from his desk and watched Hillary Greene approach. He liked her figure and he liked redheads. He didn't so much like her warrant card.

'Inspector Greene. Help you?'

'We want a word with Jason Vaughan.'

'He's out. In the van.'

'Do you know what route he's on?'

Wallace sniffed, rose and went to the filing cabinet. He had a computer on his desk but it was silent, and Hillary guessed the old man preferred the old-fashioned methods. He withdrew an itinerary, glanced at his watch, then said reluctantly, 'He should be in Witney about now. Then he's off to Brackley.'

'Does he have a mobile number?'

'Must have.'

'Can you find it for us please?' Hillary persisted patiently. Beside her, she could sense Mark Chang begin to shift edgily.

Jack Wallace delved into the filing cabinet for yet another folder, took his time finding it and running his finger down a list, then recited a string of numbers so fast that Chang wasn't able to get it down first time, and had to ask him to repeat it.

When Hillary thanked him and they left, Jack Wallace went back to his desk and sighed heavily.

He had several buyers lined up for the business now. Abruptly he reached for the phone. He was going to accept the best offer. The sooner the contracts were signed, the better he'd like it.

Outside, Hillary let Chang phone Jason Vaughan and arrange a meeting at a services station just outside Oxford. Hillary drove in silence, thinking things through.

By now, she should have had a better handle on the case, but this one seemed to be something of a non-starter. There was no prime suspect as such, no helpful forensics and not even a clear-cut indicator of what sort of crime she was looking at. Crime of passion was probably the best bet, given Mike Ivers's penchant for the women. But it could equally be money-related, if the casino angle was anything to go by, with a revenge killing running a close favourite. She'd bet that Jason Vaughan's wasn't the only life to have been ruined by Quixote's allure.

And why was old man Wallace being so obstructive?

'When you've got time I want you to concentrate on Wallace Deliveries. Is it solvent, making a good profit, anything known against it. That sort of thing,' she said to Chang, who instantly made a note in his book.

Jason Vaughan was already in the services cafeteria when they arrived, a plate of half-eaten burger and chips in front of him. He seemed to have difficulty swallowing the mouthful of food he was chewing when he saw them, and he reached for his mug of coffee and took a good slurp to help it down.

He recognized Chang at once, and his eyes briefly met Hillary's before moving away again.

Hillary asked Chang to bring them both a mug of coffee, and approached Vaughan. She introduced herself, and was about to show him her ID, when Vaughan glanced around nervously and held out a hand to stop her.

'That's all right. No need to go flashing around the cop card.' He smiled as he said it, but his pale-green eyes flickered nervously.

He was a sandy-haired lad, with a smattering of freckles. Not particularly young though – he was probably nearly thirty, Hillary gauged. Old enough to know better, one would have thought. But then, when did human weakness ever reach an age limit?

Chang quickly joined them and reached for his notebook.

Jason watched him miserably.

'I believe, when you first talked to the constable here, that you were somewhat less than honest, Mr Vaughan,' Hillary began mildly, stirring her coffee with a plastic spoon, and hoping it wasn't going to taste as foul as it looked.

'What do you mean?' Vaughan hedged. 'I never lied to him.'

'You told him, I believe, that you never saw Mr Ivers outside of the office. But we now know that you were seen together at a gambling establishment in Chelsea called Quixote. Ring a bell?'

'Oh that,' Jason mumbled. 'That was nothing. He took me to this club once, that was all.'

'Once?' Hillary pressed sceptically.

'I only went there with Ivers the once,' Vaughan insisted. It was a clever prevarication, but Hillary saw through it instantly.

'Ah. But you went by yourself many times after that, I imagine?' Hillary guessed, and took a sip of the coffee.

And shuddered.

It was far worse than it looked. Still, she found it very hard to abandon a cup of coffee and took another sip. The second sip never seemed so bad.

Well. Nearly never.

'It's not against the law is it?' Jason Vaughan asked angrily. 'What I do with my money is my affair isn't it? I earn it, I get to spend it.'

'And does the CSA agree with you, Mr Vaughan?' Hillary asked, and the van driver nearly choked on a chip.

'Look, it's temporary, see. The wife ain't really left me – she's just living with her mother, like, until I can find a bigger place for us. So the CSA don't come into it.'

Hillary nodded. So the wife hadn't yet gone down the official route. She suspected that that wouldn't be the case for much longer. And from the way Vaughan's hand shook as he lifted his own coffee mug, she could tell that he had come to the same conclusion.

And what would he do then? If the CSA managed to take the money straight out of his wages before he could even touch it, how would he cope? If he was that deeply hooked on gambling, he'd have to try and find the money from somewhere else. Thieving, maybe. Mugging old ladies for their pension money.

She sighed heavily.

'Michael Ivers really screwed up your life, didn't he?' she said sadly. 'No one would blame you if you did take a length of two-by-four and whack it upside his head.'

Vaughan audibly gulped. 'I never did no such thing.'

'Tell me again where you were the night Mr Ivers was murdered,' Hillary said, and listened to the same litany that Chang had heard before.

'So your friend can't confirm that you were in his flat that afternoon,' she said, although that hardly mattered. Ivers had been alive and well until the last of the depot employees had left at nearly six.

'No, he was at work.'

'But the people at the chippie would remember you, wouldn't they?' Hillary pressed.

'Dunno. It was busy. Nearly six, just when people are turning out of work and wanna buy something on the way home. There was a big queue.'

'Don't they know you at the chippie?'

'Nah, not really. I only went there 'cause it was close to my mate's flat. I usually eat at my local Chinkie.'

'And when you got home, nobody saw you come in? A landlady, a fella in the next room to you?'

'No, I told you. There ain't no landlord, as such. And I never saw any of them who got rooms either side of me.'

'You have to see that that leaves you in a vulnerable position, Mr Vaughan,' Hillary said, trying for a third sip of her coffee before reluctantly giving it up as a bad job and pushing the still-full mug away from her.

'You had reason to hate the victim, and you have no alibi for the time he was killed.' She held up her hand and ticked off two of her fingers. 'You know the site, and could easily have watched the nightwatchman's routine and slipped past him.' Another finger down. 'You'd know that there were always pieces of wood to be had from around the builder's yard, and the victim wouldn't have been surprised to see you on the premises. Giving you ample opportunity to come up behind him and hit him over the head.'

She rested her now clenched hand beside her useless coffee and regarded him levelly.

Jason Vaughan, his food going cold and forgotten on his plate, stared back at her in dismay.

'You can't be serious.'

'Don't I look serious?'

'But I didn't do it. And since I know I didn't do it, I don't reckon you can possibly prove it, see. Isn't there forensics and all that sort of stuff nowadays? I watch the telly. You can't have found my fingerprints or DNA or what have you on Ivers, since I didn't do it. So now, if you don't mind, I've got my deliveries to make.'

And with that bit of bravado, he got up and walked swiftly away. He turned once or twice to look fearfully over his shoulder to see if they were following him, and seemed relieved to find that they weren't.

Beside her, Chang slowly folded away his notebook. He looked a little forlorn. In spite of everything, he was rather inclined to think that Vaughan had been telling the truth. But he didn't trust his instincts that much. Not yet anyway.

Hillary shrugged. 'Well, he sounded plausible,' she said slowly. 'But then, a lot of killers often do. He's got to be top of the list so far. We need to keep plugging away. Get his photograph and set up a stop-and-show on the Aynho road. Arrange it with traffic, and set it up for one night this week, at around the eight p.m. mark. See if any motorist recognizes him – and get a photo of the van he drives and his own motor if he still has one. If Vaughan did kill Ivers, he must have travelled down that road at some point that evening. And you never know your luck. You might find a regular traveller who clocked him that night.'

Chang knew a long shot when he heard one, but then he supposed they couldn't afford to leave any stone unturned. Hillary wasn't the only one who realized that the case was in danger of stalling.

Hillary checked her messages when she got back to the office, and wasn't surprised to hear her ex-sergeant's familiar voice.

'Boss, it's Janine. We need to meet again. Call me.'

Hillary sighed.

She filled Gemma in on the interview with Vaughan, and her sergeant in turn recited what she'd learned about the people on Chisholme's list so far. Nearly all of the punters whom Ivers had brought in to the casino lived locally, and it was going to be a pain pinning down alibis for the night of the murder. Hillary told her to grab as many uniforms as she could muster to help out, and then settled down to some solid paperwork.

The phone records for their victim's work phone and mobile had at last been checked out, but had thrown up nothing of interest. All of the calls made direct to his office line were legitimate business calls. And his mobile didn't turn up much of use either. There was a call from Quixote, but that had been nearly a week before his death. There was a call from the Willows Health Centre, probably where Ivers's GP was located, and she made a mental note to get in touch with him or her at some point, but it was hardly a priority. There were the usual calls from friends and one from his dentist, arranging a check-up. The only highlight was the fact that a call had been traced to Ivers's current girlfriend. But even there they were out of luck, for the uniform checking up on that one noted that the girl, a Monica Stevens, had been in South Africa since last Monday. Apparently, it was a regular annual holiday for her, since she visited her mother, who'd remarried and moved there over four years ago.

So the current love interest hadn't even been in the country when Michael Ivers had been killed.

Hillary sighed, and tossed the telephone details to one side. She'd have to get in touch with Ivers's solicitor soon, and find out the contents of his will. It would be interesting to see who benefited from all his gambling profits.

Only when Gemma and Chang had both left for the night and dusk was setting in outside, did Hillary call Janine back on her mobile and arrange to meet at her local pub – The Boat, in Thrupp.

Janine hadn't been to Thrupp for over a year and as she bought herself a vodka and tonic at the bar, she smiled briefly at the flirtatious landlord's compliments.

Hillary was outside, sitting at one of the tables beside the canal, even though it was nearly fully dark now. But with the light spilling out from the pub windows, Janine found the white wrought-iron table where her old boss was sitting without difficulty, and sat down beside her with a sigh.

Hillary echoed the sentiment.

'Bad day?' Janine asked, remembering how Hillary sometimes found a noisy pub too much if she was wrestling with a particularly recalcitrant case.

'Murder inquiry. Going nowhere fast. The usual.'

Janine nodded, took a fortifying gulp of her drink and sighed again.

'Vane found Skunk Petersen,' she said, and took a second long swallow of her drink. It bit the back of her throat and she had to cough. In the darkness, a tawny owl called and his mate answered. Something rustled nervously in a stand of reeds close by. Overhead, the stars were coming out, and it was getting just a bit too cool for comfort. Janine did her sheepskin jacket up and leaned back in her chair, which scraped noisily across the flagstone patio.

'It might be a good idea to give him a bung,' Hillary said after a moment's thought. 'Tell him to take a little holiday somewhere. Just to keep him out of Vane's orbit until he has to push off to Hull.' She didn't say it out loud, but they both knew that Janine could afford it. Mel had left her well provided for. 'A skell like that would probably like a few weeks down in Brighton.'

Janine sighed. 'OK,' she agreed wearily.

'And don't worry about Vane. I'll deal with him,' Hillary concluded. She sounded ineffably tired.

Janine took another swallow of her drink, and was glad of the darkness that prevented her from having to look her old boss in the face.

'So, you're really going?' Janine Mallow asked.

'Yes, I'm really going,' Hillary Greene replied.

## CHAPTER NINE

*The Mollern* was gleaming more silver than grey in the moonlight when Hillary returned to her mooring that night. The boat's name was an old English dialect word for heron. Consequently her uncle, the narrowboat's original owner, had had her painted in that waterbird's colours. Overall, she was a soft blue-grey, with black-and-white trim, and panels on the side with paintings of the river bird set against a pale-gold background.

It was at times like this when living on the water endowed her otherwise mundane life with a touch of the romantic. Would it really be such a wrench to finally untie *The Mollern* from her mooring and set her free to travel at last? Surely the point of owning a mobile home was to be mobile?

As she walked up the towpath towards her boat, Hillary was pleased to see that the paintings on the side were all still in good repair. She especially liked the one of the heron who was crouched over a pond, stalking a stickleback and ready to jab with its long, predatory beak.

She climbed on board, undid the padlock on her metal door and stooped to walk down the three steps that took her into the narrow corridor that ran the length of her boat. She walked right on through into the tiny galley, pausing to toss her coat on to the top of her bed through the open doorway, and put the kettle on. Next she opened up a tin of chunky soup and put it on the stove. With some bread, it was almost as good as a bowl of stew, and it was the only thing she could face cooking after a hard day at work.

Besides, she didn't have all that many saucepans to prepare a more complicated meal, and she had long since become a past master of living with just the bare essentials.

As she left her supper to simmer, she went back into her bedroom and pulled a flat A4 brown envelope from beneath the mattress. This she took forward to the main living area's single armchair and with the envelope on her lap, drew out the photograph and looked at it thoughtfully.

It hadn't changed since her old colleague had first handed it over. In it, Brian Vane, maybe as much as ten years younger than he was today, was talking vigorously to a woman whose dress, make-up, and whole belligerent stance, screamed working prostitute.

Vane had never worked Vice; this much Hillary had been able to ascertain, and so, in theory, he shouldn't have had a reason to be feeling a working girl's collar. But of course, there could be many explanations for it. She could have been a witness in a case he was working on, or maybe she'd been an informant. And the fact that Vane could no doubt come up with even more reasonable excuses for the photograph didn't help her sense of descending gloom.

She sighed and put the photograph back in the envelope and transferred it to her briefcase. Obsessing about it wasn't going to do her any damned good. At some point tomorrow, if she got the time and the chance, she'd have to confront Vane and tell him to back off from Janine, and the skell who'd supplied her with the gun. Because one thing was for sure - if he somehow managed to get Skunk Petersen to talk, Janine faced jail and she herself might just join her. Accessory after the fact could still carry a custodial sentence if the facts warranted it. And with all the media circus that had surrounded the Clive Myers shooting, Hillary knew that the Criminal Prosecution Service would have no other option but to go for the maximum penalties.

She wished, yet again, that she knew the background to the photograph, but she had no other choice but to use it blind. And she'd have to be very clever about it. If Vane even got a whiff of the idea that she didn't actually know what the threat was that it held for him, she'd really be up the proverbial creek with paddles in short supply.

She sighed, and went to eat her soup. It annoyed her that, yet again, she was being distracted from the thing that really mattered – which was solving her murder case.

Over the past few weeks, she'd been well aware of the fact that she was feeling a growing reluctance actually to go through with it and retire. Every instinct she had told her it was going to be a gut-wrenching experience, and every nerve was screaming at her not to go through with it. But now she knew for sure that she was doing the right thing. If she'd ever needed confirmation, this was it.

Even if Vane did back down and went off to Hull, who knew when the spectre of the Myers case might rise up and bring her down, once and for all? And she couldn't be a serving police officer if it did. It would disappoint too many of the friends and colleagues who believed in her. Worse, it would bring the whole of Thames Valley into disrepute.

No. She was doing what was best for everyone, whether they liked it or not. And whether she liked it or not.

The next morning, as she pushed through into the main foyer at HQ, she saw three uniforms clustered at the desk sergeant's desk shoot her a quick look, then scuttle away guiltily. It was enough to make her curious enough to go over and find out what was afoot.

'Stan,' she greeted the man behind the long expanse of fake-wooden countertop, and nodded at the disappearing backs of the men. 'Anything I should know about?'

She relied on the desk sergeants to keep her in the loop, and Stan was one of the biggest gossips in the station. He was a

large, flaccid man, who had a surprising turn of speed on the
rugby field, and regularly played for the station house against
their fiercest rivals from St Aldates nick.

Now he winked at her jovially. 'Nah. That silly sod, Wren, is
trying to set up a book, but it ain't gonna run.'

'Really?'

Hillary was surprised. You could usually rely on quite a few
at the station house to bet on whatever took their fancy. The last
punt, if she remembered correctly, was on whether a certain
very rotund female inspector in Traffic was pregnant or just
more rotund than usual. Her husband had bet against, she
remembered. And lost.

Then she frowned. 'Wait a minute. Is it about me?' she asked,
trying to mask her disbelief.

'Yeah. Well, it's daft,' Stan said, looking and sounding a touch
uneasy. 'Like I said, it just ain't gonna run, 'cause there's no one
willing to bet against you.'

Now Hillary was curious. 'So what's the bet?'

'That you won't solve your murder case before you go, but
will have to hand it over to Sam.'

'So, they think DI Waterstone's going to take it on?' she
mused. If she had to hand it over to anyone, she hoped they
were right. Not that she exactly relished the thought of going
out on a dud.

'No probs, though, ay Hill? You'll get your bloke.' Stan
chivvied her.

Hillary hoped he was right. Then she felt a soft warm glow
begin to settle in her stomach. So, none of her fellow officers was
willing to bet she wouldn't do it, weren't they? Unless Stan was
just being kind, of course.

She shrugged. 'Well, I'd better not stand here wasting police
time then, had I?' she said, deliberately cheerful. 'Just in case.
Can't have anyone winning the pool, can we?'

Stan laughed. 'Like I said, it's a non-starter. That Wren is still
wet behind the ears.'

He watched her go and shook his head. There weren't many DIs who'd take it all in such good part. He'd miss her. They'd all miss her.

At her desk Hillary tackled her ever-avaricious in tray until Gemma and Mark arrived, then for a half an hour or so they tossed the case about, swapping ideas, trading thoughts and picking it apart. Unfortunately, it didn't get them any further forward. She left Gemma to get on with tracking down and questioning those on the list of people Ivers had recruited for Quixote, told Chang to get back to the victim's office and find out how well Wallace Deliveries was doing financially, then telephoned Michael Ivers's solicitor.

For once, she was in luck. He would see her within the hour.

At the Aynho Islip Business Park Mark Chang parked his car and quickly walked across the forecourt. He was distracted from going straight to the newspaper-delivery depot by the sound of raised voices coming from just inside Unit 4.

Very much aware that the murder weapon had probably been picked up from just outside the builder's yard, he walked carefully towards it, careful to keep out of the line of sight of anybody who might be passing by the open door to the yard.

He recognized Frank Ross's voice coming from inside at once, and was surprised. He'd thought the ex-cop's shift had ended at six. Though, come to think of it, he hadn't noticed anyone manning the security booth. Perhaps he was working overtime.

'Come off it, Hodgson. I don't give a crap what you think,' Frank Ross said, now viciously. 'And you can go running off your mouth to anybody you like. You don't run things here, much as you might like to think you do.'

Chang pressed himself more closely to the wooden fencing and found a knothole in the wood. Sticking one eye to it, he suddenly felt vaguely ridiculous – like a comic book flatfoot eavesdropping on villains.

He couldn't see Frank Ross at all through the narrow aperture, but he did have a good view of the man who was obviously arguing with him. He was a pear-shaped man in his mid-fifties, Chang guessed, with short-cropped hair going grey, and was wearing a pair of old jeans and a padded check jacket. The boss himself, Chang guessed, since Ross had called him by name.

'I'm a unit holder, same as anyone else, and the management bloody well will listen to me. I'm not the only one who's made a complaint against you, Ross, not by a long shot. I'll have you out of here yet, you sticky-fingered bastard.'

With this threat, the owner of the building yard took a step forward, and Ross must have done the same, for in the next moment, the two men were face to face, and the young constable could see them both now, in profile. Chang could also feel the air bristling with aggression.

'Kiss my arse, Hodgson,' Ross hissed. 'If you can't control your boy, that's your problem, not mine. Don't be such a wuss about it. It's pathetic.'

Chang saw the other man's hands clench into fists, and he wondered, with some irritation, if he was going to have to break up a fight. He'd thought those days were mostly behind him. When he'd been in uniform it seemed he did little else but keep hotheads apart on a Saturday night. Football fans, boozed up and looking for trouble, were nothing new to him. But now that he'd made detective grade he was getting used to doing something a little more cerebral.

'Let's leave our Alan out of this, you bastard,' Hodgson yelled. Holding up his two hands he shoved Ross hard in the chest and out of Chang's line of sight. Deciding it was time to get closer to the action Chang quickly jogged to the open doorway and stepped inside.

Hodgson caught the movement from out of the corner of his eye, and his head swivelled around. Ross, who had taken a step back and was lifting his arm preparatory to taking a swing, did an almost comical double-take too. For a second the three of them formed a frozen tableau, and again Chang felt vaguely ridiculous.

Then Frank's arm lowered quickly to his side.

'Piss off, Ross,' Hodgson hissed at him quietly.

'Yeah, and who's gonna make me?' Ross jeered back just as sibilantly.

'Keep away from the boy, you hear? Or you'll be sorry.'

Chang, who couldn't quite make out what the men were saying now that they'd resorted to near-whispers, moved quickly closer.

'Why? Just what do you think your precious Alan is in to?' Ross shot back, knowing it was the man's weakness. Hodgson was nobody's fool. He knew that things were going missing regularly from his site, and he knew that there must be an inside man. Presumably he trusted his foreman, and he knew none of the casual workers would have the keys or knowledge to be of much use to a gang of thieves.

Which meant, quite rightly as it turned out, that his dear precious son Alan must be a prime contender. And Frank considered it was high time that the builder was reminded that if he went down, so too would Alan Hodgson.

'Everything all right, sir?' Chang asked blandly, then jumped as a man suddenly came up behind him. Chang hadn't heard his approach and he felt a moment of real fear. But the man, a tall, lanky man with a shock of ginger hair, was looking at Hodgson.

'Pat, those quarry stones have just arrived. You know, the ones for the patio paving for the Hilburne Hotel job. You wanted to check the quality before it was unloaded.'

'Right. Thanks, Tim. I'll be there.'

'I'm off to me bed then,' Frank Ross said cheerfully, and cheekily slapped Chang – hard – between the shoulder blades as he passed.

Before Chang could ask anything further, Hodgson too had scuttled away. Chang turned to the newcomer and smiled hopefully.

'Your boss and the night watchman don't exactly hit it off, do they?' he said nonchalantly.

The man called Tim shrugged his shoulders briefly. 'Hardly surprising, is it? The boss caught him drinking on duty one night, and tried to get him fired.'

Before Chang could ask anything more of him, he too turned and walked quickly away.

Chang wasn't particularly offended. He was long since used to the fact that most people were in no hurry to volunteer information to the police.

He went back to Wallace Deliveries with a thoughtful look on his face. It didn't take a genius to figure out that Ross must have some sort of a scam going. And since whatever it was it obviously enraged Hodgson, coupled with the fact that builders' yards were notorious for being full of goods that could easily be sold off the back of a lorry, it wasn't hard to figure out exactly what kind of scam Frank Ross was running.

He'd have to ask around and find out who this Alan fella was. But the real question, of course, was; could it have anything to do with the murder? Ivers was the kind of man who noticed things, of this Chang was sure. And he'd already proved to be a man who liked making money, and was willing to stoop to any means to get it. If he'd discovered a lucrative little scheme here at the very business park where he'd worked, wouldn't it be just the kind of thing he'd want to get in on?

Try a spot of blackmail, maybe? Or even set up a rival scheme. And Frank Ross, as an ex-copper, had a lot to lose if he was ever caught and convicted. A copper's life in jail would be one of perpetual misery, harassment and pain.

With a sigh, and feeling like a stool pigeon, Chang reached for his mobile and called Hillary's number.

Jenkins, Jones & Portland had their offices in a smart new building not too far from the famous Banbury Cross. Matthew Jones was obviously one of the younger partners in the firm, and he greeted her with a bland smile as his secretary showed her in.

'DI Greene. I have been expecting you to get in touch, ever since I read in the papers about Michael. I was really shocked to hear about his murder. I hope you're making progress in your enquiries?'

Jones was a short, dark-haired man, dressed in a suit that tried to hide his lack of inches. He wore a very slim, discreet gold-and-onyx signet ring on the index finger of his right hand, and a plain but expensive watch on his left wrist. He indicated a chair in front of his desk, and Hillary took it with a smile of thanks.

'They're ongoing, of course,' she agreed meaninglessly. 'What can you tell me about his will, sir?'

'I doubt very much that there's anything there that will be of help to you, Inspector. He made a will five years ago, leaving everything to his mother, his father having died when Michael was in his early twenties. Alas, his mother also died, and he altered the will to benefit his only remaining relative, a sister who lives in New Zealand.'

'Nothing to his ex-wife and her son?'

'No, I'm afraid there's not. There are one or two personal bequests to various friends – a rather fine Rackham watercolour sketch goes to a young lady called Lucy Kirke. His car goes to another young lady.' He named Ivers's most recent girlfriend, currently holidaying in South Africa. 'And there are two rather surprising philanthropically motivated bequests. A local donkey sanctuary gets several thousand, as does an Aids charity here in town.' The solicitor smiled. 'I have to say, these rather surprised me. Michael never struck me as a charitable type.'

Hillary smiled, but her heart was sinking. Once again, any possible motive or lead was going down the drain. She'd have to check on the sister, of course, but it should be fairly easy to check whether she'd ever left the antipodes.

'Was it a sizeable estate?' she asked curiously.

'So-so. His flat in town was mortgaged, so the equity in it wasn't as much as it might have been. But he had a very healthy bank account. Funnily enough, though, nothing in stocks or shares or other investments.' The solicitor sounded so disapproving that she suspected that he himself had a considerable portfolio of financial buffers.

'No, there wouldn't be,' Hillary voiced the thought out loud. For a man who liked to gamble, Ivers would have wanted all his assets to be both liquid and easily available.

'Did you know him well, would you say, sir?' she asked next, but disappointingly, the other man spread his hands in a telling gesture.

'Not really. We'd meet occasionally, and he struck me as a rather larger-than-life figure.' The solicitor laughed suddenly. 'I'd see him sometimes roaring about town in an open-top sports car with a pretty girl by his side, and I'd feel quite envious. And yet, you know, the few times when we actually spoke, there always seemed to me to be something, I don't know … sad about him. Or dark. Perhaps he was just lonely.'

As Hillary's mobile gave a little trill, Matthew Jones laughed a second time, looking a little shamefaced. 'Now I sound like something out of a women's magazine,' he added self-deprecatingly.

'Sorry, sir,' Hillary muttered, scrambling for her phone and feeling angry at herself for forgetting to turn off her mobile before beginning the interview. Not that it was proving very fruitful.

'Yes?' she said curtly.

'Guv, it's me,' Chang's voice cut across the solicitor's musings. 'I've just witnessed something here in Adderbury that I think you should know about. It's about Sergeant Ross, guv,' he added, lowering his voice somewhat theatrically.

Hillary sighed heavily. Great. Just what she needed right now. 'OK, I'll be right there.' She hung up and smiled vaguely at the solicitor.

'Well, thank you very much for your time, sir.'

'As I've already said, I fear there's been little to help you. Mr Ivers's will is quite straightforward.'

Hillary agreed with him. Still, it was another box ticked off.

Later, she was to wish that she'd paid far more attention to what this particular witness had just told her.


Brian Vane stared at the scruffy woman standing in the doorway, a sense of rage beginning to start a slow burn inside him. It made his normally pleasant, some would say handsome face flush an unbecoming red.

She was one of those woman who looked like a sack of potatoes tied around the middle with string. At this moment she was slouched insolently in her doorway to deny him access, with her arms crossed mulishly across her ample chest, and she was looking at him with scorn. She had deep grooves on either side of her mouth, and every now and then she'd take a deep drag on a foul-smelling cigarette. Her mouth, coloured with a bright red lipstick, grinned at him with aggravating pertness.

'Like I said, he ain't 'ere,' she repeated with mock patience.

'I was told he lodged here,' Vane pressed.

'So he does. But he left for a holiday. He got off on a shoplifting charge and wanted to celebrate, like.'

Brian Vane snorted. 'I doubt that the likes of him go on holiday,' he shot back, his voice dripping with disbelief. 'It's Mrs Rodgers, isn't it?' he said in an insinuating tone of voice. Very often women of her sort could be intimidated by showing them you knew who they were. And, by association, just how to get to them. But this one didn't frighten easily.

'Vera Rodgers, that's me,' the woman agreed without turning a hair. 'My old man's doing time up in Newcastle,' she added, showing just why the coppers held no particular fear for her any more. 'What they want to put him up there for, that's what I want to know?' she whined. 'I can't visit him much up there, can I?'

Vane wasn't interested.

'Look, tell Skunk he doesn't have to worry. I'm not here to arrest him. I just need to talk to him again. We've got business together,' he added, deciding to try a bit of wheedling instead. Sometimes it paid off.

Vera Rodgers laughed out loud. 'Come off it. Skunk and coppers don't do business. 'Ere, are you calling him a stool pigeon?' she asked with a sudden spike of aggression and suspicion.

Vane smiled, thinking fast. If this slag thought her precious lodger was an informer, she'd soon give him up.

He shrugged helplessly. 'I'm afraid I can't possibly say, madam,' he said, using his favourite weapon of reverse psychology. But Vera Rodgers was more than a match for it, because, after a moment's thought, she began to grin again and take another drag on her annoying fag.

'Nah. I reckon you just want me to drop the lad in it. But I can't, see, 'cause he really has gone. To the coast, he said, for a holiday like. Had cash and everything. Even paid up the rent before he went, bless him. He can be a bit lax in that department if I don't watch him. But he's a good lad. When he's flush, he pays up.'

Detective Superintendent Brian Vane felt the rage ratchet up another notch.

So the low-life was flush was he? It didn't take him long to figure out just who the punk's benefactor must be. Janine Mallow had somehow heard what he was up to and had paid the little scrote to get out of town for a while. *Shit!*

He didn't realize it, but his face was now so flushed with anger that Vera Rodgers was enjoying the show immensely. Her radar told her that this was no mere sergeant or even lowly DI looking for promotion, but a high-ranker. And it wasn't often that people like her got to thwart the muckety-mucks in Thames Valley.

'Did he say which coast he was off to on his hols, then?' Vane gritted.

'Nah,' Vera said. Skunk had, in fact, not told her where he was going, mindful of Janine Mallow's instructions that he should keep his head down, but she wouldn't have told Vane even if he had.

Sensing it, Vane took a deep, calming breath. 'When he gets back, give him this,' he said, taking one of his cards and handing it over. 'Tell him I'll make it worth his while to get in touch with me.'

Bribery, or the promise of easy money, nearly always worked.

Vera took the card and watched him walk away. Then she went back inside her cramped little council house, spat on the white card, and threw it in the kitchen rubbish bin.

Frank Ross walked into Interview Room 3 and had to laugh. How many times had he come in here with witnesses and suspects, and pumped them for information? He glanced at the wall to his left, a favourite leaning spot of his whenever either Hillary Greene or another of the team had taken the lead.

Now, Hillary Greene held out the witness's chair for him, and sat down opposite him. It felt so damned wrong that it gave him the willies.

Making a big show of it, he slumped down, then glanced pointedly at the mute tape recorder lying between them on the desk. 'What? No formal caution?' he mocked.

Hillary sighed. If she turned on the machine, it became official. If it became official she'd have to tell Danvers that she'd brought her ex-sergeant in for questioning, and then she'd have to admit why. After what Chang had overheard Danvers would realize that Ross was a credible suspect, and he'd yank her off the case without a qualm. Now that she had the bit between her teeth, she didn't want to get yanked.

This was her final case, and she was damned well going to solve it before she went. Just in case PC Wren or any other little toad thought about betting against her!

Now she stared at Frank coolly. If the contrary sod realized just what a bind she was in, she'd never get anything out of him.

'I can make it official if you want, Frank. But it sounds to me as if your job at the business park is hanging by a thread as it is. Do you really want the people who hired you to know you're a suspect in the murder of Ivers?'

'Oh, that's bollocks. I know why you hauled me out of bed. That little slitty-eyed pretty boy of yours told you about me and Hodgson going at it. That was nothing. Hodgson's just a pain in the arse.'

Hillary let the racial slur slide. Ross and decency of any kind, let alone political correctness, would never sound right in the same sentence.

'Just what have you got going, Frank?' Hillary said wearily. 'Not that I care, so long as it doesn't affect the Ivers's case.'

Frank Ross laughed across at her. 'Just who the hell do you think you're dealing with?' he snorted, sounding genuinely aggrieved. 'Like I'm going to admit to anything to you, of all people. You'd have me banged up faster than I could spit.'

Hillary sighed, realizing that she really was up against it this time. There was simply no way that she could persuade Frank Ross, of all people, that she had no interest in screwing him up.

It was she who'd been instrumental in forcing his retirement, after all.

'Did Ivers find out what you were up to?' she asked calmly and without hope, but, as expected, Ross merely blinked back at her, looking more than ever like a benign Winnie-the-Pooh.

'Who me?' he said with mock innocence and opened his eyes wide. 'Not me, officer. I ain't done nothing, honest.' He parodied what he'd heard every other little chiseller whinge and whine over the years, and grinned at her in defiance.

'Fine,' Hillary said wearily. 'We'll do it the hard way. But Frank, I resent having to waste my time on you when I've got a murderer to catch. So let me just say this: I hope that you covered your tracks well. And if I find out that you and Ivers had any history together, I'll be back. And next time the tape recorder will be on.'

Frank's eyes wavered for a moment, then he shrugged and sauntered cockily out through the door.

Hillary drove back to the business park grim-faced and tight-lipped. The last thing she needed right now was to butt heads with Frank Ross, of all people.

But until she could rule him either in or out, she had no other choice. It was not something she could leave to either Gemma or Chang. Chang was still too green to be able to tackle someone like Ross, and Gemma would know what it meant to have Ross in the frame. She'd go straight to Danvers. As a sergeant just waiting for her promotion to DI to come through, there was no way she would risk her future just because Hillary Greene might get chucked off her case.

It was why she'd told Chang not to mention the incident to Gemma for now, and not to write it up in the murder book until she told him to.

Chang had looked surprised, but she thought he'd obey her. It made her feel guilty having to ask him, though, and it was just one more example of why it was time for her to go. Once she became compromised, and had to start lying to her team on a regular basis, she was washed up as a serving police officer. It was as simple as that.

And it was damned well time she faced up to that once and for all. There could be no more prevaricating.

A week next Friday, and she'd be gone. And that was that.

'Mr Hodgson? DI Greene.' She held out her ID badge. 'I'd like a word please, sir.'

She'd found Pat Hodgson in a small Portakabin office, and was thankful that he was alone.

'Oh right. Sorry about Mike Ivers, but I didn't know the man all that well. And I don't think I even saw him on the day he died.'

'Yes sir. I've read the interview you gave with the WPC who took your statement.'

Hodgson looked at her warily. 'So what else can I do to help?'

'I understand that you had a violent argument with Mr Frank Ross, the night watchman here, sir. Can you tell me what that was about?'

Hodgson slowly sat down behind his desk. He licked his lips, which suddenly felt dry, then he said slowly, 'That had nothing to do with Mike Ivers. Ivers worked at Wallace's.'

'Yes sir. And you, and all the other units here, share Mr Ross's services. If you have a problem with Ross, then perhaps Mr Ivers shared your concerns. And I'm sure you can appreciate that, as the officer assigned to find Mr Ivers's killer, I'd be very interested in anyone who might have a grudge or dealings with the dead man.'

Hodgson shrugged. 'I know that Mike caught him out drinking one night. He told me that Ross was drinking from a hip flask, bold as brass in his cubicle one night, when Mike was doing the annual inventory. He said he'd driven past his cubicle about ten o'clock at night, and the man had to put the flask away in order to press the buttons that raised the barrier on the main gate. Did it, as bold as brass, according to Mike.'

'And did Mr Ivers take exception to this?' Hillary asked curiously. She was beginning to get a feel for the victim now, and something told her that a man like Michael Ivers would have found such a scene more amusing than annoying.

Hodgson hesitated, obviously tempted to say yes, but in the end he just shrugged.

'Mike was a bit of a one, Inspector. He liked the ladies, and I heard it said that he liked to gamble too. I never thought he was one for the drink himself, in particular, but he liked fast cars and the good life all right. So finding the night watchman having a nip from the flask wouldn't have worried him much. I think he made some sort of comment like 'good on him' or something like it, and never gave it another thought. Of course, he only manages Wallace's, he's not got his own money invested in it, otherwise he wouldn't have been so cavalier about it,' Hodgson added bitterly.

'But you yourself reported Frank Ross to the people who lease the units?' she pressed.

'I did,' Hodgson said. 'Much good it did me. He's still here, you notice.'

'Because, unlike Mike Ivers, you store some quite valuable commodities here, and need good security at night?'

Hodgson tensed, but nodded reluctantly.

Hillary nodded. 'Do you have any other reason to believe that the night watchman was, let us say, rather lax in his duties?' she asked delicately. Her witness was obviously getting very antsy, and it made her wonder why.

Hodgson licked his dry lips again, then shrugged. 'The man likes to take a drink. I'd rather he was sober. I told the lease-holders committee I'd rather he was replaced. So far, they haven't done so. And that's really all there is to it, Inspector,' Hodgson said determinedly, rising to his feet. 'So if that's all?'

It wasn't, Hillary thought grimly. Not by a long shot.

'Had you noticed Mr Ivers and Frank Ross talking together much – in the past few weeks, say?' she pressed, making no move to rise herself, and this time Hodgson didn't have to fake surprise.

'No,' he said at once. 'I don't think they ever met all that much. There was no reason for them to. Mike wasn't an early riser, nor one to stay late. Ross was usually gone by the morning when Mike came in, and Mike had usually gone before Ross got here at night. Most of us were.'

Hillary nodded. So the likelihood that Ivers had somehow managed to stumble on to Ross's little rip-off scheme was fairly low.

'Did Ivers ever give any hints to you that he knew what Ross was up to?' Hillary pressed. Hodgson was already shaking his head before he realized that, in doing so, he was silently acknowledging that there actually *was* something going on in the first place. And that he, Hodgson, knew what it was.

'Did you ever hear Ross threaten Ivers in any way?' Hillary persisted. 'Or have you heard rumours that he and Ivers were either pally with one another or had a problem with one another?'

'No. Like I said, I don't think they really knew one another.' Hodgson was sounding impatient now, and Hillary decided to let it go.

There was nothing more to be got from Hodgson just now. But the interview had reassured her a little. She was reasonably confident that Ross wouldn't have had any reason to fear or worry about Ivers.

Outside, Chang hovered anxiously. 'Guv. I've found out who this Alan bloke is. The owner of the yard, Pat Hodgson, has a son called Alan who works for him as chief supply officer.'

'Ah,' Hillary said. That explained a lot about Hodgson's unease.

It wasn't until she was on her way back to HQ that it hit her that she was seriously considering Frank Ross as a murder suspect.

And somewhere in the back of her mind, she could hear her late unlamented husband's mocking laughter.

# CHAPTER TEN

Back at HQ, Hillary consulted the murder book, but learned nothing new. Sometimes she liked to reread all of the team's entries, because the odd phrase written by someone else, or considering a different perspective on the same data, could trigger a chain reaction in her own mind that resulted in her thinking of something new. This time, however, she had no such luck.

She sighed and leaned back in her chair. Over in Danvers's cubicle, she could see cardboard boxes on his desk, and realized that he'd already begun the process of packing up. Soon he'd be off back to Yorkshire. She suspected he'd do well there – probably gain another promotion and, with luck, find a woman who could help him to offset the rigours of the job.

It would do him good to have someone to come home to of a night. She knew, of course, that he'd carried a torch for her for the few years they'd worked together, but it had never been on the cards. Now she wondered, idly, why that was so. He was young, attractive, and they were both free.

She shrugged.

Perhaps, now that she was retiring, she might think about looking out for a romance of her own. The thought made her smile. According to her vague plan, she was going to take her narrowboat on a tour of the country's canal system. Chug along for a day or so, then moor up, find a pub, have a meal, maybe see a few sights if she happened to be near a quiet historic town, then chug off to the next mooring point.

Just who the hell was she going to meet while doing that? The canals didn't have lock-keepers any more – well, not many. Besides, how long did it take to get a boat through a lock? Twenty minutes? Not much potential for establishing a relationship there.

OK, she might moor up one night behind a nice little boat, that also had a nice little single male owner. They might get chatting, have a drink together, discover things in common. Then what? People who lived on travelling boats, as opposed to those with permanent moorings, were, by their very nature, nomadic. In theory, she supposed, she could meet up with someone and they might, just possibly, end up sharing a boat and travelling together. But the thought of living with someone on *The Mollern* made her shudder.

She caught herself wool-gathering. She shook it off and reached for her phone. She speed-dialled the number of her young constable and waited for him to answer.

'DC Chang.'

'Mark, it's me. I want you to start nosing around at the builder's yard to see if you can pin down what's missing and, if you can, find a pattern for *when* it goes missing. Don't talk to either of the Hodgsons, and don't let Frank Ross find out what you're doing. Chat casually to the lorry drivers coming in and out, see if you can get pally with some of the staff. Nothing too obvious, get my drift?'

'Right, guv,' Chang said, sounding thrilled. He probably saw himself as doing some undercover work. Hillary hung up, still smiling. She hoped Chang retained his enthusiasm for the job for a few more years at least. After that, even the best of cops found the job more of a chore than a pleasure, most of the time.

Gemma came back from wherever she'd been, looking glum. 'That's the last of them – the casino lot,' she explained, slumping down in her chair. She was wearing a black pantsuit that showed off her pale short hair to advantage, and most of the male eyes in the room were swivelled in her direction, as per usual. Hillary wondered what a psychiatrist would make of the fact that she was marrying a blind man, then told herself it was none of her damned business.

'Sometimes I just don't get human nature,' Gemma complained, swivelling in the chair to face her boss. 'This bloke Ivers introduces them to a casino, where they lose sometimes vast sums of money and, more often than not, money they can't really afford to lose. And do the majority of them blame him? Do they hell. Most of the pathetic losers I've been talking to still admire the man, and seem genuinely sorry he's dead.

'The general consensus of opinion seems to be that he was a real man. He showed guts at the tables, whatever that means, and was attractive to the ladies. He drove a great car, and could tell a good story, never get drunk or not so's you'd notice no matter how many brandies he drank – which was his preferred tipple, apparently. And mature Cognac naturally, none of the cheap stuff. Everyone seemed to admire him as a jack-the-lad living the kind of life they envied. When I pointed out that he lived in a common or garden market town, and worked at a newspaper-delivery depot it just got shrugged off.'

Hillary smiled. 'That was just what he did, not who he was,' she explained drily. 'To them, he was good-looking, single, devil-may-care and the world of mortgages, bills, and every other damned humdrum thing that the rest of us have to put up with never touched him. And I imagine that that was an image he was careful to maintain.'

The pity in her voice made Gemma look at her quickly. 'Feeling sorry for the vic, guv?'

'I always feel sorry for the vic,' answered Hillary. Although soon, much sooner than she'd expected, she was going to find those words very hard to live up to.

Alan Hodgson was not happy. He was sure his father suspected that he was behind the goods that were going AWOL, and just this morning he'd learned that he and Frank Ross had been heard arguing. If his father knew that Ross had been the one to approach him, what else did he know? It was Ross who had introduced him to the rest of the lads, and pointed out just how easy it would be to earn a little extra cash by redirecting some of the yard's inventory.

After all, Ross was the night watchman, so he could just wave the van in. And Alan knew all the alarm codes at Hodgson's and, even more important, was in a prime position to fiddle the invoices. All he had to do was turn the odd nought into an eight, or add a one here or there, and he could order in goods that, in theory, never even existed. All that was needed then was a man with a van and a couple of strong backs to help load the gear, and Robert was your mother's brother.

And so it had proved, at first. All during the first month of the scam Alan had been nervous, and sure that his old man must catch on. But he hadn't. Ross had shown him how to be clever about it, and taught him never to be greedy. The odd cans of paint here, this batch of nails and carpentry equipment there, wood that could be written off as damaged by weather or loading accidents. By the time the second month had passed Alan was getting used to the extra cash. He could dine out with his girlfriend more often, go clubbing, have a bit of fun for a change. Buy good quality booze, go to the cinema more often or get the latest computer and games package. Simple stuff like that that made life just that bit sweeter.

And why not? His old man didn't pay him any more than he paid the rest of his staff, and that wasn't right, was it? He was his son and heir, after all.

He'd always admired Michael Ivers, and the lifestyle he led. Well, Alan wasn't going to waste his money by throwing it away at the casino, even though Mike had tried to get him to go along with him a few times. But Alan wasn't *that* daft.

But then, after the third month, some eagle-eyed clerk in admin noticed a discrepancy. Luckily he'd come to Alan with it, and not gone to his father, so he'd been able to gloss it over. But then, just last week, he'd caught his father looking at him oddly, and then someone had killed Mike – and on the very same night as they'd made a run, too. Suddenly, the cops had been swarming all over the place, and everything seemed to be coming down around his ears.

Alan was an only child, and his mother had died when he was twelve. He'd always been what most people would call a screwed-up kid, and prone to self-pity and impulsive behaviour.

He'd never done well at school, but he knew that he could run a bloody builders' merchants, no problems. If only his father would pay him a decent wage! And if only Frank Ross wasn't such a devious bastard. He didn't trust the ex-copper not to drop him in it, if things got tough.

Now he sat in his office, his hands shaking, wondering whether he should confess everything to his father and hope for the best. Living with all this uncertainty was driving him mad! Never the most stable of men, or the most self-aware, it never occurred to Alan that his father kept him close, and on so tight a leash, in order to keep an eye on him.

But the truth was, nobody knew how weak and easily led his son was better than Pat Hodgson. Now, as the son sat in his office, worrying and working himself up to the point where he felt he could scream, his father also sat in his office and thought about things.

Then Pat Hodgson nodded.

It was time he dealt with Ross once and for all. And he knew just how to do it. He'd been planning this for some time now. He'd put it off whilst the cops were still thick on the ground, but most of the forensics work was done now, and only the odd member of Hillary Greene's team came and went. Even the constable guarding the gates had been called off.

Now was as good a time as any.

*

Mark Chang heard about the special consignment of Italian marble within the hour. It was a man called Bill Billings who told him. Chang, who on being introduced to the site foreman at Hodgsons had to wonder what parents thought they were playing at when they named their children, quickly managed to fall into conversation with him.

He was a fifty-something, comfortably married man who was by nature gregarious. Within minutes the young constable had learned all he needed to know about life at Hodgson & Sons. First that there were no sons, plural, only the one. And that Alan was a nervy sort of kid, and you had to always check up on what he told you since he often got things wrong. That drove a lot of the workers at the yard barmy, but what could you say? He was the boss's son, and the apple of the old man's eye.

"Course, I don't know why this order's come out of the blue like,' Billings was saying now, scowling at the spot in the yard that he'd ordered to be cleared. 'This Italian marble's worth a fortune. Must be some special order just come in. It's not like the boss to specialize, though. Still, he says to clear room for it, so I clear room for it. I wouldn't be surprised if it's destined for that that swanky new hotel they're building. We're one of the lucky ones who got a contract. Funny though – I thought marble would have been more likely to be handled by the interior decorating lot, rather than us.'

Chang dutifully noted it all down, and would report it to Hillary later. He didn't find it particularly noteworthy himself, but then he lacked Hillary Greene's experience.

Before the park closed down for the night everyone at Hodgson's, and quite a few in the surrounding units, knew that expensive marble, worth near nigh-on a hundred grand, was due to be delivered the next morning.

Pat Hodgson had set his bait. And, as bait went, it wasn't any too stingy. But then, it needed to be good Cheddar in order to lure out the mice.

*

That afternoon, Hillary had gone over the list of casino suspects with Gemma, and had to agree that they could probably all be struck off the suspect list. All but four had good to solid alibis, and those few that didn't weren't very promising.

One was a sixty-eight-year-old woman with slightly arthritic hands. Another was a female advertising executive, probably with a coke habit, and Gemma, reading between the lines, was convinced that she was stoned out of her mind on the night Ivers died. One was a respectable upper-middle-class man who was patently gay. According to Gemma, he was lying about where he was that night, not to cover up the fact that he'd gone out and killed Michael Ivers, but to conceal the fact that he'd almost certainly gone out to find a rent boy.

The last of the possible candidates, Gemma thought, simply hadn't either the brains or the gumption to carry it out. Besides, he lived furthest away, and didn't own a car – he'd lost it in a bet the week before. And since the killer of Ivers had almost certainly arrived at the business park in a vehicle of some sort, that more or less ruled him out.

'And I just can't see our killer arriving by taxi, guv,' Gemma concluded glumly. Then laughed. 'You know. Keep the meter running, mate, I won't be long. Just gotta go and bop someone over the head.'

Hillary obligingly smiled. 'He could have borrowed a car from a mate.'

Gemma snorted. 'Right. I'll bet he's up to his ears in mates who'd be willing to lend him a car.'

'Bad as that, huh?'

Gemma snorted again. 'Even I knew he'd sell any car he got his hands on and be off with the money to the nearest racetrack. And I'd only spent two minutes talking to him. I guess his friends and family could have told you which car dealer he'd have used.'

Hillary had just reluctantly told Gemma to wind up that avenue of inquiry when her telephone rang.

'DI Greene.'

'I bet you thought I'd emigrated and gone to Australia.' Steven Partridge's voice came cheerfully to her over the wire.

'Oh, not Australia, Doc,' she parried swiftly. 'Not enough culture for you. Now if you'd said Canada maybe, or Vienna, I might have agreed.'

'You know me so well. Seriously though, my apologies. I've just finished with your man, Ivers. Thought you might like to know the news straight away.'

Hillary sat up a little straighter. If Steven Partridge thought she needed to know something before the written report could wing its way to her desk, then it meant something interesting or unexpected had come up during the autopsy.

'Don't tell me blunt force trauma to the head wasn't the cause of death,' she said, making Gemma perk up and move closer.

'Nope,' Steven said at once. 'As far as the actual death goes, it turns out to be just what it looked like. I think it was probably the second blow, rather than the first or third and incidentally, last blow, that killed him, but I can't be sure, and anyway that's semantics. Basically, his brain was bashed in. Three distinct blows.'

'Charming.'

'Not much in the way of finesse, I grant you, but it got the job done,' the medical man agreed crisply. 'There were no defence wounds on the hands or arms, by the way, so I don't think he saw it coming. Or if he did, he didn't have time to do much about it.'

'So why the heads up?' Hillary asked curiously. 'Did you find traces of dope? Was he high? Drunk?'

'None of the above. But what he was, most definitely, was HIV positive. And, from the state of him, well on the way to developing full-blown Aids. Although I can't say that with one hundred per cent accuracy of course, until the results of some tests come in.'

Hillary blinked. Thought about Ivers's lifestyle and all those women, and swore softly.

'Oh shit.'

'Yes, that's what I thought,' Steven Partridge's voice said softly in her ear. 'From what I've heard on the grapevine, your vic wasn't exactly short of the odd sexual partner or two.'

'Or three or four,' Hillary said grimly. Then 'Oh shit,' again. Opposite her, Gemma was watching her intently, and Hillary absently wrote HIV on her pad and turned it round so that her sergeant could read it.

Gemma's eyebrows rose.

'Would he have known about it?' Hillary asked sharply. 'I mean, would he be feeling ill?'

'Oh, I would say so – that he knew about it, I mean,' Steven said at once. 'Until I've got the tox results back, I can't say for sure that he was taking the proper medication for it, but the signs are that he must have been. And as for feeling ill – probably not. Well, not so's that it would put a real crimp in your day-to-day routine. Mind you, he'd begun to lose some of his body mass. There were signs of ...' and here he went into a medical spiel that Hillary barely listened to.

'So you think he was probably seeing a doctor?' she summarized, and nodded at Gemma, who quickly began to sort through the file for the name of Ivers's GP. 'That makes sense. One of the listings on his mobile phone shortly before he was killed was from a GP's surgery,' she said to the pathologist.

'You'd better start contacting all his partners,' Steven said grimly. 'And I can't say as I envy you *that* job. There isn't much in the press nowadays about Aids and HIV but it's still out there – and thriving. If that's the word I want. And it's still a potential death sentence, in spite of all the advances they've made.'

Hillary felt a chill go through her. 'But he'd have used condoms, right?' she said. But of course, it was a question that Steven Partridge was in no position to answer, and he made no attempt to do so.

'I bloody hope so,' was all he could manage before promising to have the full written report on her desk by the morning.

So when Chang came back and reported on what he'd found out at the site, Hillary's mind was on other things. Nevertheless, it gave her pause.

'And you say this marble delivery is worth a bit?' she asked, when he'd finished.

'More than a bit I'd say, guv. Nearly a hundred grand, or so I heard. 'Course, that might be an exaggeration.'

'And things have definitely been going missing from the yard?'

'Well, I couldn't get anyone to say so out loud, guv, but I reckon nobody would be surprised.'

And with Frank guarding the yard at night, it was all but a certainty, she mused grimly. It was like setting a fox to guard the henhouse.

'What the hell is Hodgson playing at?' she asked, then looked up as Gemma shoved a piece of paper under her nose. It was a long telephone number, longer even than that of a mobile.

'What's this?'

'The phone number of the current girlfriend in South Africa, guv. Do you want to call her and tell her to get herself to a doctor pronto or do you want me to do it?'

Hillary sighed heavily.

'No, I'll do it. You need to get a list of all the others Ivers has seen in – oh hell, I don't know. Say the last five years? What's the incubation period, or whatever the hell it's called, for HIV anyway?'

'Dunno guv. I'll look it up on the net. Don't tell me,' she added gloomily, 'you want me to phone around everyone else and tell *them* to get checked out. And to get *their* partners checked out, and whoever they might have been seeing on the side. Boy, am I going to be popular. It's a bloody nightmare! With the way Ivers put it about, I'll be here until next Christmas.'

'Get Chang to help you,' Hillary said, then instantly changed her mind. 'No wait, Chang. I don't like the sound of this sudden delivery of marble. It sounds to me like Hodgson's deliberately putting temptation in Frank Ross's way. Not that Ross will be stupid enough to fall for it.'

And then she wondered. He wouldn't, would he?

'Boss, I think we should prioritize this HIV thing first,' Gemma said. 'This is literally life and death.'

'You're right,' Hillary said. 'Chang, help Gemma, she'll fill you in. I'm going to see the ex-wife and Lucy Kirke myself. Oh, and the Welleses, both man and wife. Find out whether any of them knew about this. We might just be reading it wrong. Maybe Ivers told them about it.'

From the look on Gemma's face, it was clear just what she thought the chances of that were.


Hillary drove back to Bodicote, and the home of Michael Ivers's ex-wife. This time, however, she was out of luck, and nobody answered the doorbell. With a sigh, she drove on into Banbury and to the shop where Madeleine Ivers worked. The manageress there was both a curious and a friendly soul, who quickly agreed to Madeleine taking a half-hour break.

They walked to a nearby café, where Hillary indulged her coffee habit and ordered the biggest, strongest brew they had. Madeleine settled for a diet fizzy drink.

'Madeleine, I don't want to worry you,' Hillary began carefully, after taking a sip of her brew. 'But I've just had your husband's medical reports back.' She deliberately didn't use the word 'autopsy'. This was going to be tricky enough without using such emotive words. But there was simply no easy way of sidling into it, so in the end, she just asked quietly, 'Did you know that Michael was HIV positive?'

Madeleine took a deep breath, and then smiled shakily. 'No. Not really?'

'He never mentioned it?'

Madeleine gave a shaky laugh. 'Not to me. But then, he wouldn't, would he?'

Hillary nodded. 'You need to make an appointment with a doctor. I have the numbers of some helplines that you might like.' Before she'd left the office, she'd asked Gemma to run off a whole printed page of data and helpful numbers.

But to her surprise, Madeleine was already shaking her head. 'There's no need.'

'But Mrs Ivers, you can't just ignore this. I know it's a lot to take in, but it's not just about you. I don't mean to pry, but if you have another partner now, or just someone you're seeing casually, you might be putting them at risk too.'

'Oh, it's not that,' Madeleine said, twirling her straw in her drink with swift, angry, agitated flicks. 'I'm not trying to bury my head in the sand, or pretend nothing's wrong. It's just that I went and got tested the moment Mike left me. For a whole range of things – herpes, crabs, you name it. Not just Aids. I was so furious you see. So upset. I suppose I wanted them to find something, so I'd be able to throw it in his face. You know. "See what your latest tart has given you? And now you've given it to me, you bastard." I wanted to see him humiliated, I suppose. He was always so smug about everything.'

Madeleine laughed, and threw the straw down on to the table. 'But I was clear. Everything came back fine. And now you tell me this. He must have got it after he left me.'

She sounded bitter about it. Almost as if he'd done it on purpose. Cheating her one last time, and this time, managing to do so even when dead.

Hillary, though, felt nothing but relief. One down, two more to go.

'Your husband seems to have blighted the life of a lot of people,' Hillary said, thinking of the poor saps he'd introduced to the casino. And of the girl she'd telephoned in South Africa before leaving the office, who'd broken down and cried anew. First she'd been informed of her lover's death. And now she was being told he might have given her a death sentence too.

'That was Mike all right,' Madeleine Ivers agreed bitterly. Then she looked up at Hillary, her thin face suddenly tense. 'Don't tell Ben about this. Ben always said Mike was a dirty sod. This'll hit him hard. He'll be sure to think that I've got it too, no matter how much I try and tell him that I haven't. He's only fifteen after all, though he tries to act so tough. Something like this will be bound to scare him. You know what teenagers are like. Always making a drama out of a molehill. He'll be convinced that he's going to lose his mum, and he'll be watching me like a hawk, wondering every time I get a cough or something.'

Hillary privately thought it would probably do the young lout good to get a scare; it certainly wouldn't do him any harm to show some concern for his mother. She smiled briefly.

'I wasn't planning on telling him anything,' she said, truthfully enough. She made a mental note to herself to make it a priority to try and establish just where the stepson had been on the night of the murder.

Madeleine sighed and took a sip of her drink, and Hillary gratefully finished her coffee. It was getting late. She'd save talking to Lucy Kirke and Honor and Harry Welles until tomorrow.

That night, Purple Pete and his father Ollie had a long chat. It hadn't taken more than a few hours for news of the delivery of Italian marble to come to their ears.

'It's the jackpot, boy, that's what it is,' Ollie said gleefully now. They were sitting in their favourite pub, talking with their heads bent close together. The pub was busy and nobody paid them the least attention.

'A hundred grand easy,' Ollie continued. ''Course, we won't get that much for it. And we need the right fence, but your Uncle Johnno has already said he knows this bloke.'

'But Dad, you and Frank agreed we had to lie low while the cops were still snooping around.'

'But they've more or less finished up at the business park,' Ollie said. 'There's usually only this one young copper about now, sniffing around. Besides, not even the cops will be around in the small hours of the morning, will they?'

'I suppose not.'

'And even with a fence, I reckon we can get seventy thou for it. Split just four ways, that's nearly twenty grand each. Think what you could do with that, eh?'

'But what if we get caught?' Purple Pete whined.

'Well, what if we do? We'll tell Hodgson his son goes down with us. Simple.'

Pete brightened at this thought. He had personal experience of how fathers felt about their only sons. 'That's right. He won't shop his own son, will he? And Frank will let us in just as usual. Yeah, you're right. It'll be a doddle.'

Ollie shifted a little uncomfortably on his seat. In fact, he hadn't even approached Frank Ross, but that shouldn't be a problem. If he and his usual driver just turned up, Ross would have no other option but to let them in. He might cut up about it, but he'd have no choice. He could hardly call the cops, could he?

'And Alan will show us just where it is, so we'll be in and out real quick like. Isn't marble heavy, though?' Pete frowned.

Ollie nodded. Sometimes, his son surprised him by saying something that was actually bright, for a change. 'We'll have to use a loader. But there's one at the yard.'

'Right. That'll be Alan's job as well,' Pete agreed happily. 'To have it ready and waiting, like.'

Ollie again smiled warily. Just as he hadn't approached Frank Ross, so he hadn't approached Alan. In fact, he doubted that the boss's son would even be on the premises.

But Ollie and Jim, his driver, had been very observant over the past few months, and Jim reckoned they no longer needed the boss's son to help out on the runs. He had seen Alan enter the codes on the interior alarm systems, and had memorized them. And how hard could it be to find a hundred grand's worth of fancy marble amid a pile of brick and wood?

No, the fewer in on this the better. It meant that Alan's share went straight into their pockets. And if Frank Ross didn't play ball, they'd have his share as well.

It *was* a final raid, when all was said and done. The scam at Hodgsons had run its course. And this would make for a nice little retirement present. A one off, and a big payload. With nobody in a position to go squealing to the rozzers if it went bad, it was as sweet a deal as you could ask for.

'We'll do it earlier tomorrow night. Say ten o'clock.' Their usual time in the small hours wouldn't do for this job. It would take longer than usual to load the marble, and Jim had to get the special lorry back by four. Reinforced, it would take the weight of the marble all right, but it had to be back in the yard where he was 'borrowing' it from before it was missed. Besides, going in at an earlier time would help to throw Frank Ross off his stride.

Purple Pete wondered why they wouldn't be doing it at their normal time, but his dad was looking so happy that he didn't want to put a damper on his mood by asking about it.

Besides, his dad knew what he was doing. He always did.

# CHAPTER ELEVEN

Hillary got in bright and early the next day, although she was not looking forward to doing the rounds of Michael Ivers's womenfolk and breaking the bad news. As ever, when there was an unpleasant task ahead of her, she wanted to get cracking, get it done and dusted and behind her as soon as possible.

It wasn't to be.

Before she'd taken two steps into the main foyer the desk sergeant spotted her and called her over. 'Hey, Hill, Donleavy wants to see you soon as you get in.' He saw her grimace, and grinned widely. 'Whatcha been doin' then? And was it legal?'

Hillary smiled grimly. 'No idea, but I daresay I'll soon find out.'

She climbed the stairs but bypassed the doors to the open plan offices where she'd worked for nearly ten years, and went on up to the top floor instead. After tapping on the outer office door she went in, and felt her jaw clench as Donleavy's secretary gave her a sympathetic look.

Her spirits abruptly dropped. There was only one reason she could think of that would merit her being in Donleavy's bad books; as soon as she walked in and saw a grim-faced Paul Danvers already seated before his desk she knew her chickens had come home to roost.

Or rather just the one. A big pain-in-the-neck-Leghorn called Frank Ross.

'Hillary, sit down,' Donleavy said abruptly, but she noticed as she took her seat that the commander had that rare twinkle in his eye which told her he was more amused and secretly pleased than truly reproving.

'Something has come to DCI Danvers's attention that rather surprised him. And when he told me, it rather surprised me too. It seems you forgot to mention something rather significant in your reports on the progress of the Michael Ivers homicide?'

Hillary let her face remain blank. After all, at the end of next week she was out of here. What could they do to her? Fire her a week early?

Her mute belligerence made the twinkle in Donleavy's eye grow ever brighter.

There was no doubt about it, Marcus mused silently. He was going to miss her. There was no other officer under his command who had quite her style. Or brains. Or experience.

Well, he'd miss her in the short while it took for her to come to her senses and return to Kidlington, he modified his thoughts hastily. Having her work as a consultant on the cold cases wouldn't be quite the same thing as having her as a fully oper-ational DI, but it was better than nothing, and he'd settle for that.

It never, for a single second, occurred to him that she wouldn't return. Now he watched her with a sense of pleasant anticipation to see what her next move would be.

'Oh?' she asked mildly, turning to glance at Paul Danvers with a look of superbly vague innocence.

Paul swore under his breath. 'How come I only hear that Frank Ross is a night watchman at Ivers's place of work, now, nearly a week into the inquiry?' he gritted.

'Oh that,' Hillary said mildly. Donleavy leaned back slightly in his chair and rubbed his hand over his mouth to hide the grin that sprang up on his face.

'Yes that!' Danvers repeated grimly, holding on to his temper with difficulty. It wasn't like Hillary to play silly buggers, and with only a few days left to go before he went back to York, he didn't want any complications that might force him to postpone the move. 'You should have told me the moment you saw him at the park. You know damned well it could constitute a problem with conflict of interest.'

'Oh, I have no interest in Frank Ross, Paul, you should know that,' Hillary assured him with a gentle smile.

Donleavy coughed behind his hand, and turned his head quickly to look out of the window.

Danvers forced himself to relax, knowing when he was beaten. 'OK, let's have it,' he demanded wearily. 'And all of it this time, in all its grisly detail. And then we'll have to turn it over to the legal eagles to see what they make of it.'

'There's not all that much to it,' Hillary continued to reassure him. And herself. 'Frank Ross, on retiring from the police force, did what a lot of ex-cops do, and took a job in security. He's been night watchman at the Aynho Islip Business Park for the past nine months or so. He comes on in the early evening, and leaves at six in the morning. He was questioned, along with all the other members of the business park. He knew the victim only very slightly, since their paths seldom crossed. As finder of the body, he was closely scrutinized, just like any other potential suspect, but forensics found no suspicious traces of him on the body, and Ross himself says he never touched Ivers once he saw him lying on the ground. And, let's face it, even Frank knows better than to contaminate a crime scene. There's nothing on the murder weapon that links it to Frank, and since there's no evidence that the victim or Ross had any connection, there's no motive either.'

Hillary sighed. 'Not even Frank, if he did have a beef with the man, would be stupid enough to attack him and kill him when he himself was apparently the only other man on the spot. Frank's not *that* stupid. He might as well write GUILTY across his forehead in permanent ink.'

Danvers hoped she was right.

But it galled him, looking back on it, how crafty she'd been.

Now that he thought about it, her reports had been very care-fully worded indeed. More often than not Ross was described as the security man, and even in the more detailed reports, he'd been listed as a Mr E.F. Ross. Apparently Frank's first name was Ernest, a name he hated. It simply hadn't registered with him that Hillary had been talking about their own albatross-round-the-neck, Frank Ross.

Until someone in admin had picked it up and brought it to his attention.

But perhaps it was his own fault. He'd been so preoccupied winding things down for his move back north that he'd hardly spoken to Chang or Gemma Fordham. Either one of them would probably have told him about Ross if he had.

'So, we have an ex-copper, and one who worked on your team for many years, finding a body. And you don't think that constitutes a conflict of interest?' he asked her sarcastically.

Hillary shrugged. 'If we'd been bosom buddies, I can see the CPS having a problem with it. But if, in any future court case, Frank Ross should be brought into it somehow, you'll have a whole plethora of witnesses who'll be able to reassure the jury that I wouldn't do Frank Ross any favours if my life depended on it.'

Paul sighed. That much, at least, was true. But he couldn't see the CPS being happy with it, nevertheless. Protocol demanded that she be taken off the case.

He glanced across at Donleavy with a questioning look.

Donleavy took over. 'How likely is it, do you think, that Ross will play a major role in any murder trial?'

'At the moment, I imagine he'll simply be called as the witness who found the body. The prosecution may try and make something of the fact that he was an ex-copper and that we knew each other, but I don't see how it'll affect the jury much.'

'Unless Ross turns out to be the killer,' Danvers put in glumly.

'I don't think he is, sir,' Hillary said mildly.

'Well, that makes me feel so much better!' Paul retaliated hotly.

Donleavy held out his hands in a placatory gesture. 'All right, all right! I think there's very little point in pulling Hillary off the case just now. If things get sticky, we can always tell the court that we were short-staffed and that, since Hillary was due to retire in a few days' time anyway, her role as SIO was only ever meant to be interim.'

Danvers nodded. 'That'll probably wash, but only if someone else takes over after she's gone. Hillary, how likely is it, do you think, that you'll make an arrest before then?'

Hillary shrugged helplessly. 'It's hard to say. We've just had what might be a significant breakthrough.' She brought them up to date on the HIV situation. 'So I'll be interviewing the main women in his life today. After that, I might have a better idea of what's what,' she concluded.

Donleavy nodded. 'Fine. We'll leave it there for the moment.'

Hearing a cue to leave, Danvers got up reluctantly, and Marcus nodded for him to go. Hillary, being given no such signal, remained reluctantly in her seat. The moment the door closed behind the man from York Donleavy shook his head at her.

'Couldn't bear to have to give up the case, huh?' he mocked.

Hillary shot him a fulminating look. 'You had no business giving me the case to begin with. Sir,' she added after a significant pause.

'In other words,' Donleavy said drily, 'if the brown stuff hits the fan, I've nobody to blame but myself.'

Hillary smiled sweetly back at him.

Donleavy nodded briefly, then his face suddenly became serious. 'Just between you and me, though, how likely is it that Ross can screw this up for us? You know how that man can usually be guaranteed to make a sow's ear out of a silk purse.'

Hillary thought about it for a moment, then shrugged. 'Rather unlikely I'd say, sir,' she said at last. But before twenty-four hours was out she would have cause to regret even that cautious optimism.

Not that Ross would, in fact, jeopardize her murder case. But he was going to make life very difficult for them.

Just not in a way that anybody could ever have predicted.

Mindful of her promise to Lucy Kirke not to go back to her house and run the risk of upsetting her mother, Hillary drove to Lucy's place of work, from where she was able to take an extended tea-break.

Instead of finding a café, they sat outside in the warm May sun on a wall in the local park, where sparrows twittered around their feet begging for bread. They twittered in vain. Both women were breadless.

Lucy glanced round her at the jubilantly colourful tulip beds and sighed. 'So, what's new? Have you found who killed Michael yet?'

'Not yet, but every day brings us closer,' Hillary said, watching a toddler and its mother play ball a few feet away. 'But there's been a development that meant I needed to see you urgently. I'm afraid it's not good news.'

Lucy looked at her quickly, and Hillary saw the fear rise up in the younger girl's face. 'Oh?

It was interesting, but not necessarily significant, and certainly didn't mean that she was feeling guilty and terrified that she was about to be arrested.

Hillary glanced at her, needing to see her face when she broke the news. If Lucy was going to lie to her, she'd have a better idea of it from her body language.

'During the autopsy it was discovered that Michael was HIV positive, Lucy. I'm so sorry.'

Lucy Kirke went deathly white. The pupils in her grey eyes contracted and for a second she swayed precariously on the wall. Hillary shot out a hand to steady her, and took a deep breath herself. Well, at least that answered that question. Lucy

Kirke, for one, had had no idea of his condition. Not unless she could give Dame Judy Dench a run for her money in the acting stakes.

So Michael Ivers couldn't have told her, for one. And if he hadn't confessed to Lucy, the chances were he'd been quiet about it all around.

'Lucy, I have to ask you this, and I'm sorry if it sounds intrusive. No, it is intrusive,' she corrected herself honestly, 'but you must see how important it is. Did you practise safe sex?'

Lucy blinked, took a few rapid gulps of air, then nodded slowly. 'Yes. I always insisted on it.'

Hillary sagged in relief. 'Good girl!'

Lucy Kirke began to cry. Hillary shuffled in her bag for a tissue and quickly handed one over.

'You need to make an appointment with your doctor and get tested right away, nonetheless,' Hillary prompted gently, once the storm of weeping had passed. 'And if there's another man in your life…?'

The pretty girl shook her head. 'No. I haven't found anyone yet.' Suddenly, she reached out and grabbed Hillary's hand in such a strong grip that Hillary felt her fingers going numb. If anyone else had done that, and in any other circumstances, they'd have quickly found themselves on the ground, with their arm twisted painfully behind their back, and a set of handcuffs on their wrists.

'Don't tell Mum about this!' Lucy begged, still white to the lips.

'Of course I won't,' Hillary said gently, and the younger girl let her go as suddenly as she'd grabbed her.

'Sorry! It's just that – this would kill her. I'm all she has left now. And she can't go through it all again. Not another lingering illness. Not another daughter lost.'

Hillary nodded. 'I understand.' And she did. But, much as the Kirke family tragedies touched her heart, she still had a job to do. 'Lucy, did you never suspect Michael might be ill?' she asked now, making her voice brisk and businesslike once more. She was relieved to see Lucy respond by stiffening her own backbone and sitting up straighter.

'No, never. He always seemed fit and active to me.'

'You never saw him taking pills or injections, and wondered what they were for?'

'No. Nothing like that,' Lucy assured her.

'Had he begun to lose weight when you knew him?'

Lucy closed her eyes for a moment, thinking back, then shook her head. 'I don't think so,' she said slowly, cautiously. 'But he did say something about wanting to lose a few pounds. Said he didn't want to give middle-age spread a chance to take root if he could help it, so he'd go for a pre-emptive strike. He made a joke of it. So if he had begun to lose weight ...'

She trailed off, sounding appalled.

Grimly Hillary finished the sentence for her, 'You wouldn't have questioned it. No. He thought of everything, didn't he?' Hillary said softly.

Lucy Kirke resumed her weeping. 'Yes,' she sobbed. 'He was the kind of man who thought of everything,' she agreed forlornly.

Except for that night nearly a week ago, when somebody killed him, Hillary added silently. That night, he didn't manage to think of everything.

She left Lucy to pull herself together in the tulip-filled park, and drove grimly to the house where Honor Welles lived.

At Hodgson & Sons, a large heavy-duty lorry pulled into the loading dock. From his office window Alan Hodgson watched it, and felt a growing sense of panic.

As he watched his father supervise the unloading of the wooden pallets that protected the exquisite, expensive marble, he began to chew his nails. Why hadn't his father mentioned this delivery to him? It was his job after all – his specific job – to order in and store all deliveries. There was something about this that just screamed trouble.

For a start, they'd never had anything like this on the premises before.

Oh, as a builders' merchant they sometimes had deliveries of expensive stone – the creamy Cotswold stone for new builds out on the Gloucestershire border edge of their market range. Some times they'd get some of the ironstone that villages like Deddington preferred, and, of course, quarried flagstones for upper-class kitchens and patios. But, expensive as some of those items could be, they were nothing, *nothing*, compared to this Italian marble stuff.

And what was it for, anyway? As far as Alan knew, they didn't have any contracts on the go that would call for it.

He watched the others in the yard, who were also observing it being stacked, quite near the entrance, and felt a rising sense of panic. Why was his father doing that? Why wasn't he putting it in one of the storage sheds at least, where it could be padlocked in? And why advertise the fact that it had just been delivered? Usually, expensive stuff came in early in the morning or last thing at night, just as a basic security precaution. It was as if his father was just asking someone to steal it.

With that thought, Alan went cold.

Then hot.

Then he proceeded to chew his nails until his fingertips bled.

He had to do something. He had to prove to his father that he could be trusted. He knew, deep down, that he'd never survive without his father's backing and support.

He must do *something*. But what?

Honor Welles was in. Hillary, coming back to the house that had so depressed her before, wondered if it would do so again.

It did.

Honor, dressed in a long floral skirt and a cream blouse, looked cool and classically chic as she showed her into the lounge and Hillary felt again a growing sense of unease. She resolutely ignored it and sat on the sofa as Honor poured them both some cold, home-made lemonade. Hillary surreptitiously glanced around the room, and wondered what it was about the place that made her feel so smothered and hemmed in.

'I'm thinking about leaving my husband,' Honor said, and took a sip of her drink.

'Now that's what's called a conversation stopper,' Hillary said pleasantly.

Honor had the grace to laugh at herself. 'Yes, I suppose it is. But I just thought I'd better get it in before you started asking me questions again. Just in case it's relevant. This is, obviously, something to do with Michael's death, yes?'

'Yes,' Hillary agreed mildly. 'And as to whether or not your marital status is relevant, it rather depends, doesn't it. Are you leaving your husband because you think he might have killed your ex-lover?'

'Good grief, no.'

'Are you leaving him because *you* killed your ex-lover?'

Honor laughed and took another sip of her lemonade. 'Nothing so dramatic or interesting, I'm afraid. It's just that, since Michael died, it's as if something's changed. Inside of me. I don't know quite how to put it. It's like my inertia has been slowly wearing off. Once I couldn't be bothered to leave Harry because it would have meant too much effort. Now ...' she shrugged helplessly, and looked around. 'I've just got to get out. Do you see?'

Hillary nodded. She did indeed see. 'There's been a development,' she said, getting down to business and putting down the half-drunk glass of sweet-sour lemonade on the immaculate coffee table.

'You've found out who killed him?'

'No. Not yet. It turns out that Michael Ivers was, and I'm sorry but there's no easy way to say this, so I'll just come right out with it. Michael Ivers was HIV positive.'

As with Lucy Kirke, Hillary watched her face closely.

Honor Welles blinked rapidly and her lower lip became slack.

She swallowed once, compulsively, then raised her glass to her lips. Her hand trembled slightly.

'Oh my,' she managed to say with a somewhat shaky smile. She took a minuscule sip of her lemonade, then put the glass down beside Hillary's on the table.

'You didn't know, I take it,' Hillary said, more as a statement than a question.

Honor smiled savagely. 'No.'

'Does it surprise you so much? I mean, given his lifestyle. You must have learned, fairly quickly what he was like,' Hillary said, as gently and tactfully as she could, under the circumstances.

Honour gave a short bark of bitter laughter. 'As you say,' she agreed. Then she shrugged again. 'But for some reason – no. I never even thought about it. I mean, it's not as if I regularly have affairs. Mike was very much a one-off, so to speak. So I wasn't really up on the drill,' she explained bitterly.

Hillary nodded. Then took a deep breath. 'You know, Mrs Welles, that if you had found out about it, and decided in a fit of rage to kill him, a jury would be most sympathetic.'

Honor looked at her for a moment with a perfectly expressionless face, then she smiled savagely again.

'Sorry,' she shook her head firmly, 'but no.'

Hillary nodded. Well, it had been worth a try. 'You will make an appointment to see your doctor straight away, yes?' she chivvied softly.

Honor Welles reached for her glass, rose, went to a drinks cabinet disguised as a large world globe, and poured an extremely generous amount of gin into the ice-cube-laden glass.

'Yes,' she said eventually, after she'd taken an enormous swallow. 'Yes, I'll be sure to do that.'

Janine Tyler sat listlessly at her desk in Witney, her current case-load of files spread out in front of her. When her phone rang, she reached for it automatically.

'Yes,' she said shortly.

'Er, is that DS Tyler?'

'This is DI Mallow,' Janine corrected, then her voice lowered to a whisper. 'Skunk, is that you?'

'Yeah, it's me.'

'I thought I told you to scarper?' Janine hissed.

'I did, I swear. I'm calling from a B and B in … well, let's just say I have a nice view of the sea.'

Janine relaxed a little in her chair.

'Normally I wouldn't make contact, like, but I just thought you should know. I called the woman where I live, just to make sure she ain't gonna rent my room out or nothink from underneath me, and she warned me that she'd had this swanky copper nosing round, asking after me.'

Janine sighed. 'We knew all that. That's why I want you to enjoy your sea view until the end of June at least, you hear me?' she warned him firmly. 'The super's off to Hull then, and he'll be out of our hair for good.'

'You sure?' Skunk Petersen's voice whined in her ear.

'Yes,' Janine said with more conviction than she felt.

'Good. 'Cause I need to get back to Oxford as some point, see. I got contacts who get nervous if I go missing for a while. And there's always someone waiting to move in on my patch, see.'

Janine sighed heavily. 'Until the end of June, Skunk, or I'll put your arse through a mangle.'

'Yeah, OK. S'long as it's all settled like,' Skunk said nervously.

'It is. Now sod off and go paddle in the sea or something,' Janine hissed and slammed down the phone.

She waited for a moment, then dialled Hillary Greene's number. She was put through to her voicemail. She hesitated about leaving a message, then said brightly, 'Hi boss, it's me, Janine. That situation we discussed the other day. I think you should go ahead soon. Real soon. OK? 'Bye.'

She hung up, and caught a curious DC looking at her. He quickly turned his head away when he realized he'd caught her eye.

Janine began to feel the familiar nibble of depression. At Witney, nobody quite knew what to make of her, and she decided, there and then, that it was time to put in for a transfer. Perhaps to the south coast somewhere. Somewhere where she wasn't quite so famous.

Or was that infamous?

When DI Hillary Greene pulled into the business park, the security man in the booth watched her curiously. He knew who she was, of course, and he watched with interest as she turned, not to go towards the newspaper-delivery depot where the murder had taken place, but instead into the unit next door. Hermes' Wings.

He wondered what she wanted there.

Unlike Frank Ross, he was not an ex-copper and he was finding it something of a chore to be in the middle of a murder investigation. At first it had been exciting in a horrible sort of way, and all his friends and even his wife had found him suddenly interesting. But as the time went on, with no arrest in the offing, things were settling back to normal.

Mandy, one of the secretaries at the garden-supplies depot had told him that the police were sure the crime had something to do with the murdered man's love life, and nothing to do with his job at all. Which meant that everyone at the park was beginning to relax a little. It obviously put them in the clear. Apart from the fact that Mr Ivers had been murdered at his office, that was.

He shrugged and went back to reading his newspaper.

Harry Welles was standing nervously behind his desk when one of the girls in the outer office showed Hillary in. He bade her sit, then sat himself, fiddling nervously with a pen.

Hillary regarded him thoughtfully. 'I've just been to see your wife, sir,' she began slowly.

Harry swallowed hard and went a little pale. 'Oh? Yes. Er, I'm sure … er …' he trailed off, obviously not knowing what he was sure of.

Hillary could see him start to sweat. It was, by now, what

she'd come to expect of him. 'Mr Welles, were you aware that Michael Ivers was ill?' she tried again, cautiously. With this type you had to be very careful.

'Ill?' Harry repeated blankly. Whatever it was he'd been dreading her saying, it obviously wasn't that.

'Yes. To be specific sir – he was HIV positive.'

Harry Welles dropped the pen he was holding. It clattered on to the desk with a noisy ping and rolled, unheeded on to the floor. 'He was what? You mean he had Aids. The dirty bastard. And he was messing about with …'

Harry Welles's mouth suddenly snapped shut. 'But that means that I might have it!' he squeaked.

His eyes rolled up in his head, and he slumped in his chair. Before Hillary could reach him he toppled untidily out of it on to the floor beside his pen.

'Oh shit!' Hillary said, then walked swiftly to the door and thrust it open. 'Would you call an ambulance please. Mr Welles has passed out.'

The two girls in the outer office turned wide-eyed faces towards her, but one of them reached for the phone.

'Would you bring me some water and a towel please,' she said to the other one, who got up, looked about vaguely, then suddenly sprinted for the door.

Back in the office, Hillary walked quickly to the prostrate man and hoped he'd only had a fainting fit. If the shock of what she'd told him had brought on a heart attack, then things were going to get very grim indeed. But, to her relief, she quickly ascertained that his breathing was regular, and when she went down on all fours to press her ear to his chest it sounded to her to be beating regularly, if a little fast.

She raised her head as she sensed movement behind her.

'I couldn't find a proper towel – they only have these grey paper things in the ladies loo. So I wet them for you. I hope that's OK?' the young secretary said breathlessly.

Hillary nodded. She took the cold and damp paper towels

and a white plastic cup of water from her, and put them on the floor beside Welles.

'Make sure the ambulance, when it comes, knows where it's needed,' she said. The girl nodded and backed out, her eyes still fixed on her stricken boss.

Hillary wiped the damp towels over Harry Welles's face. He muttered, but didn't really come round. Hillary sat back on her heels and waited. In the end, she drank the water herself.

When the paramedics arrived, a youngish man and a middle-aged woman, she moved away and gave them room, watching with a thoughtful look on her face as they put smelling salts under his nose, which brought him back, spluttering, to consciousness. They fixed little discs to his chest, arms and legs, and studied the monitor carefully.

After asking a few questions, taking his blood pressure, and pronouncing themselves satisfied that he was in no immediate danger, the man and woman helped him into his seat. The woman asked him if he wanted to go to hospital to be checked over again, but warned him what waiting times were like in A&E.

Wisely, in Hillary's view, Harry Welles declined. They made him promise to see his own GP without delay, and left briskly.

Hillary, knowing she could hardly carry on questioning him now, also said goodbye quietly, and let herself out.

In her car, she sat behind the driver's wheel and thought.

Harry Welles was obviously a very highly strung individual. He was the kind of man who brooded over grievances and wore himself out with his own nerves. He probably felt with painful intensity every slight and arrow that life's slings sent winging his way.

His wife didn't think he had in him to kill someone.

Hillary wasn't so sure.

In her experience, it was often the brooders and timid types who could suddenly explode in a catastrophic moment of madness.

Had Harry Welles done just that?

His wife gave him an alibi. But, really, how much credence could she put in it?

She was sure, well, as sure as she could be, that Honor Welles hadn't known about the HIV. Neither, from the way he'd reacted, had her husband.

But that, in itself, might mean nothing. If Harry Welles had finally decided to be a man and not a mouse, he might have decided to whack the playboy, the fun-loving and gambling womanizer, over the head with a plank of wood regardless.

And Honor Welles, who'd admitted she wasn't the sort to have affairs, might just have felt guilty enough about it to give him an alibi when he came home, covered in her lover's blood.

Maybe.

Or maybe not.

Hillary sighed, put her car into gear, and drove away from the park.

From his office Pat Hodgson watched her go with relief. The last thing he needed was for the chief investigating officer in the Ivers case to start sniffing around again.

He glanced at his watch anxiously. Just a few more hours to go before they shut up shop for the night. He walked to his desk, and stared at the large cardboard box standing against one wall.

He'd bought the equipment it contained just two days ago, and was confident that he could work it. He was sure that he could remember all he needed to know from the demonstration the man in the electronics store had given him. He'd been an enthusiastic salesman and Pat suspected that he'd sold him one of the more expensive items in the range. But he'd been clear in his instructions and the demonstration, and that was the main thing.

And for once, Pat didn't mind the expense. He needed the equipment to be top of the range and to not let him down.

And tonight, unless he was much mistaken, it was going to earn every penny he'd forked out for it.

With a grim smile, he set about unpacking it and setting it up.

# CHAPTER TWELVE

Michael Ivers's GP's surgery was a pleasant, new building, not far from the canal and the new big shopping and leisure complex. Hillary found a space in the too-small car park where shrubs bearing bright orange berries were dotted about. She got out and listened for a moment to a song thrush proclaiming his territory.

Beside her, a long, one-storey building of yellow brick sprawled away, and through the large glass windows she could see movement within. She had a glimpse of a large waiting area, and behind it a long counter; people were moving busily too and fro, but the reflection of the sun on the glass made it hard to make out details.

It was turning into another warm May afternoon. Hillary realized that, for the first time in a long time, she could plan a long, overseas holiday and not have it cancelled due to an unexpected and important case arising.

She told herself firmly that such new-found freedom was wonderful. Then she walked towards the main doors, where a large steel plate, when pressed, made the doors open electronically for her.

Inside, it was a little too warm and garish orange-upholstered upright chairs stood ranged in rows on hard-wearing beige carpet.

She approached the long reception counter but found it empty. She pressed the button for attention and heard a very annoying buzzing echoing into the office area beyond. There were stacks of files, and a computer humming, and someone, quite close, was talking on the phone. But nobody came to answer the buzz.

Behind her only two patients still waited to be seen, and she assumed the afternoon surgery was nearly over. She sighed, and walked at right angles to a smaller, glass-enclosed booth with the word PHARMACY written above it. This had a more old-fashioned little brass bell, which she lifted and rang.

A moment later a middle-aged woman with grey curls appeared behind the glass. 'Name please?'

'Sorry, I can't find anyone at reception. I need to speak to a Dr Phyllis Wainwright.'

The pharmacist glanced over Hillary's shoulder towards reception, and frowned. 'That's odd. Suzy was there just a moment ago. Sorry, patients need to make appointments at reception.'

'I'm not a patient,' Hillary said quietly, and showed her ID. 'I need to speak to Dr Wainwright on an official matter.'

The older woman blinked, then said uncertainly, 'Oh. Yes. I see. I think Dr Wainwright is with a patient just now.'

'That's all right, I can wait,' Hillary assured her. 'If you can just let the doctor know I'm here, and that I need to see her when she's seen her last patient?'

The pharmacist nodded and withdrew. Hillary could hear her whispering to someone else further inside the room. Hillary took a seat and selected a *Homes and Garden* magazine where she admired the camellias. The reception area remained unmanned, but nobody else came in, and within fifteen minutes Hillary was being shown down a long internal corridor. Off this, doors were adorned with various names, and Dr Phyllis Wainwright was about midway down on the left.

Hillary thanked the pharmacist, knocked and went in.

Phyllis Wainwright looked barely out of her teens, and Hillary had to smile at her own misconceptions. She'd imagined someone in her early sixties, thin and with a brisk, no-nonsense manner. The young woman who watched her take a seat, and then carefully studied her ID card, however, was plump, with long fair hair and boiled-gooseberry eyes.

'It's about a patient of yours, Dr Wainwright, now deceased. Mr Michael Ivers,' Hillary came straight to the point.

The doctor nodded, but, surprisingly, didn't launch into the usual spiel about patient confidentiality. 'Yes, I read about it in the papers. You don't expect someone you know to be murdered, do you?'

It was a familiar question, and Hillary gave her usual sympathetic smile.

'I've just had the pathology reports back. He was HIV positive,' Hillary said. 'Was he aware of this fact?'

'Oh yes,' the young doctor said at once. 'Mr Ivers first consulted me nearly two years ago. He became worried when he spotted lesions on his upper arms. The diagnosis was fairly swift.'

'He was on medication?'

'He was, and responded well at first. Lately …' the doctor paused, then shrugged delicately. 'I don't think I'm at liberty to go too precisely into his medical details, Inspector.'

Hillary nodded. 'Thank you, but I don't need you to. Our own pathologist can tell me anything of that sort that I need to know. What I need from you is more personal and background detail. How did he take the news, for instance?'

Phyllis Wainwright held her hands up in the air. 'Not particularly well, but then that's hardly surprising, is it? He went through the usual stages – disbelief, anger, self-pity. He hadn't got round to acceptance yet, but I daresay he would have. Eventually.' She didn't sound convinced though, and neither was Hillary.

'You told him, of course, to contact and warn his past and present sexual partners?'

'Naturally,' the doctor responded curtly.

Hillary sighed. 'I don't believe that he actually did so.'

The younger woman shook her head sadly.

'I take it you're not all that surprised,' Hillary guessed gently.

The other woman shrugged, but discretion was too ingrained into her for her to be drawn.

'Did he ever mention to you being worried about anything other than his condition?' Hillary changed tack. 'Did he mention a girlfriend who'd been particularly vitriolic with him, for instance, when she learned about his diagnosis, or who'd become threatening?'

'No. But then, if he hadn't told any of them about his infection, they probably wouldn't even know about it, would they?' Dr Wainwright pointed out with unerring logic.

'No, but he may have told a friend, a male friend perhaps, who might have let it slip to someone. So he never mentioned being followed or harassed, for example by a current boyfriend or lover of a past sexual partner? Someone who'd have a reason to bear him a grudge?'

'No. But he wasn't what you might call very chatty with me. To be honest, I always got the feeling that he resented me. As if it was my fault that he was ill. But that's not an uncommon reaction amongst patients.'

'Don't shoot the messenger, as they say.' Hillary nodded. 'Well,' she rose to her feet, 'thank you, Doctor. Is there anything that you may have noticed that struck you as odd?'

'Such as what?'

Hillary shrugged helplessly.

'No. I'm afraid not,' Phyllis Wainwright said firmly.

As she went out the reception area was still deserted; the last of the patients had left. Hillary went outside, climbed into Puff, and mentally made one more tick against her to-do list for that day.

When she got back to HQ she waded through the usual mound of paperwork, then checked her messages. Janine's was the fifth one, and she felt her stomach lurch as she listened to it. It was nearly five, and she had no more excuses for putting off her confrontation with Vane.

She reached into her briefcase and extracted the plain brown paper envelope. Then she phoned the internal number for Vane's secretary.

'It's DI Greene. Is the super in?'

'He's just about to leave, DI Greene. Is it urgent?'

Hillary bit back a bitter laugh. 'Yes. But it'll only take a minute.' Well, she could hope.

'Very well. I'll inform him you're on your way up.'

And won't that fill him with joy, Hillary thought grimly. Resolutely, she picked up the envelope and walked slowly upstairs. There was the usual foot traffic about, and more than one pair of eyes watched her curiously as she tapped on the outer door to Vane's office. Everyone knew that Hillary Greene avoided having anything to do with Superintendent Vane if she could possibly manage it. This close to her retirement, and with Vane's move to Hull imminent, tongues would be wagging the moment the gossips could get together. But there was nothing she could do about that.

Vane's admin assistant was a large woman with improbably red hair. She smiled vaguely, but her eyes were curious as she nodded at her to go through.

Hillary took a deep breath and pushed open the door. Brian Vane was seated behind his desk. His face was closed down and wary and he watched her wordlessly as she walked to his desk, but his eyes went straight to the A4 sized brown envelope she was carrying. It was not surprising. It was the only thing she'd brought with her, and so looked, for that reason, ominous.

'Brian,' she said, deliberately forgoing using his title just to nark him.

Brian Vane blinked, opened his mouth, thought about it a moment, then gave a mental shrug. No doubt he liked to pick his battles, as did she, and he didn't fancy being reduced to petty nitpicking. 'Hillary,' he said drily.

'I've just heard from my old sergeant. DI Mallow as she now is,' Hillary began, making no move to sit in one of the spacious chairs facing his desk.

He smiled grimly. 'Oh yes. The sort-of heroine. That's how I heard some women in a supermarket queue once refer to her.'

Hillary shrugged. 'Whatever. Apparently, you seem to be keen to speak to one of her sources. Odd, that. A super taking an interest in a mere skell. And not even one of his own narks.'

Vane began to smile, clearly enjoying himself. 'Oh, I think Mr Petersen might be very interesting to speak to,' he parried.

'I doubt it.'

'Now there we differ.' Vane leaned back in his chair, beginning to feel better.

She could almost read his mind. In his view, she must be here because she was worried. Maybe he thought she was on a fishing expedition, to find out just what he knew, or had guessed. Maybe, in his wildest dreams, she was here to beg him to back off.

Yeah. Right.

It was time she nipped all of that in the bud before he could start to feel too good about himself.

'You can forget about it,' Hillary told him. 'It'll do you no good, even if you find him. Besides, you'll be in Hull by next week.'

Vane winced at the thought and gave an ugly snarl. 'There are trains from Hull, you know, Hillary. I can always commute. And I may have to, if the inquiry into the Myers case has to be reopened.'

So. At last the threat was out in the open.

Hillary eyed him curiously. The man really was full of bile. All of this because she'd once caught him out planting evidence? It was not as if she'd turned him in, even. She'd been just a raw WPC, and he was already a respected sergeant. For years, they'd never crossed paths again, until he'd been given Mel's old job. And then just her presence in the same building had been enough to make him feel he needed to get rid of her. If it hadn't been for that, he wouldn't have made such a prat of himself over the Myers debacle.

And somehow it had all snowballed and brought them to this. The man hated her. It was ridiculous.

'Cat got your tongue?' Vane asked, made suddenly uneasy by her quiet contemplation.

'No. Just giving you a chance to agree with me. There's no percentage in raking up the Clive Myers tragedy,' she said evenly.

Vane snorted. 'No chance.'

'You know, Brian, I thought you'd be the last one to want to bring a fellow copper's misfortunes kicking and screaming into the open.'

'Oh? Going to plead for the poor pregnant widow, are you?' Vane sneered. 'But she's not pregnant any more, is she? She's had the sprog. And she's no longer a brand-new widow. Public sympathy will have waned for her.'

Hillary nodded. He was right.

'But Brian,' she said, shaking her head from side to side in mock gentle reproof, 'did your granny never tell you that people in glasshouses really shouldn't throw stones? After all, if you can rake up somebody else's past,' she carefully withdrew the photograph and laid it on the table in front of him, 'then somebody else can always return the favour and rake up your own.'

Vane saw the photograph and did a visible, mental stutter. His eyelids fluttered, and his breath caught. He went abruptly grey.

He reached for it and stared at it, then looked at her out of bleak, furious eyes. 'How the hell did you get this!' he roared. In fact, he roared so hard that his secretary, who'd just opened the outer door to leave, froze.

The three uniforms loitering outside also heard. The secretary shut the door smartly behind her and scurried away, head down. She knew of the gossip about Hillary Greene and her boss. But he was off to Hull, and another boss would soon take his place. She had enough sense to keep out of it.

The three uniforms lingered eagerly, waiting to see if there'd be any more fireworks.

Inside his office though, Hillary was perfectly silent. She smiled at him gently.

'Just toddle off to Hull, Brian,' she advised him quietly. 'And let sleeping dogs lie. And I'll do the same.'

She didn't wait to see if he'd agree but simply turned on her heel and walked away. She had to get out of there fast, and whilst she was still ahead. If Vane cottoned on to the fact that she didn't know the photograph's true significance, she was scuppered.

'Oh, you can keep that,' she said airily from the doorway, nodding down at the photograph. 'I have another copy,' she lied. 'Just in case the Myers inquiry should ever reopen.'

She left, shutting the door quietly behind her. Once on the other side she felt only a vast sense of relief. For she'd seen his face, and could clearly read the defeat in it. Vane no longer posed a threat. She felt her shoulders ache with the sudden release of tension, but for the first time in a long time she felt better. The storm-laden cloud that had hovered over her head ever since Janine had shot and killed Clive Myers was dissipating at last.

She knew it would be all over HQ by tomorrow that she and Vane had had one last confrontation, but she hardly cared. What, after all, did it matter now?

She stiffened her shoulders and walked to the outer door. There the uniforms scattered as she walked out, but her small, satisfied smile didn't go unnoticed.

It was getting dark, and Mark Chang was beginning to regret the impulse that had brought him back to the business park.

When he'd left HQ a few hours ago it was buzzing with speculation about his boss and Brian Vane, but for once Chang was in no mood to listen. He'd decided that tonight he was going to do a little observation work of his own.

It had been obvious when he reported on Pat Hodgson's activities at the yard that Hillary Greene had sensed something was going on, but that she was too ploughed under with the HIV angle of their case to chase it up.

Chang also thought that something was definitely up. It was obvious that Frank Ross was involved up to his neck, and that Hodgson was at the end of his tether. Chang was eager to find out what was afoot. So a little unpaid overtime, keeping watch on Hodgson's, had seemed like an ideal plan. He could report to Hillary in the morning on any suspicious activities, and earn brownie points for his initiative and dedication to duty.

But now, as he approached the gates, it was quiet and the darkness was spooky. Even though traffic filed past on the busy Oxford to Banbury road off to his left, Chang felt isolated and slightly silly. He probably wouldn't even be able to get past the gates without the night watchman having to come to let him in. Since that would be Ross himself, the whole exercise would have failed before it had started.

But he was lucky. The gates, although shut, were not yet locked, and when he pushed them open a sliver and took a look around, he could see at a glance that Ross was not in the booth.

As quickly as he could he pushed open the gates and slipped inside. Once there, he headed for the unit nearest to him, which was Unit 6, the auto-repair shop. He stood in the shadow of its front gates. Spotting a stand of shrubs not far away, he made for those and slipped in between the foliage. From there he had a good view of Hodgson's.

He decided he might as well make himself as comfortable as he could, and sat down on the dry grass, ignoring the twigs and leaves that scratched his arms and legs. It wasn't yet ten o'clock and he expected that if something was going to happen it would probably take place in the early hours.

He was wrong.

Frank Ross was the first to hear the rumble of a heavy lorry, and he was out of his booth the minute the front gates swung open. Since he knew he'd not yet locked them for the night, he swore and began to move cautiously forward.

It was barely eleven, and he wasn't yet afraid. It wasn't beyond the realms of possibility that one of the units had a late delivery scheduled and had just forgotten to notify him. But when he saw Ollie pushing open the gates and waving an obviously reinforced truck into the yard, he swore under his breath.

Inside Hodgson's the boss of the outfit gave a small smile of satisfaction and turned on the camera he'd set up in his office. It had an infra-red gadget that allowed it to film in darkness, and had a sweeping view of his yard – with the load of marble almost centred in the viewfinder. Pat Hodgson could hear a reassuring drone as the camera began to record the activities outside.

In his own office Alan Hodgson started in dismay as the doors to the builder's yard opened, and Ollie's son, Purple Pete, began to wave his arms about, directing a truck that was backing into the yard.

The bastards! Just as he'd thought, they were going to steal the marble. Although none of them had said anything to him about it. Frank Ross had looked through him as if he didn't know him from Adam when he'd first come on his shift.

Alan got more and more worked up as the red light from the truck's reversing lights glowed gently in the dark.

In the bushes, Mark Chang felt his heart pound, and he hit Hillary's number on his speed dial.

Frank Ross ran over to the lumber yard and grabbed Ollie's arm. 'What the hell's this?' he hissed.

Ollie beamed at him. 'We've hit the jackpot, mate. Didn't you hear about the fortune in marble old man Hodgson's got stacked in here?'

Frank had. Of course he had.

'Are you out of your bloody mind!' he hissed. 'You can't do a heist of that size! It's way out of our league! This is serious time if we get caught. Which is why you didn't tell me about it, you—'

Frank Ross threw a punch that landed squarely in Ollie's face. He went sprawling.

On her boat, Hillary Greene was just stepping out of the tiny shower when she heard her mobile ring. She sighed, wrapped a towel around her and went through to the bedroom, hunting for it in her bag.

'What the hell was that for?' Ollie whined. He'd fallen on his backside, and it was stinging.

'Dad? You OK?' He heard his son's voice call loudly behind him, and Frank cursed.

'Tell the fool to shut up!' he hissed nervously.

In the bushes, Chang hesitated uncertainly, wishing Hillary Greene would pick up the damned phone.

In his office, Alan heard angry voices and moaned. He then went through to the small supply shed, and selected a large nail gun. Something like a glue gun to look at, it had a rectangular box attached to the handle, which held nearly 200 nails. Carpenters used it a bit like clerks would use a stapler. Only this fired six-inch nails. Very fast, and with enough force to drive them deeply into wood.

Hefting it into his hand, and feeling a bit like a gunslinger from the Wild West, Alan Hodgson slipped quietly outside. He'd teach these thieving sods that he couldn't be taken lightly. Not even telling him about it! And trying to do his dad out of nearly £100,000. Just who the hell did they think he was? Some little kid who could be pushed around?

In his office Pat Hodgson looked through the night-camera viewfinder and frowned. Just what the hell was going on out there? Why had Frank Ross just punched one of the thieves?

For a moment, a nasty feeling snaked down his back. Surely

he hadn't got it wrong? Was the ex-copper really trying to do his job and prevent the robbery?

On her boat, Hillary Greene found her phone and pressed the button. 'DI Greene.'

'Guv, it's me, Chang. I'm at the business park. Something's going down.'

Hillary found it hard to hear him, since he was whispering, but she caught the gist of it.

'At the park. What for?'

'I thought I should keep watch, guv. Something was obviously off at Hodgson's. A lorry pulled in a few minutes ago.' Chang rattled off the facts so fast he had to stop to remember to take a breath. 'Frank Ross has just thumped someone. I think I need back-up guv,' he added nervously.

Hillary went cold. 'You're there on your own?'

'Yes guv.'

Hillary wanted to blister his ears for being so stupid, but knew that now was not the time. 'All right, I'm on my way. Stay out of sight if you can, and keep out if it as far as possible. Is the main gate open?'

'I think so, guv.'

'Right. Sit tight.' She hung up and hit Gemma's speed dial number. At the same time she frantically began to dry herself on the towel and stepped over to her wardrobe, pulling out the first clothes she came to.

'Gemma Fordham.'

'Gemma, get over to the business park fast.' Even to her own ears her voice sounded tight with tension. 'Something's going down and Chang's on his own.' She hung up and pulled on her clothes, swearing at they way they stuck to her clammy skin.

At least she knew she could rely on Gemma not to need the situation spelled out for her and to act fast. She ran down the towpath, praying that Puff would start first thing. It would take her at least twenty minutes, if not longer, to get to Adderbury.

'What you doing down there?' Purple Pete said, staring at his father who was rolling around on the ground and struggling to rise.

'Don't be such a prat and help me up,' Ollie said angrily.

The driver of the truck climbed down and stood watching them nervously. 'Hey, are we going to load this gear or not?' he whined.

'Not,' Frank Ross snarled. 'Get back in the cab and get that truck out of here.'

'No!' Ollie snapped, holding on to his son's hands as the lad levered his father, with some difficulty, back on to his feet. 'Pete, help Darren load the marble. You'll need the forklift. Darren, you said you can operate one, OK?'

'Just lead me to it,' the driver said, eyeing Frank Ross curiously.

Chang left the bushes and crept closer to the outer wooden fence, the better to make sense of the angry but lowered voices he could hear. He crouched up against it, feeling tense but calm.

'It's by the loading bay,' Purple Pete said, stepping between his father and Frank Ross. The night watchman was breathing heavily, and was clenching and unclenching his fists in impotent rage. Pete could feel the anger emanating off him in waves.

'What's up with Mr Ross,' he hissed at his father, who shot him a quick angry look. 'Just help Darren,' snarled Ollie. 'Me and Mr Ross need to have a quick chat.'

'The hell we do,' Frank Ross began, and then stopped as another, totally unexpected voice joined in.

'What are you bastards doing here?' Alan Hodgson said, his voice squeaky with nerves and cracking with false bravado.

In his office, Pat Hodgson's eyes widened behind the viewfinder. He lifted his head abruptly. Alan? What the hell was his son doing here? He felt suddenly sick. He'd known that

Alan must have been the one supplying the thieves with the info, but he'd never suspected his son of actually, physically, being in on the raids.

This was all getting out of hand and fast. Nothing was going according to plan. He stepped quickly to the door and slipped out into the darkness.

Mark Chang carefully worked his way towards the open doors of the yard. Hillary Greene had ordered him not to get involved, but surely she'd expect him to watch?

Hillary Greene drove towards Adderbury, breaking as much of the speed limit as Puff could manage. It wouldn't have surprised her to be overtaken by Gemma's more sporty and larger-engined new car, but her sergeant had further to come. When she hit the traffic lights at Hopcroft's Halt, there was still no sign of Gemma.

Hillary scraped through on amber, and wondered, with a grim laugh, why there was never a copper around when you wanted one. She could do with a few patrol cars to back her up. She reached for her mobile, called HQ and ordered some.

If Chang had got it wrong, and it was a false alarm, she'd have egg on her face, but so what?

She was retiring in five days' time.

In the yard, Alan Hodgson stared at Ollie and Frank Ross belligerently. 'You're not taking that marble. It's worth a mint. It would ruin Dad!'

'Don't be daft, son,' Ollie said impatiently. 'It's insured, innit?'

'That's not the point. Nobody will trust Dad with a big order again. I'm not letting you get away with it.'

Just then, the sound of a forklift engine starting up made Alan Hodgson jump. He half-turned his head, trying to see where the sound had come from, and his finger on the nail gun jerked. And with a hissing sound, a sudden volley of tiny, sharp missiles shot into the air.

One hit Ollie in the leg and made him yelp and hop around

comically. Most went into a pallet of wood just beside where Frank Ross was standing. But three went into Frank Ross.

The first one hit his shoulder and sent a shaft of painful fire down his arm. But it hit no major organs or arteries and did no permanent damage.

One grazed the side of his neck, making it bleed, and landed harmlessly in the ground behind him, its force spent.

But one hit him squarely in the throat.

Frank's hand flew up to his throat, and he tried to swear. But then found that he couldn't speak. Then he realized that he couldn't breathe either. A tight, hard feeling shot across his chest as he tried, in vain, to suck in air. He heard a strange gargling sound, but didn't realize that he was making it, then he felt his knees buckle.

Pat Hodgson stepped into the scene, and stared as Ross went down on all fours, his back arching as he tried to drag air into his lungs. Ross's face felt hot and painful. He clawed at his throat.

Alan Hodgson stared at him, puzzled. 'What's he doing?'

Ollie, who was holding his bleeding leg, sat down abruptly. 'Somebody call an ambulance, for Pete's sake!' he moaned.

Chang, who'd been peering through a crack in the fence and had seen it all, pressed three nines on his mobile and requested an ambulance. He then took a deep breath and walked boldly into the yard. 'DC Chang,' he announced, and everyone turned to look at him.

All except for Frank Ross. Panic was setting in now, and he could feel his head throbbing, as if it was about to explode. He felt something cool on his cheek and realized that his face was on the ground now. He was shrieking, *I can't breathe! I can't breathe!* but he knew the desperate noise was only in his head.

He was vaguely aware of someone beside him, turning him over, a hand on his throat trying to stop the blood.

He thrashed in panic but no matter how hard his labouring lungs tried, they couldn't summon air. Lights began to flash in front of his eyes and he felt true dread.

Mark Chang looked down into his eyes, which were beginning to bulge and felt suddenly very scared.

'He can't breathe,' Chang said helplessly.

'What's the matter with him?' Alan Hodgson asked, still puzzled. 'Is he having a heart attack?'

'No, you silly sod. You've shot him,' Ollie yelled.

'Huh?'

Pat Hodgson was suddenly at his son's side. 'Give me the nail gun, Alan,' he said, his voice so cracked that his son had trouble understanding him.

'What do you mean?' he asked.

From the side of the yard, Darren suddenly appeared behind the wheel of a forklift, with Purple Pete loping along side him.

He saw Chang and froze. 'Dad?' he called uncertainly.

'You there. Turn that machine off,' Chang said with all the authority he could muster.

But Darren left the motor running, and sprinted to his truck. He pulled out and headed for the main gates. Chang briefly considered chasing him, but Frank Ross, who was now going purple, was clinging to his arm, his fingers scrabbling against his biceps, as if trying to pull him down.

'You're a copper, don't you know CPR,' Ollie yelled. He was sweating and looked terrified.

'I do, but I think his windpipe is crushed, not blocked,' Chang said, but he bent down and tried to blow air into Frank Ross's lungs.

But the ex-cop was beginning to convulse now.

'Where's that ambulance?' Chang groaned.

Darren pulled the lorry to the outer gates, then rammed on his brakes as a nifty little car blocked the way. Gemma Fordham jumped out. She'd passed Hillary Greene as they'd been speeding through Deddington, and now she ran to the lorry and jumped up, opening the door and reaching into the cab. She deftly turned off the ignition and pocketed the keys.

'Where are you off to in such a hurry, sunshine?' Gemma asked cheerfully.

Darren stared at her. She was gorgeous. And that sexy voice! Like some actress off the TV.

When Hillary Greene pulled up on the side of the road, she saw the situation at a glance and nodded at Gemma as she passed. 'Back-up's on the way,' she called. Then she glanced around the yard and frowned. 'Any idea's what's up?'

'No guv, just got here. But I can hear the cavalry.'

But she was wrong. It was the siren of an ambulance, not a squad car.

Hillary hurried forward, not liking the fact that Chang must have summoned it, whilst Gemma cuffed the driver and made him scoot along so that she could restart the lorry and reverse it back into the park, so that it wasn't blocking the entrance.

The first thing Hillary saw on entering Hodgson's were father and son, standing close together; Pat Hodgson was holding something against his thigh. Next she saw Chang on the ground, doing CPR. Behind her, she heard the ambulance pull in. Quickly she beckoned the paramedics over.

It wasn't until Chang got up to give them access to the patient that she saw Frank Ross lying on the ground.

He didn't look good.

'He's not breathing,' Chang shouted to the paramedics, who ignored him and got frantically to work.

Hillary's heart lurched at the young constable's words. Behind her, several police cars poured into the park.

'Just what the hell is going on, Constable?' Hillary asked grimly.

# CHAPTER THIRTEEN

Hillary walked wearily through the door and into the open plan office. It wasn't yet eight o'clock in the morning, but it had been gone three before she and her team had left the business park, and although she'd been tired, she hadn't managed to do more than catnap for what had remained of the night.

She walked straight to her desk and stood staring down at it listlessly. It was the usual mix – overflowing in-tray, and folders from other cases packed in piles, the top layer being the most urgent. She had notes to go through for an upcoming court appearance that really couldn't wait, and she probably had a stack of e-mails and text messages to go through before she could even think about turning her attention to her murder case.

She sighed, and got to it.

Gemma came in next, looking bright-eyed and bushy tailed. Chang followed closely behind, shooting Hillary a nervous glance as he did so. He was not quite sure whether he was going to be congratulated or dragged across the carpet for what had happened last night, and his tension showed. Before Hillary could say anything, however, the door to Danvers's cubicle opened and he walked out, closely followed by DI Sam Waterstone.

Hillary knew and liked Sam – they'd even collaborated on a few cases in the past.

She was aware of curious eyes following their progress, for the news about what had happened last night had already circulated. And the news that Frank Ross had been seriously injured, and was being operated on right now at the John Radcliffe Hospital, had set the station house ablaze with gossip and speculation.

'Draw up a couple of chairs, Constable,' Hillary said. Chang leapt up and did as he was told. Danvers looked at him levelly for a moment, until the youngster began to blush and look uncomfortable, then the DCI sat down. Beside him, Sam Waterstone shot a crafty wink at Chang, who looked a little relieved at the silent support and encouragement.

'Right. Last night's fiasco,' Danvers began crisply. 'Let's go over it again, and I've a few updates to add that should prove interesting. DC Chang – since you were there, on your own, and without your SO's knowledge,' Danvers said cuttingly, 'why don't you begin?'

Miserably, Chang related why he'd decided to do a little off-the-cuff observation, and then proceeded to give a very good description of the events. He missed out no details, but he wasn't long-winded, and as far as Hillary could tell, had forgotten nothing of importance. His account was clear and lucid, and his time-frame seemed to be spot on.

When he'd finished, he swallowed hard and waited for whatever was to come.

Hillary sighed. 'You should have told me what you were doing, Chang,' she said. 'But your logic was good, and so were your instincts. But if things had turned out differently, it could be you undergoing surgery right now and not Ross. Or worse. You could be dead.'

Chang paled.

'Let this be something you learn from,' Hillary continued. 'There are reasons why we very seldom work solo. And observations at night, when a situation is at best volatile, is not one of those times. Understood?'

'Yes, ma'am,' Chang responded quickly.

Hillary nodded, then turned to Gemma. 'The man in the lorry

– good work with that, by the way – quick thinking. You booked him and questioned him – anything useful?'

'Clammed up, guv, and asked for a solicitor,' Gemma answered. 'His name is Colin Forrester, and he works in a heavy-goods depot out by Didcot. I reckon he "borrowed" the truck from his firm. I'm going to get on to them first thing, but I doubt whether they knew one of their trucks went missing last night. He's got no form, but I reckon he'll talk when he realizes that his mates are falling over themselves to spill the beans. The ring-leader, the fat man called Ollie, and his son Purple Pete,' (at this Danvers's eyebrows rose, and Gemma shot him a grin,) 'I didn't ask how he came by the nickname,' she admitted, 'are both falling over themselves to drop Alan Hodgson firmly in it. Mind you, Ollie was in the emergency room having a nail pulled out of his calf, and his brief might try and claim he was doped up on pain meds or whatever, and didn't know what he was saying.'

'But there's no doubt that the younger Hodgson was the one who shot the nail gun off?' Hillary asked.

'No, guv – though both his prints and those of his father are on the gun. But all the witnesses agree that Patrick Hodgson took the gun off his son after he'd fired it.'

'About that – there's been a development. Oh, by the way, Sam's here because I'm handing the robbery and wounding incident over to him. I take it we're still working on the theory that the two cases aren't linked?' he asked, looking between Sam and Hillary, who'd only had a brief liaison last night to discuss matters.

'Not that we can see at this stage, sir,' Sam said cautiously.

'I'll let Sam know if I can find any link between our murder victim and the scam Ross and his pals were pulling, but I doubt we'll find one. Stolen building material would have been a bit small-scale for Michael Ivers. He fancied himself a bit of a James Bond character – I can't see him wanting to sully himself with something so petty and sordid.'

'Right.'

'You mentioned a development, sir?' Gemma prompted Danvers.

'Oh yes. It seems that the entire incident has been caught on film. Or in this day and age, I suppose I should say caught on disk.'

'Oh? I didn't think the site had sophisticated CCTV,' Hillary said, nonplussed. If it had, it certainly hadn't been brought to her attention, and it bloody well should have been.

'That's not it,' Danvers said. 'According to a technical officer, they found a recorder running in Pat Hodgson's office. It had an infra-red camera and everything, and was filming the middle area of the yard. It got the whole incident. They're checking it over now.'

'How come?' Chang asked, but it was Hillary who answered.

'I get it. Pat Hodgson knew, or suspected, that stuff was going missing from his yard, and he suspected Frank. That's what the argument was about. And he decided to catch them red-handed.'

'But the poor bastard caught his son instead,' Gemma said, not sure whether to laugh or sympathize. 'I take it that it did show Alan Hodgson wounding Frank?' she asked Danvers, who nodded, then shrugged.

'Yes and no. It shows him jumping and half-turning, we think because of the sudden noise of a forklift starting up,' Danvers explained. 'He obviously wasn't even looking at Frank when the gun went off, and forensics have recovered nails from all over the place. It looks pretty accidental to me – well, apart from the fact that he was holding a deadly weapon at the time.'

'So it won't be malicious wounding then,' Gemma said thoughtfully. 'GBH?'

'It'll be up to Sam and the CPS what charges are brought against Hodgson,' Danvers pointed out. 'I think it's clear that this man Ollie and his son will try and get a lesser sentence for dropping Ross in it.'

'He's going to go down then, sir?' Gemma said, rather

subdued now. Much as she and everyone else at the nick loathed Ross, nobody liked it when an ex-copper got busted. It made the villains cheer and soured the atmosphere in the affected nick for months, sometimes even for years to come.

'It looks like he'll serve some prison time, yes,' Danvers said. But in that, as they were all soon to learn, the DCI was wrong.

Hillary and her team worked steadily until mid-morning. Hillary cleared her backlog and refamiliarized herself with the court case in which she was due to testify. So it was nearly midday before she turned her attention once more to Michael Ivers.

She cleared her desk and leaned back in her chair, feeling weary and discouraged. Now that Sam had been given the Ross case, she'd have to bring him more thoroughly up to speed with the Ivers's case as well, since it was looking increasingly likely that he was the one who was going to have to close it. She had only four days left before she was gone for good.

She forced thoughts of defeat away, and tried to focus.

OK. What had she been doing yesterday, before the debacle at the yard had intruded? She went over in her mind all the interviews with Michael Ivers's women, but nothing stuck out in her mind. She couldn't see Lucy Kirke killing Ivers, and surely his ex-wife, if she were going to do it, would have done so long before now. And Honor Welles...? Hillary sighed. She wasn't sure about Honor Welles. Or Harry Welles, come to that. She'd have to have another crack at them at some point.

What else? Oh yes, the trip to Ivers's GP. Although Phyllis Wainwright had tried to be helpful and honest she hadn't really told Hillary anything she hadn't already known.

Hillary was about to move on when something pinged on her radar. Something about her visit to the GP. She'd had that eerie and weird sensation before, and she knew what it meant. Her subconscious had noticed something that she hadn't taken proper heed of. Something important.

Carefully she went over it again, but nothing the GP had said seemed significant. She went over her notes, but again nothing. Again she started to move on, but again she received that little mental kick that reproached her.

Hillary frowned, and began to twiddle her pen. Gemma, who was on the phone to the haulage firm confirming that one of their reinforced trucks was missing, saw her, and quickly concluded the conversation. She then sat watching Hillary closely. She'd observed this phenomenon before, and she felt her blood begin to race.

Chang, who noticed his sergeant's sudden alertness, followed her gaze, and looked puzzled.

Hillary continued to frown, but indulged her instincts by going over the visit to the GP's surgery again, this time from the very beginning, trying to see what was nagging at her.

She parked the car. Modern building. Bird singing. Went in. Only two patients. The receptionist Suzy was missing. Went to pharmacy and … Stop!

She sat up straight in her chair. Suzy.

The missing Suzy.

'Oh shit, it can't be,' she said, not realizing she'd spoken out loud, until Gemma pushed her wheeled chair a little closer.

'Guv?' she asked urgently, her excitement catching. Chang glanced at his guv'nor and saw her eyes widen slightly.

'Oh damn, it's been staring me in the face and I didn't see it,' Hillary groaned. She'd been too distracted by other things. 'Gemma, phone Ivers's GP's surgery. Don't tell the receptionist who you are. Insist you speak to the practice manager. Then find out the full names of all their receptionists.'

Gemma nodded, and reached for the phone. Hillary watched tensely as her sergeant spoke, listened, then wrote down three names in rapid succession.

When she turned back to Hillary Gemma's face was grim.

'You were right, guv,' she said simply.

*

Hillary Greene was waiting in Interview Room 1, and stood up when Gemma came in, with Suzanne Kirke. In the observation room Paul Danvers sat with Chang; they were joined, a moment later, by Marcus Donleavy.

Chang shot to his feet.

Danvers smiled at the commander knowingly. 'Couldn't bear to miss her swan song, guv?' he asked softly.

Chang, not sure what to do, watched Donleavy take a chair, then decided to hover against the far wall, where he'd be – he hoped - out of mind and out of sight.

'Did you know there's a pool going around on whether or not she'll solve the case before she leaves?' Donleavy asked mildly. 'I saw quite a few long faces when it got around that she'd pulled somebody in.'

Danvers shook his head, but said nothing.

In the interview room, Hillary smiled gently at Suzanne Kirke and indicated a seat. 'Please, take a seat, Mrs Kirke. Gemma, start the tape please.'

She explained to Lucy Kirke's mother why the details were being recorded, then asked her whether she wanted a solicitor.

In the observation room, everyone held their breath. If she said yes, the interview would be terminated before it was even started, and then the rigmarole would begin. But Suzanne Kirke shook her head.

She was wearing a pair of beige slacks and a beige, apricot and white-patterned top. Her hair was up in a neat bun, and Hillary guessed that Gemma had brought her in from her place of work.

'Mrs Kirke, as you know, I'm investigating the murder of Mr Michael Ivers,' Hillary began carefully.

'Yes.'

'I first met you a few days ago now, when I went to interview your daughter, Lucy. Do you remember that?'

'Yes.'

'You were there as well. I believe that at the time you had the afternoon off from your job. Where you worked at a local surgery,' Hillary continued coolly, but inside she was giving herself a good kicking for not picking up on that right away. She should have checked where Suzanne Kirke had worked. How much time would she have saved if she had?

'Yes, that's right.'

'Your daughter, Lucy, used to go out with Michael Ivers, isn't that so?'

'Yes.'

The monosyllabic answers were beginning to worry Hillary a little, as they were her listeners. She needed to get Mrs Kirke to open up a little. So Hillary deliberately asked a question that required more than a one-word answer. 'How did you feel about that situation, Mrs Kirke?'

'I didn't like it. From the moment Lucy first brought him home one night, I didn't like him. He was too anxious to charm me. Too smooth. I could tell he was looking down on our house, and on me. He thought we were provincial, and not good enough for the likes of him. But Lucy is beautiful, and young, and men always get what they want, don't they?'

The words were bitter, but Suzanne's face was oddly expressionless. She seemed defeated, and Hillary guessed that there was no fight left in her.

It didn't make what she had to do any easier. But it was her job. Well, for the next four days anyway.

'I see,' Hillary said slowly, still trying to work out the best and least painful way to go. Beside her, Gemma shifted restlessly. She had read the murder book and knew all about Suzanne Kirke's recent tragedy. Like Hillary, she wasn't feeling her usual sense of triumph about bringing a case to a conclusion.

'It must have made you angry,' Hillary said quietly.

Suzanne shrugged slightly. 'Girls don't listen to their mothers nowadays, do they? Not about anything. I warned Lucy what he was like but she just wouldn't believe me. I expect, like all young girls, she thought she could change him.'

'So when he dropped her, you were angry?' Hillary asked.

'I was relieved,' Suzanne Kirke corrected her at once. 'I thought she'd get over him and see that I was right, and be more careful in the future.'

Hillary nodded. 'I understand,' she said softly. 'You thought it was all over. That must have been a relief. So it must have been all the more awful when you realized that it wasn't over at all. That the nightmare was just beginning in fact.'

Suzanne Kirke looked up at her with bleak eyes. 'It was as if a bomb had gone off under me,' Suzanne said. 'Or an earthquake. I actually went down on the floor,' she said, as if surprised at the memory. 'Luckily no one saw me, though. I just picked myself up and went on as if nothing had happened.' She shook her head in wonder, as if unable to believe her memory.

'You were working in reception at the time? You do work at the surgery where Michael Ivers was a patient, don't you?' Hillary clarified, for the benefit of the tape.

'Yes.'

'So he wasn't a complete stranger to you when your daughter first brought him home?'

'I knew his face, vaguely,' Suzanne confirmed. 'But we have hundreds of patients at the clinic. I didn't think anything of it.'

'But you deal with the mail and the filing. And when you saw Michael Ivers's name on some test documents you were understandably curious?' Hillary said, careful to keep her voice level. She mustn't spook her now.

'Of course I was. It was only three days after he'd dumped my girl, and she was still sitting at home crying over the heartless pig every night.'

Hillary nodded. 'So you read it?'

'Not all of it. Not at first. Just a line or two,' Suzanne said at once, then managed a bitter laugh. 'Me and the other girls on reception do take patient confidentiality seriously you know,' she said. Then sighed. 'But I recognized some of the words, and I knew what they meant.'

She paused and swallowed hard. 'So I read it all, and realized that he was HIV positive. And that he'd given it to my girl. My lovely Lucy.'

Tears began to roll soundlessly down her face, but she made no sound. Her shoulders didn't shake, and she made no signs of sobbing. There was just an outpouring of salty tears that had Gemma shifting uncomfortably on her seat beside Hillary and reaching for a tissue from her bag before handing it over.

Suzanne took it but simply held it, scrunching it in her hand.

'You don't know that, Mrs Kirke,' Hillary said gently. 'There's every chance that Lucy's fine,' she said. She could only hope that it was true.

'I lost my other daughter to illness,' Suzanne said simply. 'And the moment I read those words, I just knew I was going to lose Lucy too. I felt it. Mothers do. We know.'

Hillary licked her dry lips, hating what she had to do next, but knowing she had no choice.

'So, after a while, when the shock had worn off, you decided to confront him. Isn't that right?'

'Yes,' Suzanne said, and suddenly wiped her damp face with the tissue. 'He was the sort who just breezed through life, leaving broken hearts and broken lives behind him without a bloody care in the world.' She spoke with real hate in her voice. 'And I just thought to myself, not this time, you rotten pig. Not this time. But what could I do?'

Hillary nodded. 'It took you some time, but eventually you decided to see him face to face. You called him on his mobile, that night, didn't you?' She deliberately didn't add words like 'the night he died' or 'the night he was murdered.' She wanted Suzy Kirke to remain calm and focused.

'Yes.'

'Yes. From the surgery. It showed up on his mobile phone records.' Again Hillary was speaking for the tape.

'I told him I was going to see him. He tried to put me off, of course, the coward. But I told him I'd camp outside the door to

217

his flat if he didn't see me, and he eventually told me I could come to his office that night.' Suzanne laughed grimly. 'I suppose he didn't want me in his home. I might meet up with his latest girlfriend, poor cow, and tell her what he was like.'

'You drove to the park?' Hillary asked smoothly, keeping her focused.

'Yes. I parked out on the road, though. I didn't know whether there was parking inside.'

Hillary nodded. 'You walked to the front gates. Weren't they locked?'

'No. I thought they would be, but when I pushed on them, they were open.'

'What time was this, can you remember?' Hillary asked.

'It must have been about a quarter past eight,' Suzanne said. She sounded exhausted, but was obviously in the mood to tell everything, and Hillary felt some of the tension leave her.

Suzanne Kirke had been living with the weight of her knowledge for some time, and, like most normal, decent people who found themselves doing extraordinary things, her conscience must have been giving her agony. The urge to talk about it, to confess and remove the secret burden of it must have been overwhelming.

'There was no one in the little booth thing either,' Suzanne confirmed, 'so I just walked on past it. That man had told me how to find the depot where he worked.'

Hillary nodded. At a quarter past eight, Frank Ross would only just have come on duty. It would be just like him not to bother to check whether the front gates were locked. He had probably been holed up in a nice cosy corner somewhere, drinking or relieving himself, and so could easily have missed the unexpected visitor.

'So you went to the depot where Michael Ivers worked?' Hillary pressed her gently.

'Yes. I knocked on the door. He answered. I told him what I knew. He laughed at first, tried to brush it off. I was so angry.

He'd given Lucy a death sentence and it meant nothing to him! I told him I was going to tell everyone what he was and what he had, and then he got angry. He threatened to sue me, to sue the clinic, if I did. He threw me out. He literally threw me out, like I was rubbish.'

Suzanne Kirke's voice rose a notch, and she rubbed the top of her arms as if still physically feeling the touch of his hands on her as he'd thrust her out through the door.

'I started to walk back to the gates, but then I stopped,' Suzanne said. Her voice was quieter now, almost lifeless. 'I just couldn't walk away like that, all defeated and useless. I just felt so worthless. Mothers are supposed to look after their children. But I had had to stand by and watch my beautiful girl die. And now I was going to have to do the same with Lucy. And that man just laughed at me and threw me out.'

Suzanne looked at Hillary with large, bleak eyes. 'I looked around and saw this plank of wood. It looked strong and heavy and it was. I picked it up and walked back to the depot. Then I tossed some pebbles at the window. Eventually he came out. I was standing beside the wall, and when he opened the door it went in front of me – covering me. When I pushed it back, he was already walking across the grass towards the window. Trying to see what had made the noise, I suppose. I didn't think about it. I didn't stop to wonder what would happen if he heard me and turned round. I just went after him, and lifted the wood and hit him on the back of the head.'

Suzanne stared at Hillary as if puzzled. 'He went down, just like that. He gave a sort of grunt, and I hit him again, when he was on the ground. I think I did, anyway. I'm not sure how many times I hit him.'

Hillary knew from the autopsy that it had been three times, but she didn't want to interrupt the narrative now.

'He just lay there. Not moving,' Suzanne Kirke continued. 'And for the longest time, I just stood there, watching him.' She was sounding puzzled now. 'I still don't know what I was expecting to happen.' She looked up at Hillary, her eyes baffled, as if expecting Hillary to be able to tell her. 'But I kept thinking that something should. You know? Something should happen now. But nothing did. It was nearly dark, and quiet, and he still lay there. Eventually I just dropped the piece of wood and walked away.'

'You went straight to the front gate?'

'Yes.'

'Did you see the night watchman?'

'No.'

'You drove straight home?'

'Yes. I had a shower and threw away the clothes. I put them in the rubbish bin.'

The bins would have been long since emptied, Hillary realized, but she hoped that the lack of forensic evidence to back up Suzanne's confession wouldn't be necessary.

'Suzanne, I'm going to have to charge you now with the murder of Michael Ivers,' Hillary said quietly. 'Do you understand?'

'Yes. But I don't care. I mean, at least in prison I won't have to watch my Lucy die, will I?' Suzanne Kirke said sadly.

Outside the interview room Gemma drew a deep breath. 'Bloody hell, I can't say as I enjoyed that, guv,' she said shakily.

'No,' Hillary agreed, pushing on through into the observation room. 'What struck me was that she was so convinced that Ivers had infected Lucy. But I'm not at all sure that he had. When I interviewed Lucy Kirke, she told me that she'd practised safe sex. She was going to get tested right away. Let's hope she's given the all clear.'

'I hope so, guv,' Gemma said, then almost cannoned into Hillary's back as she stopped abruptly.

Facing her in the observation room, Danvers, Donleavy and Chang all looked uneasy.

'What?' Hillary said, a cold fist clutching her heart. 'The confession was solid, wasn't it?'

'It's not that, Hill,' Paul Danvers said quietly. 'We just got the word. It's Frank Ross. He didn't make it out of surgery.'

Everyone agreed that the bride looked stunning.

It was hot, almost the last in day May, and Gemma Fordham wore a white dress that stopped just short above her knees. It was cut on a bias that showed off her slender waist and made the most of her breasts, and with it she wore a large, lacy veil that seemed to accentuate rather than hide her short, spiky, blond hair and high cheekbones. She clutched a bouquet of simple pinks, and more than one person inside the cool church in North Oxford caught their breath as she walked down the aisle.

Hillary Greene smiled at her as she walked by on the arm of her proud, firefighting father.

The ceremony was solemn yet joyous, and it went off without a hitch. Afterwards Hillary didn't stay long at the reception. The bride and groom left at just gone six for their honeymoon in the Seychelles, and within the hour, Hillary drove back to Thrupp.

Danvers was in York, and Brian Vane was in Hull. Janine Tyler had put in a transfer request and would soon be in Plymouth.

Mark Chang had asked to be seconded to Sam Waterstone's team, and had been accepted. And she'd walked out of Thames Valley HQ just over two weeks ago, after enduring a riotous leaving 'do' that would probably be remembered for years to come. She hadn't stepped foot inside the place since.

Now, driving past the entrance to the station house on a mellow golden evening, the scent of flowers still in her memory and the taste of wedding cake still in her mouth, Hillary didn't even turn her head to look at it.

Instead she drove Puff to the car park of The Boat pub and climbed out of him for the last time. She'd sold him three days ago to the pub landlord's teenage son, but he'd let her borrow him one last time for the wedding bash.

Now she locked the door, left the keys behind the bar and said goodbye to the landlord. Several regulars wanted to buy her drinks, but she lied and told them she was still half-sozzled from the wedding party.

On board *The Mollern*, everything was ready and waiting. She'd had her overhauled and cleaned, and the water tank was full, the toilet tank empty, and the full gas cylinders were neatly lined up aft.

It was barely eight o'clock at night when she slipped off the mooring rope, stepped on to the stern, and turned over the engine.

She had barely an hour of daylight left in which to travel. It would make much more sense for her to stay one last night in Thrupp and then set off in the morning.

But she was scared that if she did that, she would never go at all.

So she turned the tiller and took *The Mollern* out into the centre of the canal. The narrowboat's nose happened to be pointing north, and Hillary could think of no good reason to turn around and head south.

Overhead, the sun began to lower towards the horizon, and a moorhen family darted into the reeds to avoid *The Mollern*'s modest wake.

Hillary Greene headed off into her new life at a sedate three miles an hour. The speed limit on the canal was actually four miles an hour, but she had nowhere in particular to go, and was in no particular hurry to get there.